FORSAKEN TRUST

By the Author

Crossed

Forsaken Trust

FORSAKEN TRUST

by
Meredith Doench

2017

FORSAKEN TRUST

ISBN 13: 978-1-62639-737-8

This Trade Paperback Original Is Published By
Bold Strokes Books, Inc.
P.O. Box 249
Valley Falls, NY 12185

First Edition: May 2017

CREDITS
Editor: Ruth Sternglantz
Production Design: Susan Ramundo
Cover Design By Jeanine Henning

Acknowledgments

Thank you to my family, both immediate and extended, for their continued support and encouragement. A special thanks to Uncle Dave who has claimed me as his favorite thriller writer. I hope this novel doesn't let you down!

A very big thank you to Xiamara Hohman and Lindsey Light for slugging through the early drafts of this book. I appreciate your willingness to offer editorial guidance and keep a sense of humor at the same time.

Thank you to the members of the English department at the University of Dayton for their support. Special thanks to Andy for providing Writing with Friends; Patrick, Kara, and Liz for writing alongside me in various locations around Dayton; Rachel and Dan for discussions of whether "this could really happen;" Laura and Bryan for their encouragement and advocacy of my work.

Thank you, BWR, for our discussions of loyalty and justice while also showing me these two don't always go hand in hand.

Thanks to Nancy Zafris for her continued support.

Many thanks to Bold Strokes Books and to Ruth Sternglantz for all the writing advice and a close eye with the final edits.

Last, but certainly not least, a big thank you to the readers of *Crossed* who regularly nudged me along to find out what happens next to Special Agent Luce Hansen. I appreciate your support!

Dedication

This book is dedicated to my mom
who has never forsaken me.

And for my furry companions, Joey and Tayo,
who have taught me the meaning of loyalty.

PROLOGUE

A va Washington loved nothing more than kayaking down the Powell River, eventually landing in the vast waters of Wallace Lake. Every Saturday at six a.m., rain or shine, Ava loaded her truck while her mother and younger brother slumbered on. She made her way down to the water's stony edge where she paddled until the Ohio winter months stopped her. It wasn't just the promise of a solid upper-arm workout that kept Ava coming back every week. It was the silence and the way she could hear the sounds of her own breath, the pound of her heart inside her ears, and the slice of the paddle through the current. It was how she felt when the water rushed about the bobbing kayak bringing with it the smell of the surrounding river and woods. Unlike the other kayakers she encountered on the waterway, Ava used no music. She despised those tiny earbuds that drowned out the sounds of nature, particularly in late October when the river and all its inhabitants were preparing for a long winter. Ava's life during the week was so noisy; she wanted nothing but quiet. Despite the thick fog that coated the land and wafted off the river today, Ava hoped the sun would burn the fog away, allowing her to stay on the water until sundown.

Ava was a sophomore at Wallace Lake High School and had never enjoyed school. She wasn't an athlete or the cheerleader type; she fell somewhere on the spectrum between the smart kid with no social skills and the talented but low-achieving student. Then, a few months ago, everything changed.

Ava went to her first bodybuilding practice with her best friend, Sadie Reid, mostly because Sadie had begged her to. Bodybuilding wasn't something Ava would have ever thought of trying on her own, but everyone had a crush on the new coach, Mr. Allard. She wanted a chance to check him out, and now that Sadie had a job helping out the team, Ava could do so with her friend at her side. Joining the team also meant Ava could be around Sadie even more, and truth be told, this was the real motivation for her joining the team. Ava knew that Sadie had it rough. She had been taken from her mother, a heroin addict and rumored prostitute, and had lived with her grandmother ever since Ava met her in second grade. Since then, there were two rules that Ava's mother regularly pestered her with. One, stay away from heroin, that insidious drug which had sucked the life from their town ever since the factory jobs left. And two, stay away from Sadie Reid.

The oaks, elms, and pines were losing their summer greens and exploding with oranges, yellows, and reds. Ava wound the paddle in the figure-eight motion. When she hit a patch of rushing water, she let the paddle rest on the rim of the kayak and took a deep breath while the water around her burbled and tumbled on itself. The thick morning fog allowed her to see only a few feet ahead, and she let the crests of the river waves and the swelling movement of the water pull her along.

Eventually, the water slowed to a crawl as Ava neared the bend in the Powell River. Beyond was the junction, the place where the river met Wallace Lake. The locals called the point of the river's connection to the lake Dead Man's Point, mostly because of the road that ran along the waterway. The site of many auto and motorcycle accidents, the road had a hairpin turn that froze easily in the winter and covered with water in the summer, sending cars hydroplaning to crash through the guardrails and into the river. Many had lost their lives on that turn, and it was a popular spot for ghost stories around Halloween.

The water level was low, and when Ava rounded the corner, she saw the twin land bars, one mass in front of the other. She'd heard a teacher describe them once as the broad, mossy-brown backs of two hippos cresting the water, and she now understood that image. Most days, Ava couldn't see so much of those higher patches of silt, rock, and sand; today, they took her by surprise. Something white caught her eye, something so white it nearly glowed. She looked hard. Then again. There, spread-eagle on top of one of the bars, was what looked like a person lying facedown.

Ava shook her head. She told herself it was only the fog playing tricks on her eyes. *I've been watching too many of those crime shows.* No matter how many times she shut her eyes and reopened them, though, the figure was still there. Maybe, she reasoned, it was a mannequin or some sort of sick joke meant to scare people on the river and carry on the haunted name. But it certainly *looked* real. Ava pulled the paddle back hard to stop the forward motion of the kayak. She fought to cross the current over to the exposed bar of land.

"Hello?" Ava called. "Do you need help?"

The body was naked—a white woman with her heavy breasts shoved into the earth of the sandbar. Dark shoulder-length hair was strewn across her face. Ava docked the kayak and climbed out, but the boat's rocking motion left her balance unstable. When Ava took a step, her knee gave out. She fell forward, her hands breaking the fall not far from the woman's leg.

The woman didn't move. Slowly, Ava reached out her hand. *Just a quick touch,* she told herself, *just to make sure it's real.* The woman's skin looked so pale and hard. Ava's fingertips grazed the cold calf before her. The breath seized in her throat, and she felt the heavy pulse of blood thumping in her head. A strange voice echoed in her mind and it took a minute before Ava realized it was her own: *Take a deep breath, stand up, and call for help.*

Ava pushed herself up to her feet and rushed back to the kayak. Her cell was strapped to the waterproof compartment on the side of the boat. As Ava's foot sank into the sand next to the kayak, she saw it—a gray, lifeless hand floating just under the water's surface. Ava's eyes followed the hand to the bend of the wrist and forearm.

She saw the tattoo, that wavering image dulled by the river's water. Her eyes followed the arm to the shoulder of the submerged body below.

Ava screamed, and her heart felt like it could rocket out of her chest.

Was it her? My God, Ava thought, *could it really be her?*

CHAPTER ONE

Day One: 8:30 a.m.

I held the pillow over my head and tried to will the incessant banging on my front door to go away. It was a cop's knock, that loud fist bang we all learned in the academy. Dammit, I wasn't in the mood to be around cops so early in the morning. I'd fallen asleep in my clothes and on the couch again. Judging from the sunlight seeping through the only window in the apartment, it had to be before nine a.m. Much too early for me to be up and about during my weeklong vacation.

"Come on, Hansen." That familiar fist pounded against my door again. "I know you're in there!"

"Vacation," I shouted. "Come back next week!"

"No such thing as vacation. Open up!"

I tossed the pillow on the floor. Colby Sanders was not only one of the most stubborn men I knew, he was also my boss: Director of the Ohio Bureau of Criminal Investigation. He'd also been a close friend of my father's before my dad passed on. My dad always told me Sanders was a good man, someone I could trust.

"This better be good," I mumbled, one socked foot stumbling over an empty cardboard case of beer. I twisted the two dead bolts and swung the door open.

Sanders grunted hello as he pushed past me into the apartment. He'd just taken a shower; the scent of aftershave and shampoo trailed after him. He wore his standard work uniform: black suit pants, a short-sleeved white button-up, and a black tie. This wasn't just a friendly house call.

"Come on in." I shut the door, my sarcasm lost on him.

Sanders stood inside my TV room/ dining room/ den, only about five steps from the front door, and reached for his cigarettes. "You mind?"

"Go ahead." I knew Sanders couldn't go more than an hour without a cigarette. There were no ashtrays in the apartment, so I grabbed an empty beer bottle from the floor.

"Jesus, Hansen." He lit the cigarette. "I heard your new place was a dump, but come on. You can do better than this."

"It's not the best area in Columbus," I agreed, "but it works." In truth, I hated the apartment and the undergraduate neighbors that came with it. It was nothing like the home I'd left, a place that felt comfortable and safe.

"Huh." Sanders turned to me, his thick white eyebrows squinting together the way he does when he's putting a crime scene together in his head. His eyes gave me a good solid look up and down. I definitely didn't look my best: I'd been wearing the same worn and wrinkled Fleetwood Mac T-shirt for a few days, complete with remnants of a recent meal dribbled down the front. My cutoff jean shorts were so desperately in need of a laundry cycle, they could probably have stood on their own. In my bare feet, I suddenly felt exposed like I was naked; I crossed one leg over the other and my arms over my chest.

"What's going on here, Luce?"

I couldn't look Sanders in the eye. He was seeing me at my worst, and I didn't like it. "You could have called." I pushed a thatch of greasy hair away from my eyes. God, when had I last taken a shower? I'd lost track of time.

"Goes straight to voicemail. Where's your phone?"

I picked up a towel on the couch along with a few stray socks and located the cell that was stuck between two cushions. Dead battery.

Sanders asked again, "What's going on here, Hansen?"

"I'm fine," I tried to recover. I pulled my mass of hair up into a knot at the top of my head in an attempt to hide its rattiness. "I wasn't expecting anyone."

"You're in a bad way," Sanders shook his head. "You should have told me."

I almost laughed. Me call him for help? Maybe in some other lifetime. I tried to explain. "When your girl leaves you and takes everything, there aren't too many options."

Sanders blew a stream of smoke through his nostrils. "It's been months since you split with Rowan."

"Only seven," I said, more defensively than I meant to. Then, as if it could make the sorry fact that I was still devastated any better, I added, "She kept the dogs."

"I'm sorry," Sanders said in a soft voice.

His sudden stroke of kindness brought on the sting of tears collecting in the corners of my eyes. I willed them not to fall.

"You haven't been eating," Sanders said. He nodded at the empty cases of beer scattered around the room. "And you've been drinking too much."

"A regular Sherlock."

Sanders reached out to me then, his warm, solid hand surprising me. He gave my shoulder a quick squeeze. Although Sanders was never a man who was good at expressing his emotions, concern laced his touch. I waited for him to pull away; his touch felt strange, foreign. Other than running into the random person on the street or nudging up against someone on the public bus, his touch was the first I'd felt in weeks. I almost forgot that I was mad at him.

Almost.

"Why are you here, Sanders?"

He took a drag on his cigarette. "We might have something."

I perked up. "A serial killer?"

He nodded. "Two bodies were found this morning along the Powell River. Two more were found a few months ago in the same location, where the river meets with Wallace Lake."

"Let me see the file."

Sanders shook his head. "We need to get to Wallace Lake. Shower, and we'll talk over breakfast."

"Tell me about the case first."

Sanders held firm. "Shower. Make it fast." He reached for the TV remote and flipped the channel to the morning news. "And pack a bag. You'll be there a few days."

The morning news anchors squawked as I closed the bedroom door behind me. I knew what Sanders was doing—scanning the stations for any breaking reports on the murders. Once the media caught hold of a possible serial killer, an investigation could descend into chaos in a matter of hours. Sanders's actions told me one thing. This case at Wallace Lake was going to be a big one.

Inside the bathroom, I peeled off my well-worn clothes, ignoring my image in the bathroom mirror. It alarmed me to see myself; I looked a whole lot like a woman who had nothing left to lose.

The shower stream of cool water felt good—the smack of it against my bare skin—and I let it run over my face until it warmed up. I reached for the gold Irish cross that was always around my neck to make sure it was still there, and then let the water pound against my breastbone. The collection of rowdy undergrads next door took about fifteen showers a day and sucked up the majority of the building's hot water. Every day, I missed the house that I'd been in the process of renovating with my ex, Rowan. Every day, I missed the land that surrounded our house, the quiet of suburbia that bordered on country. And every day, my heart ached for the dogs I'd left with Rowan, Toto and Daisy. Leaving them with her was the right thing to do; the Labs wouldn't be happy without their yard, and they had bonded more with Rowan, who stayed home most days to do her artwork. After all, I'd bought the dogs for her when we first moved in to the house. *An added layer of safety*, I told Rowan. *Criminals stay away from homes with dogs*. She'd reached for me then and smiled. *I have a strong detective to protect me, but I love the dogs*. Nothing made the pain in my chest go away when I thought of the dogs and the home I'd left behind. And Rowan.

I scrubbed clean my hair that stank of stale beer. I'd let it grow since Rowan and I split, giving my brown hair and everything else in my life very little attention. It had grown down to the middle of my back. Rowan would like it, I thought, fingering through the dirty strands. What did my hair or anything else matter, anyway? Rowan was gone. She said she couldn't compete with what she considered to be the other woman in my life any longer—my job as a special agent with the Ohio BCI. Rowan might have thought the other woman was my job, but what really held my heart was the water. It had saved me once from a serial killer and had been saving me ever since.

I toweled off and wrapped myself up to move to the bedroom. The towel went around my body farther than usual. Sanders was right; I hadn't been eating much. I also hadn't been keeping up with my exercise routine. I always swam three miles in the morning before my shift, but I hadn't been in a pool in over two months. My nights had been filled with bad TV and cheap beer or boxed wine. I'd gotten soft and thin. I stood still for a few moments, took a long, deep breath, and finally listened to my body for the first time in months. I found that I was hungry. Starving, actually.

I dug into the closet for some work clothes. The apartment was small, and outside my closed door, I could hear Sanders rummaging around in the living room and kitchen.

"I'm famished," I called out to him. "What are you doing out there, anyway?"

"Just giving you a hand." Sanders turned the volume down on the television. "Did I tell you to bring your suit? I booked a hotel with a pool."

The pool. A wave of guilt washed over me. I'd been apart from the water for too long.

I pulled on my only clean work shirt, a blue silk button up, and cursed Sanders under my breath. He was trying too hard to be nice, and I could smell the stink of his guilt complex all the way in my room. I didn't appreciate him showing up at my apartment. Yes, my cell was dead, but he could have sent an agent out. He could have met me at the office. I hadn't spoken much to Sanders in months other than to discuss my weekly case reports. He knew I was angry. I knew I needed to get over it—it wasn't like I could get away from the man anytime soon unless I quit my job.

I pulled the legs of my black pants up to the knee and stepped into my Frye boots, a good luck charm I always wore to work. My dad had given me the same boots he'd worn throughout his entire career as the Chesterton Chief of Police when I graduated from the academy. It was the last gift my dad ever gave me, and I missed him every day. As I laced the boots, I thought about what had happened over the last eight months of my life.

Last January, Sanders elected me for my first serial killer case. It just so happened that case was in Willow's Ridge, Ohio, a town I had history in as a child. In the summer of 1989, my first love, Marci, was murdered. Her case went unsolved, and Sanders knew there could possibly be a connection with the current crimes. He sent me in, anyway. He used my past to unlock the case, to get in deeper and faster than any outsider could have. After the case was finally closed and the killer had been caught, Sanders promised me that my work would put me in line for a shot at the FBI. Sanders, however, had made promises he couldn't keep; he blamed it on the lack of positions in DC and pointed out regularly that he needed me on his team. I let his words run in one ear and out the other. I'd trusted him. He was my father's friend. I never thought he'd manipulate me to solve a case. Yet here he was in my apartment commenting on my struggles partly brought on by *his* actions. It didn't matter that he was now sorry for what he'd done. I'd lost my trust in him. What hurt me most, though, was that it wasn't just my exuberance for the job I'd lost after the Willow's Ridge case. I'd also lost some of my trust in the criminal justice system. Ethics and personal commitments, it appeared to me, were something of the past.

The bottom line in our business is that we are paid to catch serial criminals. How Sanders went about completing that mission wasn't really the point—it was all about the capture. He succeeded in the Willow's Ridge case by ending the reign of a murderer who'd killed seven young lesbians, and those who helped the killer were now in jail awaiting prosecution. Job done and done well. In the grand scope of things, it didn't really matter that Sanders used my past as a way into the case or that he'd put me in harm's way, both emotionally and physically. He got the job done. There wasn't much room for sensitive feelings and hurt egos when it came to catching serial criminals.

My father always told me I needed to toughen up if I wanted to go far in the Bureau.

"Think Ice Queen, Luce," he told me. "And always remember, there's no crying in baseball."

I missed my father. While he'd been gone for a few years, his ghostly image hadn't. He had regularly appeared when I worked tough cases. He'd been a huge help to me on the Willow's Ridge case, the one who helped guide me through those explosive minefields of my past. Since that case ended, though, I'd rarely sensed or seen my father's presence.

My fingers reached toward my neck again for the confirmation of the Irish cross. It was still there, the sharpened edges of the cross dulled with time. I hadn't taken the necklace off since the day Marci's brother gave it to me in memory of her. I'd been touched beyond words at the family's generosity when we closed the Willow's Ridge case. I'd always felt like they blamed me for Marci's death; in fact, it was me who couldn't stop blaming myself. Marci's Irish cross provided me with comfort—a physical reminder that she was always with me.

I unlocked my safe and clipped the badge to my belt, now a few notches tighter on my shrinking waist. I checked the gun's safety lock and pulled on the shoulder strap, a device I was forced to use given my boyish not-there hips. I reached for the black suit coat next to my mirror and caught sight of my hair. It would take too long to dry. Instead, I brushed through it and weaved one long braid down my back.

In the other room, I heard commotion. I opened the bedroom door and found Sanders standing at a kitchen sink full of soapy water, holding an overflowing trash bag. He wore my purple dish gloves that came up to the middle of his forearms and smiled at me. "You have a lot of dirty dishes, Hansen."

I stared at him for a long minute. Could I really be seeing this scene correctly? Sanders doing my dishes and collecting my trash? In *purple gloves*? Once I started laughing, I couldn't stop.

❖

I followed in my truck behind Sanders's beige sedan, a ride he thought was completely nondescript but actually screamed *cop*. He took a no-name exit, and we wound our way through rural routes where the woods grew thick and road signs warning of deer and animal crossings ticked past every few miles. Lucinda Williams had been on constant spin in my truck's CD player since my split with Rowan. Her songs spilled from the truck speakers about the need for love and forsaken trust. There was something about Lucinda's throaty knowledge that I recognized, truths that resonated deep within me. I was almost disappointed when Sanders turned and we rolled into the battered and pitted lot of The Breakfast Nook where the sign promised locally grown, homemade food.

The waitress dropped off a bowl of oatmeal for Sanders and a heaping plate of scrambled eggs and waffles for me. Sanders loaded his oatmeal with pepper and then handed me the shaker. "You sure you're ready to get back on this horse?"

"What horse is that?" I filled my mouth with a forkful of syrup-dripping waffle. "A serial killer?"

Sanders nodded. "You know how dark these things can get. You're the best I've got, Hansen. I just want to make sure you're up for it."

"I've been cleared by counseling. I'm good to go."

"You know that's not what I mean. I need to hear it from you."

I took a deep breath and savored my bite. Real food—fresh and homemade—not the take-out crap I'd been surviving on the past few months. I didn't want to talk about counseling or the state of my mental health. Sanders knew I'd completed the required counseling that all law enforcement had to participate in once they shot or killed anyone while on duty. I'd killed Nick Eldridge, the serial killer in the Willow's Ridge case, not because he deserved it or because I wanted to, but because there was no other choice. He would have killed me if I let him live a second longer. I never let on that the death of Nick Eldridge bothered me, but I wished the outcome could have been different. Death was the easy way out for him since he didn't have to face any jury members or survivors of the victims. There would be no long hours in the prison cell for him to contemplate his actions. He checked out far too early, and I'd wanted the man to face justice. Instead, *I* was left to contemplate his death and what I could have done differently and why it took me so long to find him. That didn't feel much like justice to me.

"I'm sorry things didn't work out, Hansen," Sanders started.

I shrugged. "You made promises you couldn't keep."

Sanders nodded and swallowed a mouthful of coffee. "For what it's worth, the DC gig isn't all it's cracked up to be."

"Maybe not. I should have been given the chance to figure that out for myself." I leaned against the back of the chair and considered Sanders across from me. It was much easier for me to confront him about the job rather than the real violation I'd suffered. He'd never apologized for what hurt me most—the exposure of my past for his gain and the trust I'd lost in him because of it.

"I need to know something," I said.

"What?"

"Did you really send a letter of recommendation to DC for me? Or was that your way of appeasing me after Willow's Ridge?"

He almost dropped his fork. "Are you serious? Do you really think I wouldn't send a recommendation letter for you? I gave you my word," Sanders said. "I have it saved on my computer if you'd like to see it."

I said nothing. A letter from someone as respected as Sanders carried a lot of weight. I wanted to believe he'd supported me but wasn't sure I could completely trust him.

"Hansen, I'm sorry it didn't work out, but it had nothing to do with me."

An awkward silence settled between us until I finally broke it. "You know as well as I do what makes me tick," I said. "I have to work. If I don't, I'll drown in whatever is going on back there in my apartment."

Sanders stirred his oatmeal and considered me across the booth. Finally he said, "It's a lonely life. We're hunters, Hansen. Not many can survive the sidelines in our lives."

"Is that why you've been single forever?"

Sanders chuckled. "There have been a few women here and there. It's hard, though, to be the ones who watch us become so obsessed and climb inside those dark minds in order to capture them. It's the rare woman who can stand us, I tell you."

I thought of Rowan, along with the many arguments we'd had over my obsession with work and the late nights.

"I can work on it," I tried to promise her.

"I don't think so," Rowan said. "You'll never be able to leave a case at the end of the day, come home to me, and really be here. *We just don't fit together, Luce."*

"There are always the times I'm in between cases."

Rowan shook her head. "I'm nobody's backup plan. I won't be anyone's second choice."

I realized then that Rowan had always had a plan in mind, an image of what we would be like together. She wasn't willing to alter that image in any way—something I admired and hated her for, all at the same time.

Sanders wiped his mouth and pushed his plate to the side of the table. "You ever been out to Wallace Lake?"

"A few times. One of Rowan's friends had a boat, and we went waterskiing with them on the lake."

"They're nearing the end of their busy season. The water sports and camping might be the only things keeping that town afloat. They tried to put in snow skiing a few years back, but it never really took off."

I'd heard about many of the factories closing up that way and leaving so many in the rural areas of Ohio without work. "So, fill me in. What's waiting for us in Wallace Lake?"

"I'll spare you the photos while we're eating. Basics—four bodies dumped in the Powell River and Wallace Lake area. White females all over the age of fifty. Only the first two victims have been identified."

"No strong leads?"

Sanders shook his head. "Nothing has panned out."

I opened the file and picked up a crime scene photograph. A much-too-pale body was lodged on a log at the river's edge. Facedown with her arms spread too wide, her long, thin fingers pointed downriver.

"Who were the first bodies found?" I asked.

"Betty Geiger, fifty-eight, and Mary Kate Packard, sixty-two. Drifters, as far as anyone can tell."

"What ties the bodies together?" I asked. There had to be something more than location that connected these four dead women to the same killer. Rivers and waterways were notorious dumping grounds for all kinds of killers, particularly in the Midwest.

"Besides the location, gender, and age, they all have signs of drug abuse—track marks and decayed teeth."

I loaded my fork with another bite of waffle. "This part of Ohio is notorious for opiates. Drug deaths can be slippery."

Sanders agreed. I watched him closely; he was holding something back.

"Come on, Sanders. There has to be something more for you to come knocking on my door and drag me out of my vacation."

Sanders twisted his near-empty coffee cup between his hands. "There are tattoos."

"Matching?"

Sanders grunted a yes and reached for his bag.

"Interesting."

He pulled out two photographs, close-up shots labeled *left inner wrist*. The tattoo featured two plump bright red hearts seated side by side, with the right edge of the left heart spilling over into the left edge of the right heart. In that shared space of the two hearts was a black number 2.

"No connection to any groups or churches in the area?"

"Not that anyone has found so far," Sanders said. "All the victims have them in the same spot. Those photos have enlarged the tats. They aren't any bigger than a half-dollar."

"Could it be a marker for human trade?"

"They've looked into that, but no known runners use the hearts. Besides, these women are older and wrung out with drug abuse and prostitution. Not the sort of girls the runners are looking for."

"Anything else?"

"The two earlier victims died of ethylene glycol poisoning. We're waiting for toxicology on the two found this morning."

Antifreeze poisoning was a very painful way to die as the body shut down, organ by organ. Since the liquid was odorless and sweet tasting, it could easily be masked inside a soft drink or sports drink, a favorite method of poisoners who don't want their victims to know they are dying until it's too late.

"There's also a change in the murder method. The two women found today were stabbed from behind. One has multiple stab wounds. She put up a real fight, apparently."

The violence against the victims was escalating, a telltale sign that the killer was gaining confidence and possibly spinning out of control.

"We're up against a clock here, Hansen. You know as well as I do that once a killer gets a taste for violence and power, it's only a matter of days before another victim is killed. Everything inside that person needs to match that first perfect high."

Addiction, I'd found, took many forms including murder. It drove so many of the crimes we worked, leaving destruction and loss in its wake. "No signs of sexual assault?"

"Not on the first two victims. No word yet on the two found this morning."

"Wallace Lake is a small community. Has the local PD turned up anything?"

"Wallace Lake PD started locally with the drug angle," Sanders said. "They've looked into a few known dealers in the area, a pimp or two. I guess the latest excitement with the heroin epidemic in the area is to lace the drug with propofol. The dealers are making money hand over fist."

"Propofol. That's the drug that killed Michael Jackson, right?"

"That's it," Sanders said. "It's what they use in hospitals to knock people out before surgery."

"Jesus."

"It's something, isn't it? I mean, what twisted thing will dealers think of next? Anyway, the local PD came up empty. Our best chance is for something to hit on the two women found today. We need an ID on them, and hopefully, some evidence will be found at the scene."

"So we're heading into this case with next to nothing."

"That's why they need us," Sanders said. "That's why they need you, Hansen."

Sanders didn't need to convince me to work the case. My mind was already circling with possible profiles for this killer. Before I realized it, the hooks of the case had already sunk into me. I couldn't have stopped the pull toward these women if I tried. For the first time in months, I'd forgotten about Rowan and the disappointment in my job.

My body was on high alert with a sort of vibration pulsating through me, my breaths deeper, my heartbeat stronger. I was ready for the hunt. I was ready for the chase. And I was more than ready to go into that dark place once again.

I felt alive.

CHAPTER TWO

Day One: 10:45 a.m.

The day was warm, a perfect seventy degrees, and the blinding sun reflected off the large tent that had been erected at Dead Man's Point. The thick white cover helped to shield the bodies and slow down their degeneration. It had already been more than four hours since the bodies were found. Local police, however, could not remove them until the chief medical examiner arrived. Because violent crime was rare in these parts of Ohio and funds were low, multiple rural counties shared the services of one medical examiner. The doctor had been detained at another death site in a neighboring county, and the delay was a rare stroke of luck for us. Crime scene photographs and videos always help, but I'd always been a visual investigator. Nothing got my gut instincts going like seeing the full crime scene before the body has been removed.

Orange barrels and cones cut off access to parts of the two-lane road while Wallace Lake police officers detoured traffic through town. Sanders and I couldn't get very close to the crime scene—all sorts of emergency vehicles were parked in a large bubble around the side of the river. We parked out by the barrels and hiked in. The beautiful fall weather had brought everyone out to the river and lake, a high volume of hikers, kayakers, canoeists, and those out for a scenic drive to see the leaves changing colors. The warm afternoon sun glistened off the water's current and the canopy of trees that surrounded it. Stones of all shapes and sizes lined the river's edge, a collection of muted colors against the bluish-gray water.

And then there was the crime scene—it seemed that most humans couldn't help themselves from gawking at the sight of death. Officers had to be planted at various locations along the river to direct canoes and kayaks away from the scene. Crime scene investigators canvassed the water surrounding the land bars, inching their way downstream. They combed the area for anything out of place or any object that could be related to the crimes. There were boots in the water and divers scanning the bottom of the river. Initial photographs and videos had already been taken of the scene, and neon-yellow tented markers littered the area where the bodies had been outlined. At least this small police station was following all protocols, dotting their i's and crossing their t's.

I followed Sanders down the muddy embankment to the river's stony edge as a rubber rescue raft pushed off the land bar to come for us. Our paper-like booties made it even harder to keep hold of our footing. Cool river water lapped against my covered boots and shins. The land bars were approximately fifty feet from the shoreline, but we'd been advised the water depth was well over four feet in some places.

Captain Tom Riley pointed the tip of his canoe near us and stepped out to secure it to the land. Since the bodies had all been found in his jurisdiction, Wallace Lake County, he'd been the one to call us in. "Glad you made it," he said, giving Sanders and then me firm handshakes. Riley wore a sheriff's hat with a large bill to keep the sun off his face.

"Glad to help." I climbed into the boat.

"Any new developments since we last spoke?" Sanders asked.

Riley's strong grip on the paddle told me he wasn't a stranger to rowing. He guided us quickly through the water's strong current. "We've been fighting the gawkers like crazy, but you know how that goes."

Despite the fact that we were outdoors and odors could easily dissipate, the smell of death surrounded us. Many of the officers had white paste smeared under their noses to take the odor away. I immediately began breathing through my mouth—a lifesaving trick I'd learned early in the academy.

"Who found the bodies?" I asked.

"A local girl out kayaking the river this morning. Scared the bejesus out of the poor thing."

"I bet. We'll need to talk to her."

The two large humps of land in the middle of the river were larger than I expected, one following the other. Both had enough space for minimal equipment and a few people. Sanders stayed in the canoe to get more details from Riley while I stepped out and squatted next to the body on land. Her wide back was a sickly white, and a shock of dark hair spilled over her ears and the sides of her face. I used the tip of my pen to get a closer look at her scalp. She'd recently dyed her hair much too dark for her skin tone. Her roots, more than an inch long, were a solid iron gray. She was flabby along the back and buttocks, her naked skin white and puckered from the elements. She'd been stabbed twice between her shoulder blades. There were two wounds lower on her back, within the liver and kidney area, and it looked as though the killer pulled down once the blade was inside the body, damaging internal organs. Most who killed with a knife stabbed quick and hard and then pulled the blade directly out of the victim. This difference and the damage that came with it could indicate the victim struggled; perhaps she tried to get away, and the killer wouldn't let go of the knife.

The body couldn't have been on the land bar for more than a couple of days, but the wildlife had already found her. Chunks of the woman's flesh had been torn away, leaving behind masses that looked like raw crabmeat. The woman's face had been partially planted into the sand, saving it from the hungry animals. Outside crime scenes could always be messy, but I despised the scavenging of animals on a body. While the animals were only doing what came naturally to them, it seemed like such a violation. Not only did the victim suffer a violent and painful end, but her body was also desecrated in death in a way that sometimes made it difficult for us to catch the killer. Not one iota of fairness in this scenario.

With my gloved fingers, I followed her pale thick arms down to the hands and fingers hardened with death. The nails had been polished a bright pink, but the polish had chipped away in the elements leaving only swatches of color on each nail. No jewelry. I turned over her left hand and found the tattoo centered at the bend of her wrist. The coloring was strong; the tattoo was relatively new and hadn't had time to naturally fade. I made my way back up to the woman's face and used the shaft of the pen to pull back more of her hair. Her face was pitted and bloated with death, one eye open just enough to gaze out at me with a glazed brown iris. I looked into her open eye and thought about how someone somewhere must have loved this woman. Addict or not, she was someone's daughter, sister, cousin. She could be someone's mother or wife.

"The second body is submerged over here."

The sound of the woman's voice surprised me.

"Over here," she said.

I looked over my shoulder to see a tall woman behind me. She was on the other side of the land bar's hump. I waved and made my way over to her.

"I'm Harper Bennett. Medical examiner for these parts."

Dr. Bennett stood close to six feet and towered above my small frame. She was athletic, with the long, lean body of a beach volleyball player. She looked down at me through dark frames, her brown eyes warm and alert. "It's good to meet you, Special Agent Hansen."

I shook her hand. "Likewise."

Bennett's hand wrapped around mine. Once she let go, she tucked her dark hair behind an ear. Cut in a bob, thick, natural curls fell perfectly around her face.

"I figured you'd want to see the scene as police found it. I arrived not long before you, and I haven't moved either body. The submerged body has a leg caught on a log. Otherwise, she probably would have been carried out into the lake by the river's current. She's been lodged here approximately three days."

I squatted down at the edge of the land bar next to the woman whose body floated face up just beneath the water's surface. She looked boneless and serene in the weightlessness of the water, and she reminded me of an old painting I'd seen in one of Rowan's books. A woman had committed suicide and lay just under the water's surface inside a creek: *Ophelia*. This particular woman looked equally ethereal. Only visible up to her breasts, the long bleached hair swam about her face in a sort of halo, and I could make out a slight grin on her lips.

"Strange," I said. "The killer used two different methods to dump the bodies."

"Yes," Bennett said. "The other body was clearly placed on the land bar. There's no evidence of water exposure. No footprints, but the rain in the last few days would have washed those away."

I thumbed over to the body on the land bar. "It took some time to pose that body. This one, though," I pointed to Ophelia, "is different. The killer might have been seen so the plans were thwarted—he had to dump that victim fast, probably over the side of a bridge or boat."

"There is a bridge a few miles up the river," Bennett offered.

Anyone who dumped a body had a lot to lose. And a lot to hide. "You mentioned the recent rain. The water level is higher than normal?"

Bennett nodded. "I kayak these waters regularly. I haven't seen the levels this high in over a year."

A kayaker. That's what gave Bennett the strong, defined shoulders of a swimmer.

Bennett gave me a few moments to examine the body while it was still underneath the water. Then, she called for two techs as Sanders and Riley joined us. Bennett and the techs hoisted the submerged woman's naked body up onto the land bar, placing her faceup. Any dead body was heavy, but a bloated waterlogged body was worse. Water poured from every orifice, and the putrid odor of decay smacked all of us in the face. Bennett and a tech struggled to dislodge the victim's leg from the log. Once it came free and the woman was fully placed on the land bar, we all saw it—both her legs had been multiple meals for the local turtles, frogs, and fish.

"Jesus," Sanders said, beside me.

"Not very pretty, is it?" Bennett said. She punched the pointed end of the thermometer through the body's skin above the hip to get the liver's temperature. It was a sight that always turned my stomach. It reminded me of a cook checking a turkey's temperature before a Thanksgiving dinner. "This river is full of snapping turtles. They might be keeping their distance from us now, but the turtles are rabid feeders at night."

"Must have been a smorgasbord for those critters," Sanders said. His hands were restless, his fingers tapping against his thumb. He was jonesing for a cigarette, but he couldn't smoke at the crime scene and risk contaminating it.

The victim's skin looked rubbery, whale-white, and pruned from the water. It would be difficult at best to get any reliable prints from her bloated fingers.

Bennett examined the stab wound to the neck. "She bled out through the carotid artery. That's about all I can tell you at this point. I'll run toxicology today."

"What about all these scrapes and bruises?" I pointed to the contusions on her knees and thighs.

"Most likely postmortem," Bennett said. "Help me turn her."

I held the dead woman's shoulders and pulled her to me while Bennett pushed her from the back. "There are the same types of scrapes on her shoulder blades. I need to run tests, but I'd guess these are from the killer pulling or dragging the dead body across cement or blacktop."

Sanders and I followed Bennett to the other body and watched while techs turned her over. The woman's face had been preserved in the earth while the rest of her body had deteriorated considerably. Bennett examined the head and opened the woman's mouth. "Meth teeth. She also has the pitting in her cheeks and jawline. No active sores, although some of her arm veins have been blown. Looks like she hasn't used for a while."

"Possibly new to recovery," I said.

An officer in a wet suit and snorkel gear stood up a few feet from us in the shallow water. "Baggie!"

Water ran in rivulets down the officer's black bodysuit, her strong leg muscles rippling against the fabric. Riley met her at the edge of the land bar, and she dropped an object into the bag. He sealed it as the snorkeler pulled off the hood and mask, shaking out a mop of short blond hair. She flashed a perfect white smile.

"Detective Alison Harvey. She's lead on the case along with Sam Richardson." Riley thumbed over to an older man scouring the shoreline with a trash pick. "Richardson's a whiz on the computer. He'll help locate anything you need in the databases or online."

Harvey pumped my hand a little too hard and long, and I guessed this handsome woman to be in her late twenties. She spilled over with enthusiasm while rattling on about the Willow's Ridge case. I tried to smile. It was always hard for me when people brought up what happened in Willow's Ridge. The case had been very public with an onslaught of media once reporters smelled the possibilities it had for sales, but the case had been deeply personal for me. I didn't like to be reminded of it.

Sanders chuckled. He loved that his lead agent had such a following, but I also sensed it was more than that. Comments and reactions from people like Harvey reinforced Sanders's ideas that using my painful past to solve the crimes in Willow's Ridge had been worth it.

It struck me then that Harper Bennett hadn't said a word about Willow's Ridge. Given her profession, she would have recognized my name. She might have even been involved in the autopsies and medical testing of victims who were eventually sent to the state crime labs for further investigation. Many Ohio medical examiners were called in to work the case. I admired Bennett for focusing on the case at hand and not bringing my grisly past into the present.

Working with others wasn't my strongest asset, and I still mourned the death of the last partner I was placed with, Cole Ainsley, who was killed protecting me in Willow's Ridge. No matter where this case led, I didn't want to connect with anyone on this team the way I did with Ainsley. I didn't have it in me to survive another partner's death.

When Harvey finally took a breath, I was able to get a word in edgewise. "Any leads on the tattoo?"

"Nothing so far. We ran an image search through the databases for tats on inmates and victims. We've had a lot of hits featuring similar designs but nothing identical."

All four of the victims had the identical tattoo in the same body location. My gut told me that if we could unlock the meaning of the tattoo, the rest of the case would fall into place.

CHAPTER THREE

Day One: 6:00 p.m.

Ava Washington gave me a weak smile while her mother went to the kitchen for some iced tea. The teen looked tired. Her eyes were bloodshot and puffy from tears. Ava's untouched dinner of salad and fruit sat on the kitchen table.

"I'm sorry to bother you, Ava. I know you've had a long day."

"That's okay." She tucked her bare feet underneath her, all knees in her too-short shorts. Her long hair was tied in a knot at the top of her head with chunks of blond coming loose, and it made her look much younger than fifteen.

"How long have you been kayaking?"

She shrugged. "About a year."

"You must like the water." Beside me, Harvey cleared her throat. She wasn't convinced Ava could offer us any information that wasn't given to Captain Riley earlier in the day. She was anxious to move on, but I insisted on the meeting. In the process, I'd come up against Harvey's impatience. Like a lot of rookies, Harvey thought she knew everything. Listening was not her best asset.

Ava nodded. "It always calms me down. Plus I need the workout for weightlifting."

"Ah, you lift?" I asked.

Ava's face lit up with a big smile. "I'm on the team at school. Coach Allard says I've got a good shot at the championship this year."

Judging from Ava's size, she'd be in the lightweight category. "That's exciting. I guess it wasn't too calming to see those two bodies today, though. Tell me how you found them."

Ava took a deep breath and recounted for me the story she'd probably already told twenty people.

"Was there anything covering the body on top of the land bar?"

"You mean clothes?"

I nodded. "Or leaves and sticks. Anything that made it look like someone was trying to hide the body."

"No. She was naked."

"Anything around the bodies?"

Ava shook her head.

"What about along the shore? Did you hear anything unusual in the woods?"

"No, it was just me," she said. "And them."

Ava's mother smiled and handed us all glasses of weak tea. She was dressed in clean professional clothing, but the edges were frayed from long-term use, similar to the furniture inside the trailer. She was a woman who didn't have much money but took good care of what she had.

"You must have been terrified."

Ava's eyes grew big. "Especially when I thought I might know one of them."

I set my glass down on a coaster. "Know them? What do you mean?"

Ava shrugged. "There can be a lot of drugs around here."

"You think this is related to drug use?"

Ava nodded. "It's the druggies that end up killed in the river."

"Ava," her mother cautioned.

A strange silence settled in the room as if someone had said too much or a secret might have been given away. Ava's mother's tone rang of *We don't talk about those things*. The heightened level of drug use in the Wallace Lake area, however, was no hidden detail. In fact, most people familiar with the area probably would have guessed that these crimes were drug related.

"Why did you think you might have known one of them?"

"I was wrong," Ava shook her head. "I thought it might be one of my friends' mom. But it wasn't."

"The woman on the land bar?"

"No, the one in the water."

Ava's mother grabbed her hand. "Sadie's mother? I told you to stay away from that girl!"

"Mom! Relax, okay?"

Ava's mother ignored her and turned to me. "I've warned Ava a million times. But she won't stay away from Sadie. I swear, that girl leads to nothing but trouble."

"You don't even know her!"

"Ladies, please." I used my best calming voice. "Can we focus on what happened this morning?"

Both grumbled an apology, but I could tell this wasn't the end of the argument between the mother and daughter.

"Ava, that woman was submerged in the water. How did you see her face?"

She stared at me incredulously. "I didn't."

"Then how did you know it could be Sadie's mom?"

"I saw her hand and part of her arm. Sadie's mom has long nails and she paints them wild colors. The dead woman's nails were bitten down below her fingertips."

Ava's mother scoffed. "How do you know what Sadie's mom's fingernails look like?"

Ava ignored her mother.

It seemed odd that the teen could recognize her friend's mother by her fingernails. Then I thought of something. "I just have one more question." I pulled up the picture of the victims' tattoos on my cell phone screen. "Have you seen this image before?"

Immediate recognition flashed in her eyes. It was the tattoo made her think of Sadie's mother.

"Tell me, Ava. Where have you seen this before?"

Ava's mother watched her daughter carefully.

The teen shook her head. "I haven't seen it before."

I set the cell phone down on the coffee table between us. "Ava," I said, "we need to know everything to help these victims."

"Jesus, Ava," her mother said. "If you know something, tell them."

Ava suddenly burst into tears. When her mother didn't move to comfort her, I nudged Harvey to remove the mother from the room. It was clear we weren't going to get anywhere with her hovering over her daughter's every word. Once Harvey had the mother in the kitchen and out of earshot, I moved over to sit beside Ava. She took the fresh tissue from me.

"My mom would kill me if she knew some of these things."

I made an *X* over my chest with a fingertip. "Cross my heart, Ava. I'll do my best to keep everything you say between us."

She sniffled and dried her eyes. "I saw that tattoo on Sadie's mom. Her wrist. When I saw that lady's arm in the water, I was so scared because I thought it could be Sadie's mom. I didn't want to have to tell my best friend I found her mother dead."

A shot of anxiety ran through me. Since we still hadn't identified either of the bodies Ava found, it was entirely possible one of them *could* be her friend's mother.

"Why doesn't your mother want you to see Sadie?"

"She says they are all trash." Frustration came through in her voice. "She says they will only hold me down and get me into trouble."

"You said *they all*. Whom are you referring to?"

"Sadie, her mom, and her grandmother. Sadie's dad died, and her mom is a drug addict, so she lives with her grandma. My mom went to school with Sadie's mom and says she was trash back then, too."

"What do they do that could get you into trouble?"

"I'm not sure what my mom means by that. She thinks that since Sadie's mom is a druggie and prostitute that Sadie will end up the same. She won't, but even if Sadie did, it doesn't have anything to do with me."

"Have you been in contact with Sadie today?" I asked.

"She doesn't talk to her mom much, but Sadie said someone saw her mom today at that bar where she works."

The rumor mill dissolved some of my concern about the identity of the body. The last thing this girl needed was to find that her fear was a reality. I noticed, however, she hadn't answered my question.

"What does the tattoo mean?"

Ava shrugged. "I don't know."

"But you remember seeing it on Sadie's mother."

"I saw it when she handed me something." She wiped her nose. "I thought it was cute."

"Have you ever seen this tattoo on anyone else?"

Ava shook her head. She watched me quietly while I scribbled a few notes. Then she added, "I want to help you catch this killer."

"I appreciate that, Ava. You've already helped us quite a bit. Thank you."

"I want him out of my town."

"Him?" I questioned.

"You know. The killer."

"I'm curious—what makes you think this is a male killer and not a female?"

Ava looked at me like I was the dumbest person on earth. "All the serial killers in shows and movies are guys. Women can't do that stuff."

I chuckled. Nothing like the mass media dictating the profile for a serial killer. "Fair enough, Ava."

When Harvey and I walked out of the Washingtons' trailer, though, I'd learned two valuable pieces of information. One: the tattoos weren't only located on dead women, but on living women as well. Two: Ava Washington knew a lot more than she was letting on.

The nostril-burning odor of fresh chlorine. My body sank into its watery depths and into a safety beyond measure. It had been too long since my last swim. For years, water had been my refuge from panic, the place I went in my mind when I felt the crippling seize of my breath and the uncontrollable racing of my heart. During the

Willow's Ridge case, I found out that water had been more than just the escape hatch I needed for a mental time-out; it had literally saved my life when I was fifteen. The killer had been terrified of water. Since those secrets of my past had been revealed, the role of water had changed in my life, but its purpose of safety and refuge had not.

True to his word, Sanders found a hotel for me with an indoor swimming pool near the Wallace Lake highway exchange. The block of a building was only half full of travelers who were on their way somewhere else. I appreciated Sanders's efforts. He could have set me up in the hole-in-the-wall motel near the police station and saved the Bureau fifty bucks a night.

"You need to eat and swim every day," Sanders had said once he cleared the billing at the hotel, his wallet fat with yearly school pictures of two grown children he rarely saw. "Promise me you will—every day you're here."

I nodded and patted my bag. "I have a suit, remember?"

"Good," he said tucking his wallet into his back pocket. "And consider getting some therapy when you get back to Columbus, for God's sake."

When I rolled my eyes at him like a petulant teenager, he stopped me cold in my tracks. "I'm not speaking to you as a supervisor right now, Luce, but as your friend. The body has needs and you aren't tending to them," he said. "You don't always make the best decisions for yourself. I'm only trying to help."

The problem, I wanted to tell him, was that I have never been good at accepting other people's help. I nodded anyway. It had been a long day, and I only wanted to swim.

Honestly, I was surprised that Sanders supported my long swims. Most of our team worked out in the weight room and used the track the BCI headquarters offered its employees. Because there was no pool at headquarters, I always worked out alone and was generally able to surpass most of my teammates on our yearly physical tests. Despite my physical strength and endurance, Sanders wanted me to be a part of the workouts and the team-building experience. He wanted us to *bond* over repetitions and *build community* through runs that made our thighs burn and our chests heave. I preferred to sweat alone and continually ignored those yellow notices in my box warning of the missed team workouts. Sanders never missed a chance to point out that these lone wolf moves of mine held me back and ultimately hurt my chances of promotion. Here he was, though, pushing me to swim. Perhaps he was worried I wouldn't be able to surpass my teammates on the physical tests again this year. Judging from the difficulty I was having getting back into my stroke, he could have been right.

I was also surprised that Sanders was willing to let me work the Wallace Lake case without him. He didn't hide his concerns about my mental health. Sanders, however, had many smaller cases that needed to be closed and a lot of paperwork waiting on him at headquarters. He promised to return to Wallace Lake in five days if we hadn't made sufficient progress on the case. My goal was to find the killer in less than five days, not only to save any future victims, but also because I wasn't ready to work so closely on a case with Sanders yet.

Air bubbles streamed from my nose, and the water churned past as I did a flip turn. The hotel's pool was smaller than what I was used to, and given its kidney shape, it was hard for me to calculate three miles. It didn't really matter; I'd been swimming for only an hour, and my body felt heavy and awkward. I was fighting the water rather than moving with it, struggling to carry all the cheap beers and takeout I'd consumed over the last few months. It was clear I wouldn't be able to make my usual three-mile workout, so I focused on acclimating my stroke and strengthening my kick.

Earlier, Harvey and I located Sadie's biological mother at a strip club near the freeway exchange. Records indicated that Sadie's grandmother did, indeed, take custody of her when she was eight; Sadie's mother, Wilma Henderson, did not contest the proceedings and declared herself as drug and alcohol dependent. Henderson also listed her place of employment as Gary's Girls at the time of the custody hearing. Gary's Girls, I found, was a local bar known for prostitution and a favorite of many lonely long-haul truckers on the Midwest interstate. To entice clientele, the owner, Gary, offered free overnight parking for rigs in his lot along with abundant showers and laundry facilities. According to the local PD, Gary's Girls was standing room only most weekend nights, and with its 24/7 open door policy, lonely long-haul truckers rolled in and out at all hours during the week.

Detective Richardson lived up to his stellar reputation with the search engines and databases. It only took him a few minutes to pull up police records and mug shots for Wilma Henderson along with court documents and leases associated with her. Sadie's mom had a lengthy record of drug and prostitution charges. She was what we call in law enforcement a Frequent Flyer—an individual who commits nonviolent crimes regularly. They serve their short sentences, usually no longer than eighteen months, and end up back in jail on similar charges within a year or so. Frequent Flyers like Henderson jack up the country's recidivism rates and drive law enforcement crazy. Whether it is due to lack of familial support, poverty, or addiction, these individuals struggle to figure out how to make it on the outside for long. Sometimes the entire process for law enforcement feels a whole lot like the plight of Sisyphus, the poor guy who was charged with pushing the boulder up the hill only for it to roll back down again, eternally.

I wanted to interview Sadie, but Harvey convinced me we needed to start with the woman who had a matching tattoo with our victims. I was interested in both the girl and the mother that Ava's mom deemed a bad influence. Sadie could wait, though, at least for the time being.

Ava told me she'd been terrified that one of the bodies could have been Wilma Henderson. Once I saw Henderson's most recent mug shot, I understood why. She physically resembled the type of women who'd been found murdered along the Powell River in the last eleven months in every way. I imagined Henderson would be scared of becoming the target of a killer, just like any other woman in this area matching the description. I was wrong.

Henderson wanted nothing to do with Harvey and me. We waited almost an hour to speak with her while she worked the crowd onstage. I nursed a soda at the bar while Harvey weaved through the tables to the bathroom. Songs from Prince's *1999* boomed from the stage, and I was willing to bet Henderson spent her early thirties hanging on Prince's every song and interview. Her dance moves were straight out of a Prince music video circa 1980.

I settled onto my bar stool and watched the attractive bartender mix drinks. The ponytail at the crown of her head gave the woman a punkish eighties look. She had a smile that lit up her entire face. She caught me looking and gave a quick wink as she made her way over to me.

"I'm Rhonda. What can I get you?"

"Hi, Rhonda. I'm here to see your boss, not for a drink."

She shrugged and went back to her mixing beside us. "Suit yourself." It was only when she turned to walk away that I saw the large scar running up the side of her neck from her shoulder area.

The older man beside me nudged my arm. "She's not bad, huh?"

I nodded then asked, "Rhonda or the dancer?"

He laughed. "Both."

"Are you local or just passing through?"

"Local. Been in Wallace Lake, Ohio, my whole life." He nodded to Henderson on the stage. "She's local, too. I like that Gary uses our own girls."

This man obviously spent a good deal of his time hanging out at the bar and with prostitutes. Morally, he might not be upstanding, but I could tell he wanted to talk. "Do you know her?"

"Who, Wilma? Sure. She was a few years behind me in school. We socialized together after I graduated."

I offered my hand. "I'm Luce Hansen."

"Albert Finley." His cracked, worn hand pumped mine. I took him for a woodworker, possibly a retired craftsman. His hands read of the years of hard labor and nicks from tools. "You passing through?"

I flipped my jacket open to reveal my badge. "I'm in the area to work the recent crimes."

Albert leaned back on his stool, and his eyes grew wide. "Those poor girls. What an absolute shame." He shook his head. "You know those drugs. They get into the system, and you can't live without them."

"You think it was drug related."

"Don't you?"

I shrugged. "We're looking into it."

His hand wrapped around the beer in front of him. The sight of the near-full mug made my mouth water, but I'd made a promise to myself not to drink while in the field.

"Do you think it could be someone around here killing these girls?" he asked.

"Could be."

Albert's face showed visible signs of distress at my answer. "Oh, I hope you're wrong about that. I'm not sure our little town could take that."

"Have you seen anything out of the ordinary this past year? People or events that you don't normally see?"

Albert shook his head. "We sometimes get the weird out here, you know? But nothing weirder than usual."

Harvey made her way back to my side. "Only a few minutes left in her set," she said. "Gary wants to see us."

"The owner himself," Albert marveled.

"Good to meet you, Albert." I slipped him my card, and while I was at it, I handed one to Rhonda, the bartender. She'd heard every word of our conversation, though she was good about hiding her eavesdropping. "Let me know if you think of or see anything out of the ordinary."

I followed Harvey to a side door marked *Employees Only* where a man waited for us. We followed him down a long musty hallway to an open dressing room for the girls.

Gary turned to talk to us over his shoulder. "I want you to know my club has nothing to do with the murders. I run an up-and-up business. Nothing shady about it."

Gary surprised me with his youth and fashion sense. I expected an older man in his late sixties, sleazy as all get-out with a comb-over and a polyester suit. This Gary was far from that in his Gucci shoes and hundred-dollar haircut. "We are looking into every angle of the case," I told him. "We appreciate your cooperation, and we will keep our presence here quiet as long as you do so. We'll need to talk to all the women who work here."

His shoulders relaxed when he realized we weren't there to shake the place up. He led us to Wilma Henderson's area, the room strewn with bikinis and brightly colored feathers. "Anything to help—we all want this guy behind bars," he said. "It's hard, knowing someone is out there targeting women, you know?"

I nodded and handed him my card. "How long have you owned the club?"

Gary smiled, and his tanned skin showed off his perfect white teeth. "I bought the place from my uncle. He was the original Gary, and the one who ran the finances into the ground."

Henderson exploded into the dressing room from the stage breathing heavily and sweating profusely. Overweight and soft around the middle, she hid it well with boas wrapped around her torso and a long rope of beads that settled between her heavy breasts. She stomped through the dressing area and groaned when she saw us waiting for her. She threw herself on the bar stool in front of a mirror.

Gary pulled over two stools from a neighboring station. "Give these officers your full cooperation, Wilma. Don't let me hear any different."

She grumbled something in response and leaned into the mirror until Gary left us, dabbing her sweat-filled brow with a dirty towel.

"I don't know what you all think I know," she said, licking the tip of her pinkie and smudging away black streaks from the wrinkles around her eyes as she touched up her eyeliner. "I don't have time for this." She crossed one leg over the other, and her miniskirt revealed the loose skin of her thighs. I could see the remnants of track marks on her legs, telling me that her arm veins were most likely blown.

"Make it quick," she barked.

I pulled up the tattoo image on my phone and held it out. "We've been told you have a similar tattoo."

The image stopped her a second, and then she tossed the eyeliner down. "You were told wrong."

"Was I?" A thick red bandana had been wound around Wilma's left wrist. Ava's call to Sadie had obviously done more than confirm Wilma Henderson's life; it tipped her off that we'd be coming, and the tattoo would be questioned. Sadie's mother might have abandoned her daughter, but that didn't mean the teen wouldn't do whatever she could to protect her mother.

"I've never seen that before." She looked away from the photograph and stared defiantly at me.

"You mind taking off the bandana?" Harvey pointed to Wilma Henderson's wrist.

"Not today, darlin'." Her words slurred against a chipped front tooth.

Harvey reached for her wallet and spread it wide. Henderson's hand closed over the wallet. "Girl, I'm more than you can afford."

"I'm sure," I said, and tried another angle.

Slowly, I laid a photograph of the woman from the land bar and one of the woman pulled out of the river on the dressing table. We didn't know who the women were yet—the ME had pulled fingerprints from one of the victims and Robinson had them crawling the national registries—but Bennett had confirmed that the blood tests revealed traces of antifreeze in both of the recent victims just like the two before them.

Henderson turned away from the photos of the women in autopsy. "I don't know her."

"Which one?"

"None."

I leaned in close to Henderson, so close that the edge of my shoulder nearly touched hers. "It's official, Wilma. There's a serial killer working hard in Wallace Lake."

"You don't know anything, or you wouldn't be here."

"This one"—I tapped one of the photos with my finger—"this woman looks a little like you, doesn't she?"

A visible shiver ran through Henderson, and her hand shot to her wrist where she rubbed the bandana covering the tattoo. "I said I don't know her," Henderson grumbled.

"What does the tattoo mean, Wilma?" Harvey asked. "And what does it have to do with you?"

Henderson slid off the stool and puffed up her thinning hair with some spray. "I told you, I don't know anything about nothing. I'm back onstage in four minutes."

I collected the victims' photos and tried a different route before Wilma Henderson completely shut us out. "You've heard from Sadie, then, right?"

The mention of her daughter caught Wilma off guard. She watched me close in the reflection of the mirror. "She's got nothing to do with this."

"Maybe," I said, "but it must be hard on the girl whose mom works the stage and streets every night. These killings must be making her sick with worry."

"My mom takes good care of Sadie. She's all right. Besides, she's eighteen now and not my problem."

"Sounds like you never considered Sadie your problem."

Wilma smirked.

I stood, making sure I could still see her expressions in the reflection of the mirror. "Your daughter is enmeshed in your world whether you want her to be or not, Wilma. If she wasn't, you wouldn't have gotten the call from her to hide the tattoo."

Wilma Henderson tried to ignore me as she primped one last time and then rushed toward the stage when a buzzer sounded. Loud music and the sounds of men cheering filled the entire bar.

Harvey and I watched a few minutes after Wilma Henderson took the stage. Despite her age, Henderson moved well, flipping her long bleached hair over her face and then behind her shoulders. She spilled out of her top, heavy breasts hoisted up with all the colorful fabric strings. Henderson pranced about the stage in her high heels, and I recognized a toughness in her flint-hard edges that had been formed through years of rough living. There was a loyalty to Wilma Henderson, a code of silence that I respected in some ways. Her refusal to discuss the tattoo confirmed something I'd been thinking all along—whatever the double-hearted image and its number two meant, it wasn't just a mark of loyalty among the members of the group. It wasn't something meant to give its members bragging rights, but rather it stood as a marker that told them they *belonged*. Sometimes knowing you belong to a place and to someone is all a person really needs in this lifetime. And sometimes that safety of belonging is enough to kill for.

❖

I stopped swimming in the shallow end of the pool and floated for a few minutes watching the giant light fixtures as they buzzed above me. It was after ten p.m. Exhaustion racked my body, but it felt good to be in a pool again. I let my arms and legs relax, giving myself up to the will of the water. I took a deep breath just before my face slipped under the water's membrane, and its heavy pressure encased me. My heartbeat thumped inside my ears as I sank. Down, down, down.

It was moments like these in the water when I did my best thinking, when my brain finally quieted and I felt safest. The water gave me the space to flip and turn that Rubik's Cube of a problematic case into multiple possibilities. My dad always told me it was the relaxation of the mind that allowed the pieces of a case to connect. He swore he did his best work while he jogged his daily five miles. The repetitive motion of running had done for him what swimming did for me, and I let my mind wander wherever it wanted to go. Images filtered across my closed eyelids: the women who had died, the river and its reputation for fog, the ominous Dead Man's Point where so many had died in accidents. I thought of the forest that surrounded the rivers and Wallace Lake, the coverage it provided, and the very real opportunities the forest offered to hide a body that might never be found. Over the last hundred years or so, there had been a few instances in the Wallace Lake area of a person disappearing without a trace. If these options were easily available to the killer, why choose to dump the bodies in a location they would be found by people on the water or driving the road? Three of the victims had been found on the land bars. Clearly, the killer wanted the women found and had positioned them just so, with their heads pointed toward the forest. Whoever killed them also showed the victims a sliver of modesty or respect: the victims were placed facedown in the sand hiding most of their nudity. And with the faces partially buried, the killer had saved parts of their skin from the rodents and wildlife. Such a placement indicated that the victims most likely knew who killed them. Whoever committed these crimes couldn't stand to leave the victims in the open for long. And then there was the use of antifreeze and the stab wounds to the back. All of these details led me to believe the victims trusted the killer.

I'd seen something like this before. Hadn't I?

My head burst through the surface of the water, and I gulped in a large breath of air as the sounds echoed in the empty poolroom. I nearly laughed out loud: I *did* recognize a lot of these traits.

Why hadn't I thought of Linda Clarke earlier?

CHAPTER FOUR

Day One: 11:00 p.m.

The Brazilian wandering spider is thought to be one of the most deadly spiders on earth. These little vessels of death like to hide inside banana leaves where they can plunge their venom into the unsuspecting hands that pluck its fruit. It attacks by rising up on its hind legs and lengthening its body before it lunges, sort of like a human. One of the most interesting things about this spider, though, is that one of the side effects of its venom is very painful and prolonged erections in men. Hence, Linda Clarke was dubbed by the FBI not as a black widow, but the BWS Killer, short for the Brazilian wandering spider. What can I say? Sometimes profilers' sense of humor shows and we need some way to relieve all the grizzly horror we see every day.

The Brazilian wandering spider, or the BWS case to be exact, was how Colby Sanders and I reconnected. I'd seen quite a bit of him as a child, but he hadn't been around much during my teen years once he went off to work in DC. While I was studying at the academy, Sanders showed up as a guest speaker in one of my courses. He was brought in specifically to discuss his experience on the 1976 case of Linda Clarke. Everyone had heard of Sanders—he was an Ohio native and the rock star of profiling and we'd studied his major cases in our classes. Linda Clarke had been his biggest, and he'd written a fair amount of articles and studies on the case. I watched the man who had once shared PB&J sandwiches with me for lunch take the podium looking very small under the auditorium's bright lights.

"What can I tell you about Linda Clarke?" Even then, Sanders's voice was gruff with the years of smoking menthols. He paused for the punch line. "She's one crazy bitch."

Laughter erupted, and I saw that familiar glint of a smile from Sanders.

❖

After a hot shower in the hotel room, I put on a pair of boxers and an old Stevie Nicks T-shirt. I slipped into my lucky Frye boots without bothering to lace them. I always hated walking in my bare feet in hotel rooms. No matter how clean the carpet looked, it freaked me out to think what might be lurking within those fibers. Chalk those fears up to the many joys of knowing too much about crime scene investigation.

My swim and the sudden burst of ideas had given me a much needed second wind. I'd commenced with the ritual of using a murder board to help solve the case. My father taught me the board did its best work when you weren't looking. It was all about the act of building the case and the process of pinning down each piece of evidence. My dad insisted the board should be left out in the open, in the space where you lived, because it worked subconsciously. He swore the facts of the case and the minor details seeped into your mind and somehow puzzled themselves out when you least expected it. My dad was the best investigator I'd ever met and definitely superstitious about his process. He passed those beliefs on to me as well.

I'd already pushed the desk toward the center of the room and gave myself a good three feet of wall space to use as a makeshift murder board. With four distinct columns, I tacked each of the victims' photos across the top. Along the side, I placed what I called my wild cards: information and clues that I knew would be important but hadn't quite figured out yet. I tacked in a photo of the matching tattoo and a picture of Linda Clarke from 1976 with her long flowing blond hair looking like she just stepped out of an eighties Prell commercial. Wilma Henderson had a spot there, too, along with a map and topography information about the Powell River and Wallace Lake area. Granted, this particular image-driven board was pathetically simple and lacked evidence. Like my father, though, I trusted that somehow, some way, it would all eventually come together. I felt as though I faced a gigantic jigsaw puzzle with all its tiny pieces scattered about. I sat cross-legged on the corner of my bed, my boots tucked under each knee, and considered all the long stretches of missing connections.

It was times like these I missed my father most. One of my dad's favorite parts of crime scene investigation had been the reenactment of the possible ways a murder case might have gone down. One of the worst fallouts of solving the Willow's Ridge case was that my dad's ghost had nearly vanished from my life. I'd grown used to his presence and loved the chance to bounce ideas off him just as we'd done my entire life. I couldn't make sense of why he'd left after the Willow's Ridge case. Perhaps he'd only been hanging around to help me solve the case that had been so prominent in my life. Perhaps once Marci's killer was found and killed, my dad felt at peace and was able to move on. But no matter how I tried to explain his disappearance, I couldn't picture my father *not* doing detective work—it had been such a vital part of his existence. Through his devotion to law enforcement and justice, I'd learned to love it as well.

In my father's absence, I faced my own crisis of faith. Without his help, I questioned my own abilities. Now that our partnership was broken, I'd lost confidence that I could work without him. How much of the crime solving was really me, and how much was him? The clock ticked on—this killer had already taken four lives and would certainly kill another woman. What if I couldn't stop the killer without my father's help?

I reached for a pencil and scribbled on a purple Post-it note next to Henderson's name, *Highway interchange. Gary's Girls? Long haul drivers' route?* I stared at the image of the double-hearted tattoo and listened to the ice machine down the hall gurgle out ice cubes.

Who gets identical tattoos with a group of people? I thought back to college, to the sororities and fraternities on campus who tattooed their symbol just above the ankle—I'd heard rumors back then that the body location for the tattoo changed every year, but the image remained the same. A few people from my class in the academy celebrated graduation with matching tattoos of their new badges on their shoulders. I'd also heard of friends or family members getting group tattoos to honor a promise or to remember someone who'd passed. Shared tattoos, no matter how big the group, were all about loyalty. It was that tenacious devotion to a group or a belief that bound them all together.

I'd seen strong levels of loyalty before in the One True Path ex-gay ministry. I'd been a member of Pastor Jameson's group as a teen. My father sent me to the group for help once he read my journal and realized I had feelings for other girls. Many members would have done just about anything the pastor asked, including follow him into death. And nearly all of the members would have had no problem getting a shared tattoo to declare their loyalty to the pastor and the group. At the time of the Willow's Ridge case, the Bureau had labeled some of these devout behaviors of the One True Path members as a cult. Could we be dealing here with a similar situation where one person held all the power? Maybe it was a pastor, a caretaker, a doctor, a teacher—or, given the victims' occupations, a pimp.

I searched my documents for the case studies I'd worked on in the academy. I'd snagged a one-on-one interview with Sanders about the Clarke case and had been highly envied by my classmates because of it. The truth was Sanders had only said yes because of my father. After Sanders moved on to DC, my father continued to work a few cases with him, and they shared, most importantly, good will. The interview had been part of a final project toward the end of my days in the academy and work I'd been really proud of at the time. I'd been so nervous to interview Sanders—I truly admired him and his detective work.

Finally, I found it, my recorded interview with Sanders, stuck in a file I'd titled *Spidey Sense*.

LH: Let's start at the beginning. Why were you asked to assist with the Linda Clarke case?

CS: She was apprehended in Denver, but she committed murder in six different states. It became a federal rather than a state case. They needed me to determine if there were murders committed by Clarke that they hadn't identified yet.

LH: Who was Clarke accused of killing?

CS: Her husbands. We found six, but I'm still not sure we've accounted for all of her victims. She's made comments to cellmates that indicate there could be more bodies.

LH: You personally interviewed her about the murders. What were your first impressions?

CS: She was very beautiful with long golden hair and big blue eyes. She had this pouty look about her and came across as an innocent victim. She was childlike, you know, in many ways, so people wanted to take care of her. Clarke was the last person most would expect to do something like this.

LH: She certainly had no trouble getting a husband.

CS: Not at all, which is exactly why she got the nickname of the BWS, the Brazilian wandering spider! Men couldn't seem to help themselves around her. They fell under her sexual spell, so to speak. I'm told she gets multiple letters a week in prison from lovesick followers vying for her hand in marriage. She's a temptress, no doubt about it.

LH: How was Clarke able to get away with these crimes for so long?

CS: She was incredibly methodical about her work. She poisoned her husbands slowly. Most took at least three months to die. She chose a poison that was not easily detected in the seventies. The doctors who treated her husbands wrote the deaths off as a reaction to a medication or a deadly food allergy. She was smart after the murders, as well. She completely uprooted and moved thousands of miles away. As far as we know, she never talked about the murders to anyone. Most killers can't keep their mouths shut—Clarke could. She fooled a lot of people.

LH: Until the doctor of her last victim.

CS: Yes. Thanks to this very observant ER doctor, she was finally arrested on murder charges. He recognized the odd burn pattern on the lining of Clarke's husband's esophagus and tongue.

LH: Do you believe she's mentally insane?

CS: Clarke is a sadist. She simply terrifies me. Multiple days of testimony were devoted to Clarke's insanity defense. I'm sure there were all kinds of psychologists and psychiatrists out there who would have deemed her mentally impaired.

LH: But you wouldn't?

CS: Back then, we used those big eight-track recorders to record suspects' confessions. We thought it was top-rate technology. Do you even know what that is? Anyway, I brought her in once we got that old dinosaur running. She took one look at the machine and gave me her sweetest smile. I saw a shift in her behavior. She plunged into actress mode. I could almost see the gears turning in her head. Always plotting, that one. Clarke decided with her lawyer an insanity defense would be her best bet, and she played it to the hilt that day with me.

LH: How so?

CS: Hansen, she held that syrupy sweet smile the entire time she recounted a few of the men's deaths. If you could only see her and not hear the words, you would have thought she was talking about someone she adored—her child or a beloved parent. She delighted in the pain these men suffered. She went on to explain to me that what happened with these men was only a mistake. She'd miscalculated the amount of poison in their food. The men had died much too soon. She'd hoped some of them would suffer for months. A calculated sadist, I tell you. Those men were lucky she wasn't better with her computation skills.

LH: In order to prolong the suffering, she took them to the hospital for treatment to keep them alive. Once they were on the mend, she poisoned them all over again.

CS: The medical attention for her victims gave Clarke a cover, and it also gave her the chance to begin her deadly games all over again. A black widow engages through high dramatics and will generally make her arrival into an emergency room with her victim known. Like the classic black widow, Clarke produced loud wailing sobs, dramatic prayers, and boisterous claims that her husband had been so healthy. She loved the chaos of the emergency room, the drama of touch-and-go life-saving techniques, and most of all, elaborate funerals. The black widow thrives on the knowledge that the reason people all around her suffer and grieve are because of her. It can be an enormous head-rush for most of these female serial killers, and their behavior is only fueled by sympathy and attention.

LH: Poison is considered the prime weapon for a black widow. However, Clarke's case was different.

CS: Very different in that regard. Remember, everything was about her—she wanted as much attention as she could drum up. So, rather than allowing the husband to die in a hospital or quietly at home, she broke the black widow mold by leaving her dead husbands in very public places where they would be found. One was found in his office slumped in a chair at work. Another was found in a parked car in a grocery lot. The local press picked up on some of these deaths, which delighted Clarke. She needed the bodies to be found publicly to create an exaggerated level of drama and attention.

LH: That became her MO.

CS: We haven't encountered this sort of a black widow before. Publicly planting the bodies was a new twist on this breed of a killer. Clarke also kept souvenirs, like many of the male serial killers we've investigated. She tape-recorded the sounds of some of her victims dying so that she could relive the deaths over and over.

I stopped the recording, moving the play bar back. *She needed the bodies to be found publicly to create an exaggerated level of drama and attention.*

I thought about the element of poisoning in the Wallace Lake murders. And then there was the issue of escalating violence. I found it interesting that the physical assaults and stabbings occurred from behind, which told me the killer avoided direct confrontation with the victim. But why? One element was clear: trust was involved. These female victims were comfortable enough to turn their backs on the killer.

"It's a woman," I said.

Our killer, though, was not a black widow. She broke all the molds like Linda Clarke. She killed women, not men. It was possible the killer was a lesbian; as a general rule, serial killers who are heterosexuals kill the opposite sex, while homosexuals kill the same sex. And there was something more to the location where the bodies were found. Yes, our killer dumped her prey in a place where the bodies would certainly be found—a main thoroughfare for the canoeing and kayaking community, ensuring that the victims would be found in a relatively short amount of time. Perhaps that also meant our killer was counting on us to determine these women's identities and make those findings very public through the media.

There was something more to it—a threatening element. Our killer *wanted* to invoke fear through the placement of bodies. She *wanted* the surrounding community to know she was hard at work and that no one in Wallace Lake, Ohio, was necessarily safe.

CHAPTER FIVE

Day Two: 9:30 a.m.

I waited with Dr. Harper Bennett in the Wallace Lake County morgue. Detective Alison Harvey was close to thirty minutes late for our morning briefing without so much as a text.

We lucked out—the prints Bennett took from one of the victims hit sometime before dawn. Janice Dawn Taft. Richardson pulled her arrest records and found Taft's next of kin: a grown daughter living in Dayton who would arrive in the next few hours to formally confirm the victim's identity.

"I'm sorry to take up your time," I offered Bennett and checked my cell for a message again. Even though I didn't really know Harvey, I was embarrassed and felt like I needed to make excuses for her unprofessional behavior. Partnership runs deep in law enforcement, even when you'd only just begun working together.

"It's certainly not your fault," Bennett said. "Besides, this happens sometimes with Harvey."

Bennett sat down on the other side of her state-issued metal desk after she handed me a cup of coffee. Her office was a small room adjacent to the open work area of the morgue. Like other MEs' offices I'd visited, there was a large plate glass window that served as a wall where Bennett could look out over the dead bodies. I always found these windows to be interesting, and, in a strange way, comforting. Bennett and other medical examiners served as the death keepers. They are the ones who took in a victim, generally after all sorts of untold violence has happened, and vowed to keep the body safe until it could be returned to a loved one. Medical examiners were the ones who took the time to learn every centimeter of the victim's body, to carefully record all the damage done before sending it on to people like me who worked to bring the killer to justice. Time spent with a medical examiner was like a reprieve in the chain of events for a victim. The medical examiner served as the quiet harbor after such deadly violence. Sure, the ME had to perform an autopsy, which could be violent in its own right. Afterward, though, the doctor carefully put the victim back together again, cleansing the body and hair to make it as presentable as possible to avoid further traumatizing loved ones. It was the ME who gently washed away the killer's violations and all the bloody traces left behind. And when the ME finally rolled the victim into a cooler to await its next stage, the body could finally rest in some variation of peace.

Bennett wore her oversized protective eye gear perched on top of her head like sunglasses. She reached up and tossed the clear glasses on her desk then ran her fingers through the cropped thatch of her dark curls. I found myself looking for any evidence of a commitment ring. Was there an indentation or a tan line that hadn't quite filled in yet the same way mine from Rowan hadn't?

Don't, I warned myself. *Don't go there.*

Something definitely intrigued me about this medical examiner, who was beautiful in a quiet way. There was absolutely nothing artificial about Harper Bennett—no makeup, no polished nails, and no jewelry. She had powerful features with sharp cheekbones and a squared-off jawline. Her shoulders were muscular, athletic-strong— the perfect combination for this woman who struck me as fresh and clean…so much the girl next door.

I tried again: *Don't even notice her, Luce.*

A wave of guilt pinged my heart. Not all that long ago, I'd been so wrapped up in Rowan I barely would have noticed this woman. That was then, though, and Dr. Bennett was someone I knew I wouldn't be able to easily forget.

Bennett nodded to the newspaper. "Have you seen this yet? They released the victim sketches."

Bennett pushed the newspaper toward me. "The story ran in all the papers—Wallace Lake, Columbus, Dayton, Cincinnati—all the southern Ohio towns. I heard the story and the sketches made it north. It's also in the Akron and Cleveland papers."

Murder was big news in the heartland, and the paper took full advantage of the multiple victims. Its coverage of the case took up three-fourths of the front page, complete with a timeline of when and where each of the four bodies had been found. The first two victims were named, complete with the artist's rendition of their faces, and a brief description of their lives followed. The article explained that a tip line had been set up for information and that the BCI had been called in to assist in the case. The paper featured a photograph of Sanders and me standing on the riverbank waiting for Captain Tom Riley to reach us in his canoe. The camera lens captured the features of my face all the way down to those lines I hated so much that crinkled around my eyes. I was already an outsider in this small community, and this photograph would give the locals more reason to push me out. There would be no hiding in plain sight now.

"I might as well have posed for a head shot with them, huh?"

Bennett chuckled. "Not a bad picture, though, and you never know what's going to help with these kinds of crazy cases."

"Let's hope the press drums up some information on a possible suspect." I pushed the paper back across the desk to Bennett and stood to stretch my legs.

I'd only had one experience with a high-profile case. Willow's Ridge broke me in to the chaos that sometimes followed the media. I always wanted to fly under the radar when I worked a case, to move about a town without recognition and surprise possible suspects with the BCI's involvement. Instead, the press had the power to blow my cover and gave suspects information that helped them avoid me. There could be a flip side to the media involvement, though. The press had the ability to reach the entire community with safety information and to alert them as to what they should be on the lookout for. The press also had the uncanny ability to make suspects, who always seemed to follow their crimes in the press, believe we had more information than we really did and, in some cases, lure them into speaking with us or coming forward. When done right, the press and law enforcement should work together to solve cases, but like most relationships, ours was rarely perfect and most often tense.

I paced inside Bennett's office, a space that was simple, clean, and free of any clutter. Large metal bookcases leaned against the far wall, and the books seemed to be organized by subject. There were only two framed items in the small room: a portrait of a woman I recognized from somewhere and the quote: *Arrange whatever pieces come your way—VW*. I recognized the woman the way I vaguely recognize photographs of people featured on the History Channel or in textbooks.

"Do you know her?"

"Hmm?" I asked. Bennett watched me closely. "I think I recognize her."

Bennett chuckled. "Virginia Woolf. The woman and the quote."

"The writer, right?" I felt stupid—I'd heard of Woolf before in school, but she wasn't someone I paid much attention to.

Bennett laughed. "She's my writing idol."

"You write?"

Bennett nodded. "Mostly medical science articles, but I dabble in writing some poetry and stories, too."

I've always had a soft spot for artists. Always. Something told me this amazing woman did a lot more than dabble in writing. Bennett seemed like the type of woman who excelled at everything she tried.

I noticed the oversized glass jar, chock full of colorful stones. Some of the rocks had dates written on the sides along with initials. Beside the jar sat a collection of medals and trophies.

"And these awards? Are they for rowing?"

Bennett nodded. "I competed for a few years, mostly in college. Now I kayak the Powell River and Wallace Lake. Do you kayak?"

A poet *and* a rower?

"I've never kayaked," I said, "but I'd like to learn."

I did the only thing I could think to do while in the company of a beautiful woman: I turned the conversation back to work. I fumbled with the transition, though, and tripped over my words while she intently watched me. What was Bennett thinking, anyway? It was hard to tell.

"What about the items found at the crime scene?" I asked. "Is there anything for us to go on?"

Bennett leaned against the corner of the desk, crossed her arms, and pulled her lab coat tightly around her. Her voice reverted back to its careful, professional tone. "We collected about ninety items yesterday—most of it debris and trash. There's a lot of traffic on that river with canoeing and kayaking into Wallace Lake, so it's difficult to know what could have been left by the killer or just a kayaker out for a pleasurable day." She sifted through the envelopes on top of her desk. "We did find one item that I'm not sure what to make of."

I pulled two gloves from a box on Bennett's desk. She tipped the open envelope into my open palm. A worn piece of leather fell out like a long worm. The strip, about a fourth of an inch wide, had a tie at one end as if it had been used for a bracelet or anklet. The leather had been torn open beside the tie. A thin patch in the center suggested there might have been a pendant worn on the leather strip.

"Where was it found?" I asked.

"Lodged into the muck at the bottom of the river close to the land bars. I tried it on our two latest victims for size, but it doesn't fit. If it's a bracelet, it's small. Made to fit a child or a small woman."

I rubbed the soft leather between my fingers. It reminded me of something a teenager would wear, layering multiple bracelets along her wrist. I let the worn leather strip fall back into the evidence envelope.

After a quick double knock on the heavy metal door, Harvey stepped in and dropped into an office chair. "Sorry I'm late."

Harvey wore the same clothes as yesterday, a sure sign the detective hadn't gone home last night after our interview with Wilma Henderson at Gary's Girls. Harvey gave me one of her charming smiles and finger-tousled her short, wet hair to help it air dry.

"We've been waiting for you. We've identified one of the victims from yesterday." There was an icy chill in Bennett's tone.

Harvey nodded. "I got the message."

I realized the situation as soon as I caught the edge of an annoyed smile from Harvey. These two women had a history.

Harvey used her hands to smooth out her wrinkled khaki pants along her thighs. She must have tumbled hard with a woman last night. Harvey was young in her career, and while she might have been hungry to climb the food chain of command, she hadn't figured out yet how to balance her social life with her work life. She obviously hadn't learned the Golden Rule yet: don't sleep with your co-workers unless you want to marry them.

"Well," Harvey said, matching Bennett's tone, "let's get to it."

"Sure, boss," Bennett said with a roll of her eyes. She stood, put her hands inside her lab coat pockets, and led us out to the white mound on the gurney.

Always the coldest room in any law enforcement compound, the morgue felt like a refrigerator, and I wrapped my arms across my chest for warmth.

Bennett pulled back the sheet that ghosted the body. The morgue smelled of a strange mix of freshly brewed coffee, the bitter sting of antiseptic from the sterilization procedures, and the ever-present reality of death. Both Harvey and I leaned in to get a better look at the dead woman.

"Janice Dawn Taft, sixty-one years of age," Bennett said. "Her last known address was in Akron over seven years ago. She's served time for drug possession and sales. There are multiple arrests for prostitution."

"She's got a long rap sheet with minor convictions," I said. Taft probably spent no more than a few months to a year inside at one time.

Bennett handed me the file with Taft's latest mug shot from a prostitution arrest in Dayton. The woman in the photograph and on the table had the look of what I called *rode hard*. Taft's face was pocked and wrinkled, causing her to look much older than her early sixties. She'd lived her life on a rough edge, and it had taken a harsh toll on Taft's features and body.

"What exactly killed her?" I asked. The large Y incision that Bennett used to expose the woman's sternum screamed out to me. I hated to see the work of an autopsy—I understood the process was invaluable in the search for evidence, but the act itself seemed so horrific, particularly for someone who had already been through a violent death. I always had to remind myself that this violence was measured and done with a hand in search of justice. And it was always my wish that the ME's autopsy was the last violation of the body a victim would ever suffer.

Bennett's gloved hands turned Taft's head to the right, exposing the large neck wound. "Here," she said. "The knife blade nicked the carotid artery. The pressure of the blood dumping out of the carotid ripped the artery open farther. She bled out in only a matter of a few minutes."

Bennett rolled Taft's head back to the neutral position on the small headrest. Taft's body had stiffened with rigor mortis, so it took some strength on Bennett's part. She did so with an observable gentleness, and I admired her respect for the victim.

"Along with the neck wound, Taft also has injuries to her legs and arms consistent with forced movement before death. She was most likely unconscious, and the killer dragged her to a specific location." Bennett pulled back the sheet to reveal Taft's legs from the thighs down.

I let my gloved hands float just above Taft's legs and moved down toward her feet. I called this maneuver reading a victim, a technique I'd learned in the academy that helped me to memorize the wound locations. I moved around the table and knelt near Taft's feet. The skin of both of her heels had been torn away, the right scraped much deeper than the left. The scrapes continued up along her Achilles tendon. Someone had gripped the victim under her arms and pulled her across cement or blacktop.

"She was still alive at the time?" Harvey asked. "These wounds didn't happen after she died?"

Bennett shook her head. "The wounds had time to begin to scab. She was actively bleeding at the time she was injured, which indicates Taft was alive."

"Did you find any bruising under the arms?" I asked.

Bennett nodded.

I stepped closer to Bennett to examine where she pointed—Taft's knees.

"She was also dragged facedown. See here?" Bennett pointed out the scrapes to the victim's chin and the tops of her shoulders.

"She must have given the killer one hell of a fight," I said.

"I'd say so," Bennett said. "All indications are that she fought. She knew the next step would be death."

"So the forced movement, as you call it, proves Taft didn't die at the river. She was moved there," I said.

Bennett confirmed that the river was only the place for the body drop. "We found very little blood on the land bars. Water could have carried some of it away, but if she was alive, Taft would have bled significantly into the sand. We didn't find that."

"Or any disruption to the land. Footprints. Knee prints. That kind of thing," Harvey added.

"What about toxicology?" I asked.

"Most interesting," Bennett said, "there is a connection between the victims in the toxicology. A loose one, albeit, but a connection."

Bennett had all of my attention. We needed any connection we could get.

"Both Taft and the other victims' blood work showed they were all clean at their time of death. Their bodies, though, show signs of long-term drug abuse in the past, and sobriety didn't come all that long ago for them." She guided us up to look at Taft's face. She pointed out the pockmarks I'd noticed earlier. "Look at the distinct pitting in her cheeks and around the mouth. These are consistent with meth abuse." Bennett pulled the victim's mouth open to expose what few teeth Taft had left. "Do you see these small red sores along the inside of the cheeks and the gum line? The damage is consistent with meth abuse. Some of her arm and leg veins are partially healed and were blown most likely from multiple punctures for intravenous drug use."

"The other body shows a change in the killer's MO," I said, noting the evidence of the killer escalating. "The first two were killed with poison before dumping. What about the body found in the water?"

"I ran a hair analysis on both of them found yesterday, and it shows that they had been drug-free for, at best, two months. Heroin doesn't remain in the body for long. But there is evidence on each of the bodies of damage typical to the long-term abuse of heroin. I'd say it was a coincidence, but I don't believe in them."

I couldn't help but to smile at Bennett. A woman after my own heart—I didn't believe in coincidences, either.

"These women were probably only a few weeks into recovery," I said. "Unless they were in some sort of ninety-day program that the state paid for, they were probably living with a relative or friend and doing an outpatient recovery group."

"Or a twelve-step program," Harvey said. "The meetings in this area are well attended and very popular. Even if these women were in an outpatient program, most require twelve-step meetings as part of recovery."

"Let's dig into the arrest records of those in the county dealing heroin and meth. If these women were long-term customers, their sudden sobriety isn't in a dealer's best interest. I doubt they had regular transportation, so their buys were most likely local." I looked at Harvey. "The twelve-step meetings will be a good start," I said. "My guess is you'll have better luck with this than I will, Harvey. You're a local, and people will recognize you from around town."

"Possibly, but it's a catch-22. Word spreads very fast around here, particularly about who's a cop and who isn't, who to trust and who to avoid." Harvey shrugged. "Besides, most of Ohio is infested with that shit."

Harvey was right—Wallace Lake County was notorious for its heroin addiction and meth cooking arrests. Out in these cornfields and the beautiful Midwestern scenery, there were scores of people of all ages fighting against the pipe and smoking themselves silly on Saturday night only to crawl into church on Sunday morning. The epidemic touched all in the area in some way or another, and most weren't willing to acknowledge the problem let alone talk about it.

The dealer angle could be a long shot for us. Dealing meth and heroin didn't come close to the experience of dealing cocaine. The dealers made money, sure, but not nearly as much as those who sold other hard drugs. Losing a longtime customer to sobriety might hurt a dealer's finances, but would he really be willing to kill over this loss? It didn't seem likely.

And then there was the fact that all of these women were from somewhere else. Perhaps they'd received a kinder reception into the Wallace Lake community than most, particularly if they were here for the drug trade. But I grew up in a small Ohio town and knew that outsiders aren't easily trusted, no matter what their backstories might be. Drugs, in particular meth and heroin, might be what linked these female victims together, but my gut told me there was something else going on, something much bigger and worth killing for. A secret, perhaps, or a dark truth that rooted itself into the very fabric of the town. I've learned that given enough time, the earth will reclaim everything as its own—blood and bones and, most of all, secrets.

❖

Mothers and daughters—I never understood the tight bond. My own mother left when I was two to become a famous actress in Hollywood. As far as I knew, she never became an actress, let alone famous. Once she drove out of our driveway and disappeared into the horizon, I never saw or heard from her again. My father morphed into a version of both parents, a job he devoted himself to with more determination than he gave to law enforcement. No matter how much I loved him, though, no matter how often he was there when I needed him, there were times when a girl simply needed her mother. No matter how hard he tried, he could never be the mother I sometimes craved. I sometimes wondered whether or not I would accept my mother if she suddenly reappeared in my life. Would I excuse her behavior and welcome her into my home? Or would I turn my back as if I'd never met my mother the same way she'd forsaken me so many years ago?

As a detective, I have regularly seen a strong bond between a mother and a daughter. No matter what might have happened between the two or what sort of abuse a mother might have doled out to her daughter, it was rare for one to turn on the other with law enforcement. It was even more uncommon for a mother or a daughter to completely cut off all emotions regarding the other, no matter what the past might have held in their relationship. Jill Chamberlain and her deceased mother were no different. As Jill waited to see the body and identify Janice Dawn Taft, I understood that she must have been fighting against a lifetime of emotions and betrayals from a mother she couldn't help but love.

Harvey, Jill, and I stood inside the morgue's small viewing chamber. The stark white walls and the bright overhead lighting of the morgue revealed Jill's tension. Her lips were pursed tight, and the hollowness of her cheeks accentuated the dark circles under her eyes as if she hadn't gotten a full night's sleep in weeks. Her dyed blond hair was thinning, which made her look older than her years. She clasped her hands tight in front of her soft belly as if this position somehow held her together.

I put my arm around Jill's shoulders and gave her a squeeze. "It's all right," I told her.

Tears welled in her eyes as she leaned into me. Her voice cracked when she said, "I'm not sure I can do this."

Harvey handed Jill tissues as I kept my arm around her, holding her tight. "Think of this as a way to honor your mother's life, a way to give her some much needed peace."

After a few moments of anxious tears, Jill finally wiped her eyes and blew her nose.

"You *can* do this," I said.

Jill responded with a half-hearted smile.

My cell vibrated against my hip. I ignored it. "You ready?" I asked.

Jill finally nodded.

"Your mother will look a little different under these bright lights. The doctor has brushed her hair away from her face, and you may see what looks like bruising around her cheekbones and eyes. It's a normal part of the body's death process."

Jill nodded and stared hard at a white curtain that covered the plate-glass window.

"Ready," I called out to Bennett, who stood on the other side of the window and heard everything in the viewing room. Slowly, she pulled back the heavy fabric and revealed Taft's body. A white sheet covered Taft up to her breasts. Jill took in a sharp breath of air—the first sight of a loved one deceased on a gurney almost always caused that reaction. No matter how many attempts the ME and staff took to make the body and face look presentable, there was almost always initial alarm at first sight. It took a few moments for the shock to wear off before recognition set in.

Jill finally let go of her breath. "It's Mom."

"You're sure?" Harvey asked.

"Yes." Tears welled in her eyes and spilled over onto her cheeks. "It's her."

I signaled for Bennett to close the curtain.

Three of the four victims had now been formally identified.

My cell vibrated again on my hip. This time, I pulled it from my belt and lit the screen. I almost lost my footing when I noticed the sender's name.

Rowan.

The first text read, *We need to talk,* followed by another that said, *When can we meet?*

It had been months since Rowan and I had spoken. Now, suddenly, Rowan was wedging herself into my life as though she still belonged there, as though she'd never left.

❖

Harvey handed Jill a steaming cup of coffee and shut the door behind her. We sat around the conference room table with an unused tissue box between us. Jill wrapped her hands around the Styrofoam coffee cup and tried to give us a smile. She looked as though she'd aged another year since I'd met her.

"I didn't know my mother well, you know?" She gave a laugh and dried her eyes with the edges of her sleeve. "Not at all, really. But she was my mother."

"It's quite a shock," I said, opening the fresh box of tissues for Jill. "No one expects something like this to happen to a parent."

Jill took a few tissues from me and kneaded them in her lap. "Can I ask? I mean…it's all over the news. Was my mom one of the victims of that serial killer?"

Jill paused for my response. The questions from loved ones were always the hardest part for me, particularly when we hadn't yet closed the case. Harvey's rookie status allowed her to simply observe the situation. I was the one who had to find the perfect mixture of information to give the family some level of peace without giving away anything that might compromise the ongoing investigation. Later, once the case closed, I'd meet with all the families of the victims and answer more of their questions. It was always a fine line to walk between telling the family too many details, which could cause distress, and leaving their questions unanswered.

"We don't know very much yet, Jill, but it seems likely. Your mother's death fits the pattern of the murders we are attributing to a serial killer, and she was found in a similar location as the other women."

My words confirmed Jill's worst fear. "Do you know who the killer is?"

"We are working hard on that, I promise you."

"I heard that a kayaker found my mother with another body on the river. How long were they out there? The thought of my mom dumped along the river like trash..." Her voice caught. "She didn't deserve that."

"No one deserves that." I reached for her arm. "The medical examiner thinks that the kayaker found your mother only a few days after her death."

Jill took a noticeable breath and seemed relieved.

"When did you last see your mother?"

"She was arrested in Dayton a few months ago, and she called me. I paid the bail but refused to pick her up from the jail, told her I was changing my phone number. I just wanted her gone."

Fresh tears began with Jill's admission that she wanted her mother gone. She was struggling with the same mixed feelings as so many others who love addicts: they want to support their loved one and believe all the promises that this will be the very last time, and they'll finally get clean. A person can only take so many broken promises, so many empty lies, and so many gifts of money before that reservoir runs dry. Loved ones of addicts faced a constant emotional struggle between loyalty to the addict and the tough love so many addicts needed to finally kick their habits. Jill made a common mistake; she'd paid her mother's bail because Jill didn't want her mother to suffer. The sad reality, though, was that jails provided a place where active addicts, like Jill's mother, could sometimes find protection from their worst enemy: themselves.

"I'm so surprised by her death because Mom told me she was doing better. I was thinking about that phone call on my drive here today."

"Better?" I asked.

"She called me out of the blue about two weeks ago. I picked up the cell and there she was. She said she was calling me from a bar in Wallace Lake."

"How did she get your number?"

Jill sighed. "I never changed it. I guess somewhere deep inside, I hoped she'd call me one day." Tears seeped from the corners of Jill's eyes, and I handed her a fresh tissue.

"Do you think she knew?"

"Knew what?" I asked.

"That I never really gave up on her. That I always had hope she'd get clean no matter what happened."

I nodded. "I think she did, Jill. From what I can see, she never gave up trying to get better. And she always remembered you by staying in touch."

Harvey interrupted us, clearly impatient with my coddling. She hadn't learned yet that you can get so much more information out of a person if you took the time to get to know them. "I'm sorry, but what did your mother say? When she called?"

"I assumed Mom called for money. That's what she always wanted, you know? Not this time. She said she was in recovery and wanted to tell me how sorry she was for being a bad mom. I was making dinner for my own daughter, and I didn't know what to say."

Harvey and I shared a knowing look. *Making amends*. Janice Taft had been following the twelve-step recovery program by acknowledging her wrongdoings and taking responsibility. The program suggested no one take this step until they had at least a few solid months of sobriety under their belt, but many attempted it much too early. It was a difficult step that called for recovering addicts to use a brutal honesty that didn't always have a happy, sober ending.

"Did she tell you where she was doing her recovery?" I asked.

"She mentioned a group of some kind. She said she was working with other women on her recovery and living with them. She never tells me much, you know?"

Typical behavior of an addict: telling loved ones only enough to stop their questions. I wondered if this might also indicate that Janice Taft's recovery was paid for through a donation or scholarship. Sometimes recovery centers had large donations to cover patients who couldn't pay for recovery themselves or donors who covered the costs of particular patients for whatever reason. It was possible Janice kept the location of her recovery a secret in order to protect some sort of an agreement she'd made.

"Do you recognize this tattoo?" I showed Jill the image on my cell phone. "We found it tattooed on the inside of her left wrist."

Jill shook her head. "I've never known my mom to have a tattoo."

I nodded to Harvey who then placed photographs of the other three victims on the table. "Do you recognize any of these women?" she asked. "Anyone look familiar to you at all?"

Jill leaned forward. Her fingertip caught the edge of one photograph and pulled it closer. "Are these the other women in the river?"

I nodded.

She examined each closely. "They could all be my mother."

"There are many similarities."

Finally, Jill shook her head. "I'm sorry. I don't recognize them."

As we wrapped up the questioning, I asked, "Do you know if your mom spent time with any long-haul truck drivers?"

"My dad was a trucker, but I don't know anyone else in her life that was. Then again, I didn't know anyone in my mom's life. She had a lot of secrets."

We closed up the interview with condolences and cell numbers where Jill could reach us. Captain Riley stood waiting for us in the main lobby of the police station. He handed Jill a psychologist's business card. "I know these situations can be incredibly painful. Mike's a friend of mine over in Dayton. He'd be happy to help anytime."

Jill took the card, nodded, and then pushed through the glass doors.

Riley waited until Jill had made it down the front steps of the building, then asked, "Any news?"

"We expected most of it. She did get a call from her mother, from the Wallace Lake area, claiming she was in recovery," I said.

"As is half the county. Any connection with the tattoo?"

"Not yet," I said.

Before Riley could say another word, Harvey interjected. "There might be a connection with the long-haul truckers."

"The daughter said that?"

Harvey backpedaled at Riley's question. "Not exactly. The victim's ex was a long-haul driver, so perhaps she still hung in those circles. We are located on a major thoroughfare, and the murders could be on a trucker's normal route. Easy in, easy out."

"We've examined that theory, Harvey. Officers have canvassed the lots around Gary's Girls and questioned truckers. We can't devote any more manpower until you bring me something new."

I bit back a snicker. Harvey was willing to do about anything to be acknowledged by the captain. She was full of impulsivity, and those types of acts usually came from insecure officers who weren't always loyal team players. This was exactly why I preferred to work alone. I couldn't fault Harvey for her hunger to climb the food chain of command in our business—I was guilty of that as well. But there were other ways to impress a superior, such as finding the killer. And Harvey was in my way.

"Well, then," Riley said to Harvey, "you have a day ahead of you looking into the area's twelve-step meetings. Other than the hospital, we don't have any treatment centers in the area, but look into churches and other places where people might go for help with addiction."

Before Harvey could say anything to me, I headed for the doors out of the building. "I'll regroup with you later," I called to her over my shoulder.

After I pushed through the front doors and made my way down the cement stairs, Harvey called out to me. "Hansen? Where are you going?"

I made it into the parking lot before Harvey called to me again. I needed to get far away from her. I felt that familiar surge of emotion rise inside me—some of my doctors had called them panic attacks, but I always thought of it as the moments when my bullshit meter jammed past overload. It had been difficult enough to navigate an interview with a person who'd lost a loved one to a serial killer with an impatient rookie in the room, without the added intrusion of the demanding texts to meet from Rowan. I needed to get to a space where I could clear my head and focus on what mattered most—solving the case before anyone else became a victim.

I fumbled with the door to my truck and fell into my seat as the familiar swell of water rose around me. Water, my safe space, even if only in my mind. It was the quiet of the water and its heaviness that drew me in time and again.

Sinking deeper, air bubbles streamed from my nose in the crystal blue water of my imagination. Deeper, where everything was cooler and time felt as though it ceased. I sunk like a rock until I finally settled on the sandy bottom, my legs and arms outstretched floating about me.

Breathe in.

Breathe out.

Breathe in.

I needed my father. I needed his ghost to appear and help me navigate these unfamiliar waters of the case when I had so very little to go on. Where had he gone, and how the hell could I get him to come back?

CHAPTER SIX

Day Two: 2:00 p.m.

The Powell River glimmered long and wide in the late afternoon sun. The current flowed downstream at a steady pace, and I stood at the water's edge with Bennett and two kayaks at our feet. She'd surprised me with her willingness to meet at the river and kayak alongside me to where the bodies had been found. Bennett hadn't taken part in the investigation of how the bodies were transported along the river, an oversight by the detectives. Because Bennett grew up in the Wallace Lake area, she'd been recreating on these waters her entire life and had a working expertise that neither I nor many on the local police department had. With a map of the river, I was able to determine a possible trajectory the killer took to move the bodies down the river. I hadn't figured out the killer's exact entry point to the waterway, but I figured if Bennett and I started about ten miles out from the land bars, it might give me some possible locations to look into.

I'd wanted to take a boat down the Powell River since we first visited the crime scene; I needed to see everything from the killer's vantage point and continue to work on the killer's possible pattern. Due to the regular use of the river, our team determined the killer must have positioned the bodies during the night or at daybreak to avoid being seen. A night drop would have required some sort of headlamp or spotlight since there was no lighting around the river and the killer would have been working in the black of a country night. Whether the positioning took place at night or daybreak, it would have required the killer to know the river and have experience maneuvering Dead Man's Point. And our team determined the killer most likely used a canoe rather than a kayak. The killer would have needed to work hard at getting a dead body into the seat of a kayak, not to mention that the deadweight could have toppled over the little vessel. The unnecessary work and risks made the canoe a much more viable option.

Bennett stood before me on the river's bank in skintight biking shorts that left little to the imagination and a yellow sleeveless tank. Her loose curls were tucked underneath a Boston Red Sox hat with the bill pulled down low enough to meet the top of her aviator sunglasses. With lean long arms, she showed me how to row the kayak. I followed her figure-eight movements in the air, my paddle strokes not nearly as fluid and gentle as hers.

"The river can get pretty deep in some places, above my shoulders," Bennett said. She shifted the paddle in her hands to show me how to slow the kayak down in the water.

I laughed. "For shorties like me, that means the water will be well over my head."

"You'll do fine," Bennett said in her usual confident tone. The beginning of crow's feet lined her brown eyes and crinkled with her easy grin. "Watch the current—that's what flusters a lot of kayakers in the water. It will be stronger in some places, but the motion of the water will always pull your kayak downstream."

My nervousness wasn't completely about the water. After all, I was a strong swimmer. I didn't like the small plastic kayak that looked so confining particularly in the strong current. I'd been watching the waves roll by and remembered the places I'd seen in the river where the water whitecapped with the current's force. I'd rather have full use of my arms and legs *inside* the rush of water than on top of it.

Bennett checked over each of our kayaks for possible leaks or damage. She spoke to me as she worked, explaining that she'd left the area for college and medical school. Once she graduated, she'd traveled and worked in a few different locations throughout the country, but never really felt at home. Eventually, she found her way back to Wallace Lake.

"I couldn't forget these waters," Bennett said. "It's the constant here, you know? We're lucky enough to have a substantial river and lake, and I love that you can't get away from the sounds of flowing water."

I looked out at that flowing water and felt intimidated. "I'm not sure I'm ready for this, Bennett."

She chuckled. "Come on! It will be fun, and you have a PFD on," Bennett reminded me. "The water is very calm today."

I pulled the clasps of my life jacket tighter and adjusted my Cincinnati Reds ball cap to shield the sun from my face.

"Hang on a minute." Bennett left me at the water's edge as she ran back to her Silverado pickup, its black pearl paint shining in the sun, a beautiful truck that I was very jealous of. She returned with a spray can of sunscreen. "You better coat your arms. This sun is hotter than it feels."

It was a small gesture, but sweet—something that endeared Bennett to me. I rarely thought about precautions like sunscreen and assumed my body had seen enough sun and could take it. I also hadn't spent much of my time in the presence of a doctor. I followed her orders by coating my sleeveless arms and even spread some of the sunscreen across my nose and cheeks.

Bennett set my kayak in the river, and I waded out the pebbly shore until the water rose above my knees. With one hand, Bennett held the kayak in place. With the other, she held on to my elbow and helped guide me into the little plastic boat. Her touch was strong and sure, and I appreciated her warm skin against my own.

"Enjoy the ride," Bennett called out as she pushed my kayak into the water's gentle but firm current.

"Wait!" I yelled when a sudden panic filled me. "I'm not ready."

Bennett threw her head back and laughed. "You're ready, girl. Don't worry—I'm right behind you."

At first, my kayak stalled out, almost standing still amidst the surrounding water's movement, and then my kayak slowly found its way into the river's flow. Suddenly, the front edge nudged back to the right, and I was headed back toward the river's embankment.

Bennett yelled from the side, "You have the paddle for a reason. Turn yourself left, and aim for the middle of the river."

I dunked the paddle into the water, the flat edge of it a hard line against the river's current. I pushed against the heavy weight of water and heaved the tiny boat and myself toward the center of the river. Behind me, Bennett cheered as the kayak finally fell in line with the water's flow, and I headed downstream. I let the water carry me and rested my paddle over my lap and against the kayak's hard plastic sides.

I was immediately struck by the way my body felt inside the kayak. Not for the claustrophobic—I had only enough width to shift my body a few inches either direction. Somehow, though, the kayak was comforting and safe, like a cocoon. It sat low in the water, and I felt the pressure of the water through the plastic. I had become a part of the river. I dipped my hand into the calm and lapping river—the equivalent, it felt like, of weaving my hand through the rushing air of an open car window. With the touch of the rolling water against my hand everything slowed down: my thoughts, my breath, my heartbeat. *I could get used to this*, I thought. I knew I could easily fall in love with the cool water licking the edges of my little plastic boat and the smell of the river at my fingertips, teeming with life.

Then Bennett was at my side, the tip of her royal blue kayak slicing through the calm waters next to mine. "You're a natural."

"Thanks, Bennett. I couldn't have done it without you."

She gave me one of her perfect smiles. "You know, you can call me Harper."

I evaluated her for a moment. "Yeah, somehow I only see you as Bennett."

She laughed. "The same way I only see you as Hansen."

Bennett directed me to edge the paddle in the water to keep myself in line with the current that was beginning to pick up. Then she said, "My grandmother fought hard for my name."

"Was Harper her name?"

"No, but Grandmother was a writer, and she idolized Harper Lee. She always said that she looked into my eyes when I first arrived in this world and knew I was a writer, too."

Bennett showed me how to use the paddle to weave between the small crescents of current. "Were you named after anyone specific?"

I hadn't considered my namesake in a long time, but I knew both my parents had their reasons. "My mom liked the name Lucy because of Lucille Ball—she always wanted to be an actress. My dad liked the name Lucinda because he was a big fan of Lucinda Williams and Emmylou Harris. I think he secretly always wanted to be a rock star. Somehow, Luce grew out of that."

"You do have a rocker-cool look going on."

Rocker-cool? *Really?* There had been absolutely no rocker-cool going on anywhere around me when Sanders rescued me from my apartment only a few days ago.

We rolled alongside each other while an occasional car peeked through the wooded two-lane road that followed the river's edge. We were still a few miles out from Dead Man's Point, the place the women were found in the river and that turn in the road where so many had lost their lives.

I thought about how Wallace Lake had a large missing persons cold case unit, and I wondered why such a beautiful place might have that legacy. "What's your take on why there have been so many disappearances in this area over the years?"

"If you believe the locals," Bennett said, "the disappearances are due to the ancient Indian burial grounds that surround the river and lake." Bennett went on to explain that some people believed the land and its water held power; it had the ability to claim people.

"Claim people?"

"Yeah," she said. "Some think the land selects individuals and holds them here. The earth literally claims them by burial."

"What do you say about it?"

She shrugged. "From a scientist's viewpoint, I can tell you that the earth in Wallace Lake County is soft because of the water. That softness makes it easier to hide all kinds of things in the ground."

We followed a gentle bend in the river, and my kayak nudged into hers. When I finally got myself back toward the center of the river, Bennett said, "The way I see it, we are much more connected to the earth than any of us realize. Our skeletons absorb trace amounts of the environmental toxins from where we live. We take in our surroundings."

"So, quite literally, our bones belong to the earth," I said.

Bennett agreed. "I like to think of it as the body's way of carrying a pocketful of home everywhere we go."

I couldn't help but smile. Bennett had an interesting way of looking at the world, one that I could clearly visualize.

"By the way, where is Harvey?"

"Tracking down some leads in town with twelve-step programs," I said. "We'll meet up later, but I needed a break."

"I understand. Harvey doesn't always play fair."

"How so?"

"She's used to getting her way." The sunlight reflected off the current and from Bennett's sunglasses. I tried to picture what her eyes looked like under those lenses. Angry? Irritated?

"How long?" I asked. When she gave me a sharp look, I added, "How long were you two together?"

"You don't miss much, do you?"

"I'm a special agent," I reminded her.

"A good one, apparently," Bennett said. "Harvey and I were short-lived, only a few weeks. We managed to keep it between the two of us, and as far as I know, it never got out." Bennett added, "And yes, I regret it terribly."

I laughed. "I've had a few of those, too. I think everyone has had one of those relationships at one time or another."

I thought of Rowan. I didn't regret our relationship, but I regretted the pain of our breakup. I regretted that we'd gone on together so long, even when it was apparent that neither of us would, or could, change. For the first time, I was able to see how very different Rowan and I were from the start. Perhaps those opposites were what drew me to her; Rowan's life was full of color, and she insisted on the belief that the good would always outweigh the bad with enough yoga and meditation. Despite all of Rowan's talk about balance, we never achieved any semblance of it between us. With the distance and possibly the change of scenery, I could now see that Rowan and I had been at two opposing poles while trying to communicate with each other in foreign languages.

"It's kind of funny, isn't it? Three women on this investigative team, and we're all lesbians. Knocks those statistics out of the crowd, huh?"

Bennett chuckled. "Or maybe it's just the law enforcement profession. How long have you been out?"

"Since I was fifteen or so." It was a long story, some of which I gathered Bennett knew from the press. "You?"

"College. "

Our paddles sliced through the water side by side for over an hour. With the warm sun on our shoulders, we talked about our work and our pasts. It was easy to feel comfortable with Bennett, and I had the very distinct feeling we'd known each other for years. Still, I surprised myself when I told Bennett about the breakup with Rowan and the dogs I'd left with her. I told Bennett about my inability to put work second, to let a case rest while I was assigned to it. I also told Bennett about Marci Tucker, the girl I'd fallen in love with so many years ago at the One True Path ex-gay ministry, the same girl I'd found murdered in a cave carved from limestone in Willow's Ridge, Ohio.

"Have you ever gone to those meetings with other ex-gay ministry survivors? What do they call them...ex-ex-gay ministry support groups?"

"I haven't, but there is a group meeting in Ohio now." I thought of Sanders and his insistence that I contact Eli Weaver after the Willow's Ridge case ended. Rowan had wanted me to as well. I still hadn't contacted Weaver, mainly because he reminded me so much of the Willow's Ridge case. He'd been helpful in teasing out the ideology behind ex-gay ministries and providing insight into our killer, but there was a part of me that wasn't ready for any more groups related to ex-gay ministries.

As we neared the twin land bars, the water grew deeper and darker. The current picked up, and Bennett maneuvered in front of my kayak as she jetted down the river. I followed the directions she shouted over her shoulder about how to best use the paddle. We rode over the churning water's hills and valleys until we reached the bend of Dead Man's Point. I plunged my paddle deep to slow down and struggled against the heave of the water that pushed back hard. The killer would have needed significant strength to stop a canoe in these currents, particularly given the weight of a dead body onboard. Judging from the trouble I had keeping the kayak from tipping, I figured the killer must have been a very skilled paddler and no stranger to these waters.

My kayak rounded the bend of Dead Man's Point behind Bennett's, and I heard the music and muffled voices of a party before I saw anyone. Laughter filtered through the trees. I caught fragments of movement on the forested hillside.

The land bars approached fast on my right, and I fought the current to slow the kayak and turn toward the bank of the bar. Instead, the kayak spun in the water, wild and out of my control, hurling me off to the river's stony side.

Whoever was hiding along the steep hillside saw us. The music shut down followed by the sound of movements. I looked up into the forested hillside. If this was a regular hangout, these people could have seen the killer dump the bodies on the land bar. The height of the location made it the perfect spot to see what was happening below. And, conversely, it also was the perfect location to keep watch over the bodies.

I pulled my knees to my chest and tried to climb out of the kayak without tipping it over. No luck. I was dumped into the cold water face first, just as Bennett made her way back to me. So much for rocker-cool. Kicking hard against the kayak, I also thrashed my body around in the water until I was able to break free from the little boat. I caught the tip of the kayak just before it floated downstream. Wading up the muddy bank with river water seeping from my clothing and hair, I heard someone say, "Go!" followed by the sounds of snapping branches and footfalls.

I shot into the woods and fumbled with the gnarled undergrowth and thick foliage. Finally, I found a thin path up the hillside, hidden so well, you almost needed to know it was there to find it. Branches swatted at me as the remaining river-bottom muck weighed down my feet. The hill was steeper than I expected, and the leftover water from my sandals oozed out. I slipped on the dank mud, my open palms and fingers plunging into the cool earth. Scrambling against the foliage, I followed the voices upward until I emerged into a clearing.

Below, Bennett had landed and pulled both of our kayaks safely from the water. She gave me a quick wave to let me know she'd soon follow.

The clearing was a teenager's dream party spot. The space was circular, with the remnants of a recent bonfire at its center. A thick fallen tree trunk served as a bench around the fire pit, and messages had been carved into the rotten wood about *luv* and *4ever*. Empty beef jerky and candy wrappers were lodged within the undergrowth along with crushed beer cans and empty bottles of cheap alcohol. Cigarette butts littered the area, and it still stank of pot. Hidden by the trees and foliage, the clearing made it difficult for anyone to sneak up on the group, just as I'd found out. It reminded me of the place Marci had frequented in Willow's Ridge for many of the same reasons. She'd called her space Stonehenge because it was hidden away in the limestone caves of the quarry. In either case, the point was these were secret places where teens could discover themselves and others. I was willing to bet that just as Marci named her secret place Stonehenge, this clearing also had a name that the teens used.

Whoever had been in this space couldn't have gone far. I followed the path up the steep slope where it eventually threw me onto an unpaved country road. I took in the scene from behind the foliage. A dark green Land Rover was parked along the dirt road near a faint dusty trail left by another vehicle that had already gone. A man stood with two teenage girls near the Land Rover, and he leaned forward as he spoke, looming above the girls as he held one girl's arm tightly. The girls' terrified faces reflected back in his oversized sunglasses. I couldn't make out what he said, only snatches of words and phrases, although he spoke to the two girls with the distinct air of authority.

Bennett caught up and stood behind me. "What's going on?"

"Do you recognize that man? Or those girls?" I asked.

"I don't. Do you have your badge or a weapon?" Bennett pulled her cell from a shirt pocket. "Anything on you?"

I shook my head. "Stay hidden. Take as many pictures as you can of these people and the vehicles."

"Hansen, wait!" She grasped my forearm. "They could be armed."

I considered Bennett a few seconds, and then I pushed through the thick foliage.

CHAPTER SEVEN

Day Two: 4:00 p.m.

"Ava!"

The three fell silent. The man leaned against the Land Rover and flipped a loaded key chain round and round his finger. The bill of his ball cap cast darkness across his face.

"I see you've recovered since yesterday," I said to Ava while the others stared at my wet clothes and hair. "I took a tumble in the river," I tried to explain.

"Special Agent Hansen!" Ava finally decided to acknowledge me, and then turned to the other teen. "That's the police officer I was telling you about." Her eyes lit with excitement when she looked back at me. "I wanted to show them where I found the bodies."

"I bet you were popular at school today. People love a good crime scene story." I extended my hand to Ava and then the teen next to her. Unlike Ava, this young woman gave me a suspicious look and was hesitant to shake my hand. Instead of giving me her name, she asked, "How did you find us?"

"I heard the voices from the river. It looks like you all have a regular hangout in the clearing."

I turned to the man who had yet to introduce himself and offered my hand. His cautious frown opened to a big smile. "Cody Allard," he shared with enthusiasm. "I'm not sure what you thought you saw out there, but I'm one of the coaches at the high school. I bring the team up here to run," he said with an arc of his arm.

I made a mental note of his suspicious phrase—*I'm not sure what you thought you saw*—and immediately thought of Linda Clarke. Sanders had said she was able to quickly turn on the charm for law enforcement and the courtroom. I'd just seen a similar shift in personality from Allard once he realized I wasn't going away.

"Special Agent Luce Hansen from the Ohio Bureau of Criminal Investigation," I said. "I'm investigating the recent deaths in the area."

"It's very sad," Allard said. "The entire town is mourning."

"I'm surprised to find you so close to the place where the bodies were found, Ava. It must bring back some scary memories."

She nodded and the pile of blond hair tied on top of her head bobbed back and forth. "I had nightmares last night, but I really wanted to show my friends. Sometimes it feels like it didn't really happen, you know?"

"It can be disorienting," I said. I understood what she meant—after I found Marci's body when I was sixteen, I also went through periods where it seemed like a nightmare or a horror movie I watched rather than reality. It was the mind's way of protecting itself by only giving as many images as one could mentally take. While Ava's quick return to the scene seemed odd, there was strength in numbers, particularly for teens. What interested me more than Ava, however, was the relationship between the other teen and Mr. Allard. Those two seemed to share a connection that didn't include Ava; I recognized the looks that passed between them, a communication that Ava wasn't privy to. Both the other teen and Mr. Allard looked uncomfortable. Whether that was because of my presence or simply the location, I couldn't be sure.

"Where is the rest of your team?" I asked Allard.

He shrugged and gave another million-dollar smile. "You know teenagers. They finished their run and didn't want to hang around to talk to this old man." His forced laugh only drew my attention to the fact that he was not an old man at all—he looked to be in his late twenties.

"Could I see your ID?"

Allard smiled even bigger. "Sure."

The photograph on the ID matched the person in front of me—a twenty-six-year-old white male.

Suddenly, I recognized the teen beside Ava. "Sadie Reid?"

She nodded. Here was the young woman I'd heard so much about. Sadie, the daughter of Wilma Henderson, and the one Ava had been so worried about when she found the dead bodies.

"I met your mother yesterday. We talked about the women who have been murdered, her tattoo, and recovery."

"Heart to Heart?" Ava immediately recognized she'd spoken without thinking and caught a dirty look from Sadie. In an attempt to hide her sudden blush, Ava looked at her feet. Her reaction told me Sadie was in charge and that Ava probably spent a good deal of her time trying to impress Sadie.

Sadie's body went rigid while everyone fell silent. And then she made one movement so minor most would miss it. Her left hand fell flat against her thigh, the exact same movement someone would have made to hide a tattoo on her inner wrist.

"Well, it sure is a great view from the clearing," I said. "You can see everything for a good quarter mile. Since the bodies were found right below here in the river..."

"I'm sorry, Agent," Allard said. "We haven't seen or heard anything. Like I said, the team just comes to these hills to run on occasion. We haven't been out here in weeks." He reached for Ava's elbow, leading her toward the passenger door. Sadie followed to the back door. "If there's nothing else, I need to get back to school."

"I understand," I said. "Quick question before you go, Mr. Allard. Why does a weight lifting team need to run?"

"Excuse me?"

"I don't know much about weight lifting, but isn't it a non-aerobic sport?"

"Running builds stamina," he said, and climbed into the Land Rover.

The thing was, no one was sweating. If they'd just finished their team run, as Allard indicated, I expected at least a little perspiration.

Ava gave me a little wave, and Allard stepped on the gas pedal. I stood there on the dirt track until there was nothing left to see.

Bennett stepped out of the foliage.

"You get some pictures?" I leaned down and examined the tire tread markings of Allard's SUV. Other vehicles had driven on the dirt path as well.

She nodded. "I texted the license plate to Richardson."

"Good call," I said. "Do you know where this road leads?"

"My guess is that it winds down the hill and catches up with the main road along the river. It looks like a service road to these fields." She pointed to the corn growing on the opposite side of the road. "It's really hidden. You'd need to know the path was here."

I looked over at the place where Bennett and I had come through the foliage. Just as it was along the river's bank, there was very little indication of a footpath behind the thick line of trees. No one would guess the wooded area held a clearing only a few steep yards down the hillside. Any vehicle parked along the single lane would be well hidden from anyone on the river or any of the major roads surrounding us.

"May I use your cell to call Riley?"

She handed me the phone. "What's up?"

"We've found the killer's entry point to the river," I said, and thumbed behind me into the woods. "It's the path the killer used to drop the bodies on the land bars."

It wasn't that I hadn't thought about the shared tattoo's image: *heart to heart*. However, hearing Ava say the words out loud made it seem like a concept, a very real place of gathering, rather than just a catchy phrase inside my head. I sat down with Bennett on a fallen tree trunk as *heart to heart* rolled through my mind like a mantra. I'd alerted Riley, and the team was on its way. "Don't touch anything," he told me. "You need a forensic investigation suit. The crime scene investigators need to comb through everything."

Autumn colors surrounded Bennett and me as we waited for the team, trees filled with fiery reds and oranges, bright yellows, and greens. Without a cloud in the late-afternoon sky, everything glistened with the rumbling sounds of the river rolling along below us.

Bennett gave me a solid look up and down and chuckled. I looked ridiculous; wet clothing hung from my body, and I was coated in mud from the knees down. My braid had fallen out, and I knew my hair frizzed around my face as it air-dried.

"There is a very good reason for my appearance," I told Bennett. "I'm hiding my stealth detective skills behind an incompetent veneer. No one sees me coming."

"Ah, so that's what's *really* going on here. It's quite a disguise." Bennett reached out for my cheek, and her fingers rubbed along my jawline. "I'm not sure how the mud made it onto your face."

I let her fingertips rub away the streak of mud, feeling the electricity beneath her touch.

"There," Bennett said. "Rocker-cool as ever." With the sunglasses perched on top of her head, I could see her brown eyes were flecked with gold. Kaleidoscope eyes.

Then, just as suddenly as the moment came on between us, I fell back on my usual escape: talk of work.

"Ava responded to the word *recovery*," I said. "Heart to Heart sounds like the name of a church group or some kind of recovery program. It could be a program that involved our newly sober victims."

Bennett agreed. "It's a touchy-feely title for sure, but I haven't heard of any drug rehab programs using that name in this area. It could be located out of town in Columbus or Cleveland."

I thought about my interview with Jill Chamberlain. She said her mother called from the Wallace Lake area about her recovery. She also said her mother was working with a group of women on that recovery. "Maybe it's not a recovery program but some sort of a sober living or halfway house."

Bennett considered the option and nodded. She added, "What is up with that creepy coach, anyway? He was alone in the woods with two teenage girls. Ava, at least, is his student. Sadie might have graduated, but she's still a teenager. Do you think they saw something, maybe the drop of the bodies?"

"They all are hiding something—I'm just not sure what it is."

What was taking the team so damn long? It was torture to wait so close and not be able to investigate the area. I wanted to go back to the clearing and look at its view of the river once again. I knew the damage my footprints could do, though, and the possibilities of contaminating the scene.

While we waited, I decided to test my theories out on someone new now that the ghost of my father was virtually gone.

"Did you ever study the Linda Clarke case?"

"The BWS Killer?" She waited for my nod. "Yeah, I did. We spent a lot of time on her case when I studied poisons." As soon as she said *poisons*, she gave me a quizzical look. "What are you thinking?"

"The BWS Killer case broke the mold of other black widows, and I keep thinking about where and how Clarke positioned the bodies. And her motive for murder."

"Money."

"There was a point to Clarke's murders besides money: punishment," I said. "She tortured and punished each of her victims for her pleasure. You could say she liked to play with her prey. I have a feeling our killer also enjoys the process."

"Hmm. A gut feeling."

I smiled. "Not something a scientist or medical doctor takes seriously, huh?"

"I try, and quite frankly, I'm jealous. I'd love to have instincts that guide me toward the truth. Besides, I've heard through the law enforcement grapevine that you are known for your gut reactions. In the past, at least, your gut instincts have been correct."

We both stood at the sound of vehicles climbing the dirt road. The fleet of vans rolled into view and parked along the rows of cornfields. Within minutes, the entire hillside was crawling with investigators in Tyvek suits and booties. Yellow tent markers dotted the landscape and two detectives took molds of Cody Allard's tire tracks that still lingered in the mud.

"We'll need to bring in the three people you found up here for questioning in the morning," Captain Riley told me. "Richardson's running searches on them all now, and we'll see if anything turns up." He looked around the area. "You think the killer drove the bodies up here and then carried them down the hill into the river? That method would have taken a lot of strength."

"Maybe they used something like a four-wheeler. Once in the water, the killer could have guided the floating body to the land bar."

Riley brought the radio to his mouth and told the investigators to look for evidence of a tool or vehicle used on the hillside.

"Ladies," he told us. "We are in for a long night."

❖

By the time we reached Bennett's truck and had the kayaks loaded in the back, it was after midnight. I was hungry and needed a hot shower. Clean clothes never sounded better. I rolled down the passenger window when Bennett started the engine.

Bennett turned on the interior light and held out her hand to me. In her palm lay a stone still moist from the river, rusty red and smooth as glass.

"I collect a stone every time I float," she explained.

I immediately understood. "For the stone jar in your office."

She smiled. "Observant, too." She reached for a Sharpie in the glove box and wrote on the stone's surface: *H & B Float 1*. "I have another stone jar I keep at home. But this one is for you."

I turned the river rock over in my hand, letting my fingertips trace its smooth edges. "What is a float?"

She shifted the truck into drive and we wound away from the river. "It's what we call a kayaking experience."

She'd labeled the stone as the first float. I found myself hopeful that the future held more floats with Bennett and more collected rocks for her stone jar.

While Bennett drove, I held the smooth rock in my hand and couldn't help but think of Marci. She'd given me stones as well— she called them *Marci stones* found inside the limestone caverns where we used to meet. Those stones were different, though, weak and pocked full of holes with multiple layers as thin as a fingernail width. This river stone was solid and smooth, a significant weight in the palm of my hand.

I'd retrieved my cell phone from the kayak's compartment and had four missed calls from a blocked number. I turned the phone facedown on my thigh; I'd deal with that in the morning. Bennett pulled onto a main road headed back to town when my cell rang. *Unidentified Caller.*

"Hansen."

"Special Agent Hansen?" a male voice asked.

"This is she."

"It's Gary. From Gary's Girls? This could be nothing, but you said to call about anything that seemed odd to me. I've been trying to reach you."

"Yes?" He had my full attention.

"It's Wilma Henderson. The woman you spoke to earlier?" He took an audible breath. "Well…it's just that…"

"What's happened, Gary?"

"Wilma's gone."

CHAPTER EIGHT

Day Three: 1:45 a.m.

I handed Sadie Reid a Styrofoam cup of station house coffee, which was never much better than caffeinated hot sludge. She wrapped her shaking hands around it; her black painted fingernails had been chewed down to the quick.

Sadie sat beside her grandmother, clinging to a tissue, though neither shed many tears. I was surprised they were both willing to come to the station in the middle of the night, but with Wilma missing, they both said they couldn't sleep.

"I've learned to expect the worst from my daughter," Mrs. Henderson said. "Lord knows I've done my best, but Wilma is hell-bent on destroying herself. It wouldn't be half as bad if it wasn't also hurting this one." She thumbed over to Sadie.

Sadie's dark eyes were bloodshot, and she sat across from Harvey and me in a steely posture, as if she was prepared to hear the absolute worst from us. "Sadie, we have to investigate all possible suspects. Is your father a part of your life?"

She shook her head and looked down at her lap. "He died."

Sadie's grandmother filled in the story for us. Sadie had spent a good deal of time with her father until he died in a boating accident on Wallace Lake when she was five. He'd been fishing in one of the deepest parts of the lake at night after a day of heavy drinking. He managed to fall into the water and couldn't save himself.

"I'm very sorry," I told Sadie, who wouldn't look up from her lap.

"Has your daughter disappeared before?" Harvey asked.

"Oh, sure, but not for quite a few years now. The last time this happened, she left Sadie on my doorstep with a note of apology. Wilma said she had to get away and wanted me to take Sadie. At least Wilma recognized she didn't have the ability to be a good parent."

"Is that when you gained custody of Sadie?" I asked.

She nodded. "Sadie was so young then." She reached over and rubbed an arthritic hand over Sadie's back. "Once the legal issues had been settled, Wilma came around again. She was never one for taking responsibility or for making apologies."

"That was a long time ago," Sadie said. "My mom wouldn't leave now. Something must have happened to her."

"How do you know that?" Harvey asked.

"I just know." Frustrated, Sadie dropped her head into her hands. I saw the tattoo of the connected hearts on her inner wrist.

"Because of Heart to Heart?" I asked.

She looked up at me, but said nothing. Her cell phone rang again. "Sorry." She turned it off.

"Someone is anxious to get ahold of you," I said.

"It's not my mother."

"Probably Joan," her grandmother said. "That woman is always calling."

"No"—Sadie cut her grandmother off—"just Ava. It's nothing."

Sadie's overreaction caught my attention. I scribbled *Joan* on my pad of paper. "Would Joan know where your mother is?"

Sadie shook her head. "No one knows anything. But I need to find my mom."

I nodded. "Your mother's disappearance is suspicious, particularly given the other victims we have found in the area of Wallace Lake. As far as we know, she's only been missing"—I looked up at the wall clock—"about thirty hours. We can put out a BOLO for Wilma, a be on the lookout, but that's about all we can do at this point."

"That's it?" Sadie stared at me incredulously.

"I'm sorry," I said. "This is a small town, Sadie, and the BOLO will ensure that all law enforcement will be looking for her in the state of Ohio. We'll do all we can to find your mom, but we have to follow the law."

Harvey and I escorted the scared young woman and her grandmother, who was used to dealing with the problems of her drug-addicted daughter, out of the station. Harvey stood beside me at the window, and we watched as the two made their way into the parking lot.

"Sadie knows more than she's saying," I said.

Harvey agreed.

"I have a feeling her buddy Ava plays a part in this, too."

"How are we going to get them to talk?"

"I don't think we can *make* them," I said. "But there might be another way to get the information."

CHAPTER NINE

Day Three: 2:40 a.m.

I'd been sitting in my truck for over an hour parked two homes down from that of Sadie and her grandmother. So far, there hadn't been any movement inside or outside the home. My theory was that Sadie wouldn't stay put; she'd been upset when she left our meeting, and I figured she'd soon be out looking for her mother. I was curious to see how Ava would fit in to all of this and to see where Sadie would choose to look for her mother. Rumors were already circulating that the serial killer had taken another woman. I wanted to believe that Wilma Henderson was simply out of town, but I knew there was a very real possibility that she had already been killed.

Sadie's grandmother's small ranch sat in a working class neighborhood that was quiet and well cared for. With the summer season over, the town was eerily dead. Vacant houses spotted neighborhoods as many were only used as summer cottages.

I'd splurged on some coffee from a real vendor rather than the terrible sludge at the station house, and I sipped it while scrolling through my emails. I hadn't checked my personal email account in days. While most of it was dog care coupons and other junk, there were two emails that stopped me cold. From Rowan. *Call me*, the subject line read. *I want to talk to you.*

Delete.

I needed to contact Rowan, but it would have to wait until after we solved this case. After all, she'd waited almost eight months before contacting me. It was possible I was jumping to conclusions; I didn't know what Rowan wanted, and her insisting to speak with me could have had nothing to do with getting back together. I'd been in enough relationships, though, to know that we lesbians have what I liked to call the boomerang effect. We might argue until we lose our voice. We might also break up and swear we never want to see each other again. Give it a year or so, and after another bad relationship, we generally boomerang our way back into the arms of our exes.

I wasn't ready to boomerang back to Rowan again. I thought of Bennett; I enjoyed her company, and our kayaking down the river. And there had been that touch between us. Innocent enough. Still, I couldn't stop thinking about the way her touch made me feel.

A text came through from Harvey: *No action here. You?*

Me: *Quiet.*

Harvey: *?*

Me: *Patience.*

Harvey was stationed outside Ava Washington's trailer. Since the two girls weren't willing to talk to us, I knew their behavior would. Ava was fifteen, and Sadie was eighteen—I'd been both of those ages and remembered well my allegiance was first and foremost to my friends. My guess was that both girls had secrets—don't all teenage girls?—but that Ava would have done just about anything to please Sadie. It was in the way she looked at Sadie as she stood by Coach Allard's SUV. It was in the way Ava recoiled from Sadie after saying aloud *Heart to Heart*. Sadie held all the power in the friendship; Ava was the admirer of Sadie, something of a devoted younger fan.

What did all of this have to do with the dead women in the river? And why hadn't Bennett and Richardson been able to identify the fourth victim, the one submerged in the water, Ophelia? Her body had taken the brunt of decomposition, and logically, not everyone was lucky enough to have someone who missed them when they didn't return home or missed too many phone calls. I feared that no one was looking for Ophelia, and that would make it more difficult for us to find her identity. My heart ached for people like her—everyone in this world deserved someone who missed her absence.

Headlights spilled across my windshield, and I ducked just as the lights winked out and drove past. The car slowed until it stopped on the other side of Sadie's mailbox.

I crawled over to the passenger window and peered over the lip of the car door. I saw the signal—the flicker of the light outside the garage. I scribbled down the license plate of a dark-colored sedan, silently blessing the governor who insisted that Ohio cars have plates on *both* the front and back ends. Then there was Sadie, her figure darkened in jeans and a black hoodie. She came around from behind the house and ran across the yard with a backpack bouncing against her back. She slipped into the passenger seat, and the car rolled forward before Sadie could latch the door closed. I lay as flat as I could across the front seats as the sedan rolled away from me, lightless and soundless into the night.

Once I counted to ten, I looked out my rear window to catch the red taillights turning left at the stop sign at the end of the neighborhood street.

"When Grandma's asleep, the kid will play," I said, keying my truck awake. I turned around in a driveway next to Sadie's and ran the stop sign.

I kept my distance, but followed close enough to see that the driver was shorter than Sadie, a figure who followed all of the traffic rules while driving five miles under the speed limit. These were clear signals to me that this driver was working very hard not to catch the attention of anyone, let alone law enforcement.

I followed the vehicle through what was considered downtown Wallace Lake, a whopping three lights with a construction zone outside of the Tastee Freeze. The town was silent save for a few cars on the road. We made our way to the other side of Wallace Lake where the vacation homes loomed large over the water and docks held speedboats and pontoons. When the car turned onto a street with no outlet, I parked my truck outside its entrance so I could see every vehicle that came in or out.

Slipping out of the truck, I moved closer to the house where the sedan had pulled into the drive—number 1215. These homes were newer, no more than a decade old. I hid behind a row of landscaped pine trees just as the garage door went down and hid the car. The lights flickered on inside the home, and I snapped a few photos with my iPhone.

When there was no movement around the house for a good fifteen minutes, I made my way back to the truck. I texted Richardson, *Who owns 1215 Acorn Ridge Dr?*

My coffee was gone, but I found a bottle of water under the driver's seat.

Richardson: *Seriously? It's almost 4 a.m.*

Me: *Seriously. I'm watching the house now.*

I waited for Richardson to crawl his ass out of bed and get to his computer before I sent the license plate number. Sadie clearly hadn't come to this address to party. So why had she gone so far as to sneak outside after her grandmother had gone to bed? There was no indication that Ava was in this house, and Harvey hadn't reported any movement from her trailer. The other houses on the dead end were totally dark and looked empty—no trash cans at the curb or planters out front, nothing to suggest someone lived there full-time. I guessed them to be second homes of boaters and water skiers, weekend hideaways from the city. House number 1215 basically had the street to itself.

Finally, Richardson texted back, *Two names on the house. Henry and Joan Marco. Two vehicles under Joan Marco's name, a 1999 Buick sedan and a 2007 Land Rover.* He included the plate numbers and VINs.

A Land Rover. I searched the truck for my notepad and flipped it open. The plate numbers matched from earlier today. Whoever Joan Marco was, a man named Cody Allard was driving her vehicle earlier today with Ava and Sadie near the woods surrounding the Powell River.

What the hell was going on? The more I learned about this case, the more tangled the details and its players became.

My phone beeped with a text from Harvey: *Ava's on foot.*

Me: *Tail her.*

It would be a long walk, but it was possible for Ava to be headed to this location. If that were the case, why didn't the driver pick up both girls and not just Sadie? Where would Ava go in the middle of the night alone and on foot? She obviously wasn't the least bit afraid of the serial killer prowling the area.

Harvey: *Ava @ Cody Allard's apartment. Inside.*

Me: *Stay put. Get photos when she leaves.*

I hadn't expected this development. Ava and the new high school teacher? Ms. Washington's fears about her daughter hanging out with a crowd that could get her into trouble were well founded. However, at least so far, she'd been focused on the wrong person: Sadie and not the coach.

The background check on Cody Allard came back clean. He was a new teacher and a new resident in Wallace Lake in the past year. There was nothing to alert my suspicions of him except for the fact that a fifteen-year-old girl on his team had snuck out and was now inside his home. And then there was the SUV, the dark green Land Rover that he seemed to be sharing with a married woman.

I texted Richardson, *What do you have on Henry and Joan Marco?*

Richardson: *On it. Nothing yet but retirees.*

Me: *Last place of employment?*

Richardson: *For Joan, Wallace Lake High School. Guidance counselor until 2004. Henry has been on disability since 1999.*

I texted Richardson back, *Is Sadie Reid a current student at the high school?*

Richardson: *Graduated last year.*

There was no way Sadie could be a part of the weight-lifting team other than as a mentor or an assistant to the coach. It didn't seem likely the high school would have formally hired her to assist a new teacher, particularly when Ava made it clear there had never been a weight-lifting team at the high school before this teacher arrived.

"Dammit!" I tossed the cell phone onto the passenger seat and took a swig of the warm water. The water almost came flying out of my mouth. There on the seat beside me was my dad's figure decked out in his finest police regalia.

I choked the water down. "Dad"—I coughed—"where have you been?"

"Hiya, Lucy-girl. Looks like you've caught yourself another mess of a case." He looked out the passenger window. "I always hated these overnight stakeouts."

"Where have you been?" I asked again.

He gave me one of his grins. "You haven't needed me. You never have."

I shook my head. "I'll always need you."

"You're one hundred times better at this work than I ever was," he said. "That gut of yours is dead on except when you get too many crossed signals."

"Like in this case." I added, "I hate feeling like I'm going at it alone."

"Could be your own fault."

I knew what he was referring to, and it wasn't Harvey or Richardson. "I'll get with Sanders tomorrow."

"Allies don't always make the best decisions, Luce." He gave me a hard look. "Nor do detectives."

"I keep thinking about Ainsley."

"I know you do," my dad said. "His death was a tragedy, but it wasn't your fault. Here's the thing, Luce. Refusing to trust other law enforcement officers isn't going to keep you safe from losses like Ainsley—it will only make you vulnerable. There is a strength in needing others."

I waited a few moments before I responded. "I tried to make the murder board," I said, ignoring his comments, "but there hasn't been much so far to fill in."

"The board doesn't always work the way you want it to," he said. "Sometimes it works better in the mind."

"Meaning?"

"Exactly what you're doing now, mentally pulling all the puzzle pieces together in front of you. It's not always so neat and tidy as a murder board."

"So what should I do?" Exhaustion was setting in. I realized for the first time that I hadn't slept more than a few hours since Sanders burst into my apartment and found me asleep on the couch.

"It's not so much what you should *do* but more what you should consider," my dad said. "Maybe the shape of this case isn't a rectangle."

I yawned and took another drink of water and wished like hell for some caffeine.

"Come on, Luce. Think about what I taught you." He crossed one leg over the other and rubbed his neatly trimmed mustache. "Don't forget that one of your greatest resources as a cop is your own past. Pull from your background. You grew up in a town only a little bigger than Wallace Lake. You know how these places work."

The light went out in the Marco home and I relaxed back into my seat. It looked like Sadie would stay the night, and I needed to wait her out to see what her next move would be. "What do you mean?"

He finally said, "Small towns are all about loyalty."

"Secrets."

"Yes. Cities have them, too, but not so deeply embedded into the culture. Cities build their own small towns with separate communities. It's almost like we're hardwired to stay loyal within a certain space and to the people that inhabit it."

"What are you saying, Dad? That everyone in Wallace Lake is in on the murders?"

He shook his head. "Not at all. What I'm saying is that there are two communities working here: the locals and the outsiders. You need to go at this with an us-versus-them mentality. What do the outsiders do in this town?"

I shrugged. "They keep the economy going. They buy summer cottages and recreate on the lake and river."

My dad nodded. "And then?"

"They abandon the place until the next season."

My father was right, of course. I hadn't fully considered that the strong code of silence we faced in this case was coming from the collective community, not just individuals. When in doubt, these neighbors sided with those they knew, whether they liked them or not. There was a tendency to turn away from the crimes of a neighbor or schoolmate rather than report it. Loyalty ran deep, and secrets had a way of trickling down through generations. I thought about the way my dad and his partner, Roy Tyson, both of whom grew up in my hometown, were able to pull on familial ties and crimes during their law enforcement work. I'd been present as a child around the dinner table for many of those discussions about what someone's uncle might have done and his grandfather before that. The one thing I'd learned about small towns was that they were rarely how they appeared to a visitor. All that quaint charm and friendliness fell away once an outsider tried to grow deeper roots.

"Don't you remember what happened when we suspected Billy Anderson of dealing marijuana? Why, he had himself quite a business, and we had to…"

I listened to my dad talk about his case from long ago. He explained the snare he and Roy Tyson had to climb through in order to dig and push their way into the truth. Even then, bloody and torn from the journey, the truth, my father said, was subjective and in constant shift.

The familiar sound of my father's voice was soothing, and he lulled on and on until I eventually drifted into sleep.

CHAPTER TEN

Day Three: 7:30 a.m.

I woke to the incessant ding of my cell phone. Squinting against the sun's morning light, I tried to stretch out my legs and arms inside the truck. I'd fallen asleep slumped against the door, a dangerous move on a stakeout. Thankfully, the neighborhood was barren, and the home I'd been watching was quiet.

All the muscles of my neck and back screamed with every movement. I scrambled for my cell. I'd missed a text from Bennett at 5:57 a.m. *Fourth victim identified. Old arrest record.*

Bennett, I knew, had been searching for a positive ID using DNA analysis.

A recent text from Harvey read, *Both subjects on foot. Allard left five minutes before Washington. Headed toward high school.*

Me: *Photos?*

Harvey: *Got 'em.*

Me: *The two of them together?*

Harvey: *Hit the lotto, boss. A kiss at the door.*

A kiss. I was struck by the boldness of their physical embrace outside of the home. The two had grown comfortable with each other and their surroundings—they felt safe with their secret. Allard was twenty-six years of age. Ava Washington was only fifteen years old, and although she appeared to be complicit in the relationship, she was under the legal age for consent. We now had evidence of statutory rape.

My next question was whether or not Sadie was involved with Allard. My observations when I found them in the wooded area told me the connection between Sadie and Allard was much stronger than Ava and Allard's. But that didn't necessarily mean that Sadie was sleeping with him. Somehow I couldn't picture Sadie falling for Allard's jock charm. She struck me as a young woman who was too smart for that.

My phone rang.

Richardson: *Bennett got the DNA results back on the fourth victim. Leslie Rex, age 62.*

Me: *Wallace Lake resident?*

Richardson: *Not sure. Last known address was in Jacksonville, Ohio.*

Me: *Jacksonville? That's quite a ways from here.*

Richardson: *Sure is. Something else? That house you watched last night. Joan Marco? She bailed Rex out the last two times she was arrested.*

Me: *Hmmm. Where was that?*

Richardson: *First time in Akron. Second in Columbus.*

Me: *No record of employment or arrest in Wallace Lake?*

Richardson: *None.*

Me: *Good work. Did Ava Washington's mother or Sadie Reid's grandmother report the girls missing from the home this morning?*

Richardson: *No.*

Me: *Let me know if they do. Harvey and I need to talk to Joan Marco. Email me her driver's license, would you? Arrests?*

Richardson: *Nothing. Upstanding Wallace Lake citizen.*

Me: *I bet. Keep digging.*

We'd uncovered some sort of a ring, something I didn't yet understand. Unless I'd missed it, Sadie was still inside the Marco home, which looked very much asleep. We'd determined the relationship between Ava and Allard, but what about the relationship between Sadie and Joan Marco? Or Marco and Allard? For a town synonymous with the opioid epidemic, the only evidence we'd found of its abuse was in the victims. It was true that many dealers abstained from use, but we were looking at a number of people, and it would have been difficult to regulate all of them if we'd uncovered some sort of drug dealing operation. Besides, I couldn't picture these retirees or Cody Allard dealing heroin. Allard was a creep, definitely, but a drug kingpin? Hardly.

I rolled my head back and forth a few times, letting my neck pop out the kinks and painful knots from the long night before. No, my gut told me this case had very little to do with the dealing of drugs. Surprising, yes, given the location and the epidemic. Maybe that was what had given the Wallace Lake PD so many problems: they were looking in the wrong direction.

We all needed to change our point of view and our lens of focus. We needed to let the stereotypes go; if one thing was clear to me during that morning sunrise, it was that this case was everything but stereotypical. Like the BWS Killer, this would be one for the casebooks.

Sadie emerged from the Marco home just after nine a.m. I trailed her as she drove the large sedan back to her grandmother's. She pulled the car into the driveway. I thought she'd try to hide it in the garage, but she left it out for everyone to see.

Remember, my dad had said, *you know small towns*. I knew that cars in driveways that didn't belong to the homeowner didn't go unnoticed. I knew that the neighborhood rumor mill would spread that juicy tidbit of information throughout the community within a few days. It wouldn't have taken long before someone recognized that car as belonging to the Marcos. I needed to speak to the neighbors, and in order to get a clear picture, I needed to hear about their observations of Sadie.

Yes, I knew small towns. But it wasn't until that moment in the truck parked on a stakeout that I finally understood what I was up against, that granite-hard level of loyalty I was trying to shatter.

❖

"Ready?" I asked.

Harvey nodded. "Long night, but I'm ready for more." Her short hair was wet from her recent shower, and she smelled like aftershave. Polo, maybe? Or Tommy Hilfiger? Unlike me, Harvey was impeccably dressed. Her white button-down was pressed clean and tucked carefully against her thin waist. She reached down into one of her cargo pants pockets to check her phone for messages.

I gave the thick wooden door a strong knock. While we waited, I tucked my own shirt into my khakis where the waist was too big and slipped down on my hips.

We needed to deal with Cody Allard and soon. The good news was we knew exactly where both Ava and Allard would be until the final school bell at three p.m., but we didn't know where Joan Marco would be once I left the watch on her house. Therefore, her questioning took precedence.

Just as I was about to knock again, I heard footsteps approach, the pause as someone peered through the peephole, and then a rasp as the dead bolt unlocked. The door opened to a woman who looked as though she'd just baked a kitchen full of fresh cookies and had a houseful of grandchildren. Her short brown hair was in rollers and she smelled like hair spray.

"Ms. Marco?" I asked. "Joan Marco?"

She opened the door a little farther, eyeing both Harvey and me suspiciously.

"We're investigating the recent crimes in this area. Do you have time for a few questions?" I flipped open my badge for her to see as did Harvey.

Marco looked carefully at both badges and then at our faces. "Sure," she finally said, "but I can't imagine why you'd want to talk to me."

"May we come in?" I asked.

We followed Joan Marco through her entryway and into the kitchen. She motioned to the table. "Would you like some coffee? I just put a fresh pot on."

"Thank you, yes," Harvey said as we sat down at the table.

I watched as Joan poured two steaming mugs for us. She caught me watching and gave me a big smile. "Law enforcement must be a hard line of work for young ladies," she said, handing a cup to each of us. She sat at the head of the table and pushed the sugar our way.

"We make out all right," I told her. "What type of work do you do?"

Joan stirred a spoonful of sugar, then a second into her coffee. "I'm retired now, but I was the school counselor at the high school for twenty-five years."

"You've seen a lot, then," I said. "I bet nothing surprises you."

She laughed, and I noticed a twinkle in her eye. She was a friendly older woman, unassuming in her beige outfit and rubber-soled shoes. She wore a sweatshirt jacket with Tigger and other *Winnie-the-Pooh* characters across her ample chest. I doubted many people gave this grandmotherly type more than a second glance.

"What can I help you ladies with today? Is this about the murders?"

Harvey waited for me to take the lead. "We have some questions about your car. A green Land Rover is registered to you, correct?" I showed her a photo of her SUV on my phone.

"That's mine," she said. "Has it been stolen?"

"We questioned a man yesterday who was driving it. Who is this?" I flipped open a photo of Allard that the school district had on file.

"Oh, that's only Cody," she said, reaching for her coffee. "He sometimes drives my car while his is in the shop. He has an old tanker. He's waiting to pay off his student loans before he buys something else. Did he get a ticket?"

"How do you know Cody Allard?" Harvey asked.

Joan crossed one hand over the other on top of the table, her short stubby fingers threading between each other. "I was on the committee that hired him at the high school. I showed him around and helped him find an apartment."

"Was that one of your duties on this committee?"

"Not exactly, although we were supposed to welcome and help him get situated. Cody needed a little extra help, you know, and I can't help it." She chuckled. "I'm a nurturing figure, I guess."

I nodded. "How is Allard doing so far on the job?"

"Great! I hear he's started a new weight-lifting team and the students really like him." She apparently realized she wouldn't get many answers from me. Marco turned her attention to Harvey. "Is he in some kind of trouble?"

"We're not sure," I answered. "But he was seen in your car near the site where the victims were found. He was with these two teens. Do you know them?" I split the screen to show images of both Ava and Sadie.

Joan was more hesitant this time. "Ava is a student at the high school now, but Sadie graduated last year."

"And what is your relationship with the girls?"

"I worked with both of them and have tried to offer guidance in terms of careers for after high school."

I took a sip of coffee and let Joan's words settle. She wrapped her hands around her coffee mug, appearing casual and calm.

"Do you regularly offer your home to past advisees?"

"I don't understand."

"Sadie spent the night here last night and drove your car to her grandmother's. That's quite a close relationship with an ex-advisee."

My bluntness didn't faze Joan at all; in fact, she'd been ready for it. "She was one of my best students, and I've continued to help her since I retired. She's had a rough time, Special Agent. Her mother went missing yesterday, and she needed someone to talk to."

"Sadie's grandmother wouldn't have listened to her grand-daughter?" I asked.

"She needs my help, and she trusts me. I've worked with her for five years now, and Sadie has had many problems at home. Her mother lost custody, you know the type. She didn't deserve the title of Mother in the first place. And her dad…"

I nodded. "You seem to be the person many people come to for help."

"Yes," Joan said. "It was my job for twenty-five years. I can't suddenly turn that switch off." She smiled sweetly, the kind of calculated smile someone gives before delivering a harsh put-down. "By the way, have you found Wilma Henderson?"

Harvey informed Joan that we hadn't found Wilma yet. As the search for her grew closer to the forty-eight-hour mark, we expanded the BOLO from Ohio law enforcement to the entire tristate area. We'd sent both an arrest photo along with a more recent picture provided by Sadie to all the agencies. And, as a precaution, we had local PD officers staked all along the Powell River, as well as the continuing search of the clearing and road Bennett and I had stumbled upon. Nothing had been reported yet. It wasn't unusual for sex workers and addicts to go missing for periods of time, sometimes even years, as they kicked around the country living off people's generosity. Goodwill was surprisingly easy to find, and addicts were gifted in locating it. If it hadn't been for Wilma's job and her daughter, we probably would not have heard so quickly about her disappearance. Gary most likely wouldn't have called the police if it weren't for this case.

There was something that bothered me about Wilma's disappearance, though. She'd vanished. Generally, people who know they'll be leaving for a length of time say good-bye in some sort of way to those they love and tie up loose ends. Wilma had done the opposite by requesting extra hours for the following week at work and planning to see her daughter over the weekend. It didn't make sense.

Harvey pointed to Joan Marco's wedding band. "I see you're married. Does your husband live here with you?"

"He does," Joan said. "But my husband is disabled. Henry mostly stays on the second floor, and I bring him what he needs."

"He's bed-bound, then?" Harvey asked.

"Mostly, yes. Old age can be cruel," she said, with a shake of her head.

Since Joan didn't volunteer the information, Harvey asked about his illness. Joan answered vaguely, alluding to the symptoms of both Parkinson's and multiple sclerosis.

I scanned the kitchen for any of the usual accoutrements for the disabled, for anything that indicated a bed-bound person lived here, and saw nothing. The SUV didn't have disabled plates and didn't appear to be equipped to transport anyone with special needs, nor did the sedan. Richardson hadn't reported any other vehicles registered to the couple. But there was something else I noticed about the kitchen: boxes of food in large quantities from a wholesale store.

"Is it just the two of you living here?" I asked.

"Yes. For whatever reason God saw fit, we never had children of our own."

I nodded to the large stack of food boxes in the corner: macaroni and cheese, crackers, oversized jars of peanut butter. "Are the two of you preparing for a zombie apocalypse?" I teased.

Joan looked over at the stack of food. "Oh, I've started buying food in bulk. It saves us quite a bit. The problem is the pantry won't hold it."

"Hmm," I said. "That's quite a bit of food for two people."

While Harvey talked with Joan about the murder case, I considered the layout of the house. Richardson had emailed me the architectural plans. The house had a walkout on the lower level, although you couldn't see it from the front of the home. And the house was almost 5,000 square feet. What did a retired woman and her handicapped husband need with a home this big? Something wasn't adding up.

My cell buzzed against my hip.

"May I use your restroom?" I asked.

I followed Joan's directions down the hallway and closed the door behind me.

The text was from Captain Riley. He and Richardson were finishing up at the scene along the river. He'd attached an image with the text, *Flyer found in the wooded area around the clearing.* The attached image looked to be a wrinkled nine-by-twelve sheet of paper. The flyer looked like it had been printed on a home printer. It read, *Trying to kick a bad habit? Lost all your family and friends because of drugs? Need help and support? Heart to Heart Recovery is hear for you!* Underneath the email address—a Yahoo account named *alottahearts*—was the image of the tattoo I'd seen on the victims' wrists, double hearts combined with the number two.

The email address looked suspicious to me. A lotta hearts? What kind of business would use that as an email contact? It would only take Richardson a few minutes to track down the IP address from the person who registered the email. I texted him and leaned against the sink to wait for his answer. My thoughts ran through what we'd found in the last twelve hours. Bennett and I had been right about Heart to Heart as a place for sobriety, and the flyer verified the meaning of the tattoo. Richardson, however, had found no traces of a Heart to Heart recovery center in the state of Ohio.

There was something else about the flyer: the misspelling, *hear* for *here*. A common mistake. But it seemed like a *young* mistake to me.

My cell dinged with Richardson's response. *Ava Washington. Email address was set up about a year ago from her personal laptop.*

Me: *Pull any emails sent or received from that address.*

What did Ava Washington have to do with all of this? Could she have been the one who developed the flyer for Heart to Heart? Joan Marco didn't look like the technically savvy type to me, not that you exactly needed to be in order to print out a flyer. But I couldn't let go of the spelling mistake. There was also Cody Allard to consider, since I'd seen him with the two teens. Was it possible Joan used Cody Allard, Ava, and her friend Sadie to help find women for Heart to Heart?

I looked around the corners of the bathroom and into the shower stall, kneeling down to listen into the drain. Suddenly, it hit me. Joan Marco's home could be the Heart to Heart recovery center we were searching for. It was possible she'd set up her home address as a sober living home. If that was the case, then where were the women who were supposedly recovering from drug abuse? I thought about the stacks of bulk food in the kitchen—Joan certainly could be feeding the women with that, but I couldn't get around the fact that the house was eerily quiet.

I texted Captain Riley, *Pull Allard out of class ASAP. Bring him in for questioning. Hold him until we arrive.*

The second Harvey and I left this house, Joan would warn Cody Allard. We had to get to him first. Somehow, someway, Allard was mixed up with Joan Marco. My instincts told me he'd be the first of the two to break.

"Mrs. Marco?" I called down the hall. "Do you mind if I take a look around?"

She waited to answer until I reached the kitchen. "I'm sorry, dear," she smiled. "Henry isn't feeling well, and it's not a good time."

"Another time then." Without Marco's verbal consent, I couldn't search the home. We didn't have a warrant, and anything I found would be inadmissable.

I smiled on my way out of Joan Marco's home and thanked her when she handed us to-go cups of coffee. I assured her we were doing all we could to find the killer and Wilma Henderson. Joan watched from her doorstep as Harvey and I loaded into the truck and cheerfully waved as we drove away. I waved back and realized what my dad had been trying to tell me. I'd been expending so much energy to force the case into the shape of columns in the murder board, pushing every bit of evidence into its perfect little boxes. But this case had a new shape—a circle. I couldn't shake the feeling that Harvey and I had just stepped into that ring and found Joan Marco as its center. The matriarch. All the others—Allard, Wilma Henderson, the victims, and the teens were mere satellites to Joan, her own constellation. As we drove away from the Marco home, I was certain that it was going to be a battle to take Joan Marco down. A center, however, is nothing without its constellation. If we could knock down enough of the spokes, it would eventually collapse.

CHAPTER ELEVEN

Day Three: 2:30 p.m.

I watched Cody Allard through the double-paned window of the interrogation room while he waited for questioning. The metal handcuffs chained him to the edge of the table, and every few minutes he leaned his head down to wipe away a tear. Allard had been arrested earlier at the high school for statutory rape of a minor, and Riley hadn't been kind about it. He'd cuffed Allard and paraded him down a busy hallway and out the main entrance of the school. Ava held on to her story that she was only good friends with her coach until Richardson got Ava to admit she'd seen questionable behavior between Allard and other girls on the team.

"So you probably aren't his only girl," Richardson said. "No matter what he's told you, you aren't the only one."

Ava finally confessed the affair to Detective Richardson while inside the principal's office. Once she saw Harvey's photographs, particularly the one of her kiss with Allard, she caved. Her main concern since the confession had been whether or not Allard would get in trouble. She said he didn't deserve trouble, and that he loved her. Now Ava and her mother sat in the conference room next to Allard's, neither speaking to the other. Through the window, I watched as Ava wept, and her mother ignored her.

"Do you think he thinks he really loves her?"

I turned to find Harvey behind me. "I'd say love has nothing to do with this."

Harvey stepped up to the window beside me. "She's a cute girl. This will damage her."

"How long are we making him wait?"

"Until I say so." Captain Riley came down the hall and stood with us. "Allard is nervous. I want that anxiousness to build."

Riley was in a foul mood. He'd spent the morning juggling a talk with the fourth victim's next of kin. A detective had finally located an estranged son living in Maine. He had a lengthy record and had once been arrested with his mother for drug possession. Despite the extended questioning by phone, nothing new came from the interview. No one, it seemed, knew any reason why our four victims would have crossed paths with our serial killer.

"Richardson ran a few more searches," Riley said. "Nothing came up on Cody Allard but a few old parking tickets at the University of West Virginia, his alma mater." He rubbed his temples. "I hate dealing with guys like this. I'm sure he's done this before, but there doesn't seem to be any record of it."

I understood what Riley meant—sexual predators' crimes were notoriously hard to prove and much more rampant in the American culture than the average person imagined. At least this case would be an easy one—Ava admitted to it, Allard didn't deny it, and we had Harvey's photographs. Allard was looking at prison time or a hefty fine or both. And he'd blown his expensive education—he'd never work with children again.

I still couldn't determine why Ava would have set up an email account for Heart to Heart. There was no record of her having any sort of addiction issues, and other than her relationship with Allard and friendship with Sadie, I couldn't determine her connection with Joan Marco.

"Are there any medical records to show Allard might have had drug treatment at some point in his life? Any hospital visits for overdoses?" I asked.

"I'll have Richardson look into it, but nothing has popped so far."

"It is possible Allard met Joan Marco if he needed treatment for a drug addiction. She definitely took a liking to him, and she was instrumental in getting him the job at the high school," I said. "There's no way she didn't know what was going on between Allard and Ava. Why didn't Marco report it?"

"I'll ask him about Marco and their relationship. And we can question Ava on it as well. But," Riley cautioned, "Joan Marco is a respected member of this community and has worked with generations of our local kids at the high school. I have a hard time believing she and her husband would be into anything illegal, let alone killing women."

"I understand," I said. "We need to check them out, though."

"Tread lightly, Hansen. That's all I'm asking."

Harvey, who had surprised me by remaining so quiet, jumped in. "Ava runs with this crowd, and she didn't tell us everything when we first interviewed her. Maybe she's the one we should be looking at."

"But," I cautioned, "we could have misread her secrecy as a cover for her relationship with Allard. And she knows her best friend isn't supposed to have a lot of contact with her mother. All of her suspicious behavior might be about covering for other people she cares about like Allard, and Sadie's meetings with Wilma."

"Well," Riley said, hitching his sheriff-gray pants up by the belt loop, "there's only one way to find out. Feed me any questions to my earbud."

Riley pushed into the first interview room and introduced himself to Ava and her mother. The recording light was already blinking red, and the sound of the microphones blipped on in the room.

For the next three hours, we observed Captain Riley questioning Ava carefully and hitting Allard hard, but little came from the interviews other than the two had been sleeping together since the school year began. Ava met Allard when he'd come to interview in June and then offered to help him get acclimated. According to Allard, the move had been significant, and he couldn't have done it without Ava's help. He rarely mentioned Sadie in his answers, and when directly questioned about Sadie and Joan Marco, Allard referred to them as *friends*. It was obvious that Ava and Allard had been aware of the dangers of their relationship when they both adamantly declared Joan and Sadie innocent of any knowledge.

He fit the profile of a seasoned sexual predator with a well-rehearsed excuse. He'd chosen Ava, most likely due to what her mother called a low self-esteem, and he worked it in his favor by grooming her with compliments and sexual innuendos. He'd taken time every day with Ava, seducing her until he was sure she wouldn't tell anyone. Once Ava began coming to his home, she was his—hook, line, and sinker. I wondered if Joan Marco used this secret about Allard to manipulate him into helping her with Heart to Heart.

Ava denied setting up the email for Heart to Heart. When she was confronted with the IP address that linked back to her laptop, she said Sadie and some of her other friends sometimes used her computer. It was possible someone else had set it up on her laptop, but Ava's behavior during this portion of the questioning drew my attention. She grew fidgety and couldn't hold Riley's eye contact. That could have been because Ava's mother had once again launched into a lecture about how she'd told Ava a hundred times to stay away from Sadie. There were multiple variables to consider, but my brain was tired. Exhaustion took its hold on me again, and I struggled to stay awake once Riley let Ava Washington and her mother go. He continued a little longer with Allard, pressing him for details of Heart to Heart.

Allard denied all knowledge of any recovery center or sober-living residence named Heart to Heart and claimed to have never seen the tattoo. He also claimed to have been clean his entire life. We were getting nowhere with him, but Riley railed on another twenty minutes before he finally booked Allard and delayed the bail hearing until Monday. I was willing to bet Joan Marco would be there bright and early with the bondsman to get Allard out.

"You okay?" Harvey asked me.

"I need to sleep."

She nodded. "Me, too." She'd also spent the night before in a car. "Looks like we might have a little downtime."

"Let's get some sleep and then get back to it. I'd like to head to Gary's later and interview any employees or patrons willing to talk about Wilma Henderson," I told her. "Most have been interviewed, but it's Friday night, and if the alcohol is flowing, we might get a little more from them."

Harvey agreed to meet me there. As we parted ways, I recognized that she'd become more tolerable, a change in her behavior that I welcomed.

CHAPTER TWELVE

Day Three: 11 p.m.

After a long swim and hot shower, I slipped on a pair of worn blue jeans and pulled a white cotton V-neck over my head. I braided my wet hair and let the heavy length of it fall down my back. My muscles were beginning to fill out again, and I felt stronger. It probably was all those cups of yogurt, bananas, and granola bars the hotel provided for breakfast. I loaded my bag with them every morning and snacked all day, a relief to my body since I hadn't eaten enough food for a few months. The color had come back in my face, and I was beginning to look like my old self again. That was a good thing, especially since Bennett would be joining Harvey and me at Gary's Girls tonight to help with interviews. I found myself anxious to see Bennett again, even though Gary's wasn't exactly the kind of place I pictured getting to know her better. Then again, neither was the inside of a serial murder case.

Since I'd left the station, Detective Richardson had sent me information on the regulation of private recovery facilities. Apparently, if local zoning permitted it, virtually anyone could open his or her home to people in recovery and designate it a sober living residence, as long as no actual medical treatment was offered on the premises. Joan Marco could have easily set up and used her home as the Heart to Heart Sober Living Residence.

The growing epidemic of drug addiction in America set the stage for this kind of scam to occur. Desperation left a person wide open to fraud. Had that been the case for our four victims? Had they reached the end of their proverbial ropes with nowhere else to turn?

Still, that theory left a very real question looming in my mind—who paid for Heart to Heart? I doubted Joan Marco would have taken these women in out of the kindness of her heart, but these also were women who had little to no funds. If they had health insurance at all, it was probably high deductible. So where did the money come from?

The chain around my neck caught the bathroom light. I examined the glint of the pendant as I brushed my teeth—Marci's Irish cross—and the picture of her twirling the cross back and forth along the chain was suddenly so clear, it felt like I could reach out and touch her. Since the Willow's Ridge case had closed, my memories of Marci had slowly dissipated. There were still moments when her presence came on so strong, it felt like I'd been hit by a wave—a Marci wave that had the power to knock the wind out of me.

I thought about how Heart to Heart might have some very real similarities to the One True Path ex-gay ministry. I twirled Marci's necklace around my fingers and saw the women seeking recovery as much the same as the members of One True Path. Most were there to find recovery from homosexuality, or because a parent or partner demanded it. Either way, we were promised we would be healed. And our fearless leader, Pastor Charles Jameson, was in the business out of more than just the kindness of his heart. He had a personal mission to rid his family of homosexuality. What exactly, then, was Joan Marco's personal mission with addicts?

❖

A hot pink neon sign lit up the sky along the highway. Its huge arrow pointed at the long, flat building that rambled on and on. Clearly, Gary had added multiple additions to the original building as his business grew. The bar sat on a large plot of land, at least two acres, and had the capacity to grow larger. The parking lot was filled mostly with trucks of all different sizes, with the freights lined up behind the bar like long hash marks.

"Our officers spend most of our weekends patrolling this place," Harvey said as we stood by her truck waiting for Bennett. "A lot of truckers stop here regularly. Some even sleep in their rigs for the weekend to avoid hotel costs. Since it's private property, we can't do much about it."

"That certainly helps the prostitution business here. Have you found any evidence that Gary gets a cut?"

"Not yet, but not for lack of trying. We've spent many hours investigating this place."

"Gary has himself quite an enterprise here," I said.

I leaned against Harvey's truck, which glittered under the neon lights. I tried to ignore her eyes on me rounding over my shoulders down my torso. I couldn't really fault Harvey for looking; I'd done the same to her when she stepped out of her truck. While we didn't wear uniforms for work, seeing each other in street clothes was a different experience. Harvey liked to show off her body, and she wore a black leather jacket over a tight tank top. She was attractive, and she knew it. Harvey's attractiveness, though, was too reckless for me. I didn't need the bravado, just a woman with the confidence to be herself. Where was Bennett, anyway?

"What exactly are we looking for here?" Harvey asked.

"Anyone who is willing to talk to us about Wilma or our victims," I said. "Our main job is to listen. Most likely what we're looking for won't be said aloud—it will be in the context of the answers. Stay sober and alert. Ask clarification questions. Eventually, we will find the ones who are willing to engage with us."

I saw Bennett making her way toward us across the lot. She looked fantastic, even in worn jeans and a Chicago Cubs T-shirt. The dark hair that usually fell in curls around her face was pulled back in a small ponytail. I couldn't stop from smiling as she approached.

"Let's do this," Harvey said, after our greetings.

Harvey gave me a quick wink as she pulled open the door of the thumping bar. Music and bright lights spilled out.

Harvey immediately filtered in through the crowd, which, surprisingly, wasn't all men. Most of those women, however, were there to find johns. Our clothing helped us blend in, and the lack of revealed skin told johns we weren't interested. We'd prepped for the possibility that they might not take no for an answer from us. After all, we were at least ten years younger than most of the women in the bar and much more fit. We had a signal on our cells, something to alert the others that one of us might be in trouble.

Bennett clearly hated everything about Gary's Girls. She hooded her eyes against the bright light, shrugged against the loud music and the cheers of the men lined along the runway. She turned her eyes away from the stage where women wearing pencil-thin heels gyrated against silver poles and each other. I didn't want to leave Bennett on her own while she was so uncomfortable, but standing on the outskirts of the action wouldn't work. I stood with her a while longer, scanning the crowd, looking for the person who might talk to us, the one who also looked uncomfortable. Then it became clear to me: we needed to get into the thickest mix of it all—the bar.

I leaned into Bennett so she could hear me over the music. "Follow me." I motioned to the bar, and then I did something I hadn't planned. I wrapped my hand around Bennett's. It happened so fast and naturally, I didn't completely realize we were walking hand-in-hand until we were almost to the bar. I felt the warmth of Bennett's body leaning into mine.

The bar area was slightly quieter, and we sidled up to it. The same woman who had been tending when Harvey and I had been in was working. I noticed the pert swing of her ponytail. She gave me a quick wave.

"Rhonda, right?"

She nodded. "What can I get you two?"

I ordered two beers, though I planned for the liquid to do nothing more than sit in front of us. We sat for a while, engaging men to the sides of us who regularly filtered over for drinks. We didn't get far. Most showed great interest, particularly in Bennett, until they realized we only wanted to talk. Harvey eventually texted she'd found a table of locals, but they only wanted to talk about what *we* knew.

After almost two hours of dead ends, the crowd began to thin, and I finally drank my beer. Complete sobriety didn't seem so imperative any longer.

"Finally loosening up a bit, huh?" Rhonda took my empty and replaced it with a fresh cold bottle. "On the house."

"Thanks." I took a sip. She caught me looking at her scar, a smooth hairless mass that ran along her neck and down into her shoulder blades.

"I got it when I was a kid," she said. "A fire."

"I'm sorry."

Rhonda shrugged. "Such is life. The scar has lost its red coloring over the years, so I don't get as many stares as I used to."

"What's your take on what happened to Wilma?"

Rhonda shrugged. "Everyone here believes she ran into a bad john and will end up in the river soon. There are a lot of bad johns, but we've been lucky for the most part—our guys are mostly softies at heart."

I didn't press her to find out what constituted a bad john. The truth was, I didn't want to know. "Is that what *you* think?"

Rhonda leaned over the bar. Her soft breasts fell into unstoppable cleavage, a tool she no doubt used to get better tips. She looked around, and when she was sure no one else could hear us said, "I think Wilma got into something over her head."

"But it might not have been a john?"

Rhonda shook her head.

Bennett took Rhonda's silence as a hint and excused herself for the bathroom. With Bennett gone, we had an empty bubble around the bar, a place where the two of us could talk somewhat confidentially.

"There are secrets here, Agent."

I leaned in to better hear Rhonda. "What kind of secrets?"

"Ones that have been around for a while. Ones that are a part of our town."

I took a sip of beer. "Such as?"

"There's a reason the serial killer picked here to work, you know. He picked Wallace Lake, Ohio, not a big town like Chicago or Columbus or Indianapolis."

I agreed. "It's a deliberate choice. But why?"

"Haven't we shown you? We know how to keep secrets and how to take care of our own."

"Like Wilma Henderson?"

Rhonda reached for her ponytail and wound it round her fist. She watched me closely, as if deciding whether or not to talk to me. I drank my beer and waited her out.

Finally, Rhonda leaned in closer. "The secrets at Wallace Lake aren't always buried so deep," she said. "Neither are some of the hearts."

"What do you know about Heart to Heart?"

"I know they've helped a lot of girls in our community."

"Including Wilma?"

Rhonda nodded. "And Sadie."

"Sadie?" I asked.

"And me." She held up her wrist for me to see: a faded double-hearted tattoo.

"What were your experiences with Heart to Heart? And with Joan Marco?"

The mention of Joan's name stopped the easy banter between us. I asked again, "What do you know about Joan Marco?"

"I know I don't want to get mixed up in any of this. I know that Joan Marco doesn't play, and I don't want to be the next woman found in the river."

"Wait, Rhonda!"

But I was cut off from Rhonda's attention by a group of drunken men demanding a slew of drinks. She moved away from me quickly, as though we'd never spoken.

Someone came to my side, but it wasn't Bennett. Harvey said, "It's after two," she said. "Call the night a bust?"

❖

I walked Bennett to her truck. Once we got there, I climbed in so Bennett could drop me back at my truck.

"Safety first," I teased her. Cops are always on high alert—you can't turn off that part of us. We sat for a few minutes in her truck, the heater blowing off the chill of the crisp fall night. "What do you make of what Rhonda said?"

"The bartender? She's been around here for some time," Bennett said. "Her uncle worked for the police station as dispatch. He's retired now. I remember how torn up he was when she started working at Gary's. It's not exactly the place of employment you want for your niece."

I had been wondering why Rhonda was willing to talk to me and in such a public place. Now it made sense—her uncle had been in law enforcement. On some level, anyway, she trusted us. She wanted to help. "Secrets not buried very deep. I don't know what to make of that."

"Maybe she means we're close, that we don't have much farther to dig."

"Possibly. I'm wondering if Marco uses people's addictions to get them to do what she wants. She seems to have this strong need to control the people and situations in her life. And think of all the people we've met that she's involved with—Allard, Ava, Sadie. They avoid any discussion of Marco. Her position as a counselor gave her access to many people's records. That knowledge is a level of control, and she's also had the ability to influence many young people over the years."

"Riley said she was respected for her work in the community," Bennett reminded me.

I nodded. "Most people go into counseling because they want to help others, but some go into it for the wrong reasons."

We sat beside each other, my mind turning over the possibilities a mile a minute. I thought about cases I'd read where a social worker had a savior complex and committed a crime because of the need to save the world. Was it possible that Joan believed she was saving the world by killing women who struggled with prostitution and drug addiction?

Bennett interrupted my thoughts when she pointed to the dash clock. "It's almost three a.m."

"Sorry, time has a way of getting away from me," I said. "Thanks for coming. I know spending your evening at Gary's Girls wasn't something you really wanted to do."

Bennett shrugged. "I've always been curious about what goes on inside Gary's. Now I know." She gave me a shy smile. "Besides, I knew you would keep me safe." A nervous giggle escaped her.

I said, "I want to see more of you, Bennett, after the case is over."

"I'd like that."

Bennett's soft smile filled me with incentive to get this case solved, and fast.

Chapter Thirteen

Day Four: 5:51 a.m.

My cell rang over and over until its vibration knocked the phone off the nightstand. I reached over the side of the hotel room bed. My hand finally grabbed hold of the cell just under the bed frame.

"Hansen. We got him."

"Sanders?" I pushed myself up and cracked open my eyes. "What are you talking about?"

"I'm talking about Wayne Bernard Cooper. Our serial killer."

I shook my head, trying to wake up. Was I hearing Sanders correctly? "It's a man?"

"Fits the standard profile to a T, Hansen. Cooper is a white male, age forty-five, no record, and delivers some kind of specialty filtered water for a company out of Las Vegas. He drove his delivery truck through Wallace Lake on his way to Columbus four times a month."

"Drove? He's no longer with the company?"

"No, he's dead. Cooper's body was found shot this morning. That woman you all have been looking for, the topless dancer? She shot him dead in Millard, Kentucky. I'm on my way there now."

"Wilma Henderson? Kentucky?"

Sanders chuckled. "I know it's early, but keep up, Hansen."

I listened incredulously as Sanders filled in the story for me, or at least, Henderson's version of the story. Cooper had been a regular visitor to Gary's Girls and offered Wilma Henderson a large sum of cash to accompany him on a delivery to Kentucky. Apparently, the two left directly from the bar late Wednesday night. Henderson's cell was dead, and she didn't have time to go home for a charger. She didn't contact anyone and broke the number one rule of sex workers—always give someone you trust your whereabouts when out with a john.

The trip went well until it was time to head back to Wallace Lake and Cooper didn't want to go. He'd gotten drunk at a bar with Henderson. She continued to nag him to drive back, and when he didn't, she attempted to drive in her inebriated state. She ran the rig into a wooded section at a rest stop where the two had pulled off. Cooper, enraged and with a gun, attacked Henderson and told her she would die like the other girls. They fought hard until he got his hands around Henderson's throat and choked her. She kicked him until he released her, and then once more in the jaw, breaking it. He dropped the gun. She grabbed it, firing over and over again. Henderson then used Cooper's cell to call 911.

"She's dehydrated and banged up pretty bad," Sanders said. "She'll be in the hospital a few days. Media already caught the story."

I knew that the rode-hard look of Henderson and her supposed heroic deed would draw in the press. Soon the tabloids would be fascinated with her.

"Cooper had all kinds of newspaper clippings and pictures of the four women found in the Powell River. We also found a woman's jacket in his cab with Betty Geiger's state ID in the pocket. Remember, she was one of our first victims in the case. Our guess is that it was only a matter of time until he killed Henderson, too, and then dumped her body at the Powell River on his way back through town."

How could I have been so...*off*? So much for my dad's declaration that my gut was my greatest investigation tool. "What other evidence did you find in Cooper's truck?"

"An extensive kill kit. Hatchets, shovels, zip ties, handcuffs, knives, you name it. It all fits, Hansen."

"*All* of that was found in his possession? It sounds planted."

"They've looked into it, Hansen. Cooper wasn't the smartest guy in the world, you know. It checks out. The Wallace Lake ME is on her way now to examine Cooper's body and the evidence in the truck."

"Bennett is working the case?" I asked. "I'll meet you as soon as I can get to Kentucky."

"No," Sanders said. "Stay in Wallace Lake and close up the case files. Complete the follow-ups and records. Check out of the hotel tomorrow, and let's meet at the office Monday morning."

I argued once again that the killer we were looking for might not be Cooper. "I talked to a bartender last night. There's more to look into here, Sanders."

He ignored my protests. "No more investigation. It's over, Hansen. Take that last swim before you check out of the hotel. You deserve it. And be happy for once, would you, please? The bad guy is dead, and there will be no trial. The world is safe from Wayne Bernard Cooper."

CHAPTER FOURTEEN

Day Five: 1:30 a.m.

The television filled the hotel room with background noise. I found a channel doing a marathon of old *Law and Order* episodes, a sad attempt to fill my loneliness. I sat down hard on a chair while everything spun around me. Drinking usually brought on spells of missing Rowan and sent me into the pit of feeling sorry for myself about the breakup. I was missing her and had to convince myself over and over calling Rowan wasn't a good idea.

I'd had too many tequila shots with the Wallace Lake PD at Gary's Girls. Gary himself hosted a celebration for law enforcement and for Wilma Henderson, the heroine of the hour, for ridding Wallace Lake of the serial killer. There had been a strip show or two and all the free-flowing beer we needed to fuel the loud celebration. The collective mood of the bar's crowd was celebratory, even joyous at times, for all but one person I came across—Rhonda the bartender. She avoided me all night until I cornered her at the side of the bar.

"Can we meet?" I asked. "You name the place and the time. I'll be there."

She looked around, wide-eyed, fearful.

"I need to know what you meant. We both know this isn't over. Where should I be digging, Rhonda?"

Her dark eyes were suddenly wild, almost feral. "I can't." She pushed past me and into a crowd of overweight middle-aged men who'd all had too much to drink and wanted to get way too friendly with her.

The bar TV had been set to a local station, and I had to stand below it in order to hear the breaking news. Wayne Bernard Cooper's photographs splashed across the screen, images taken from his Facebook account, as the reporter detailed what little information they had. Captain Riley had given a formal press conference where he declared very little: *Cooper appears to be involved with the murders at Wallace Lake.* Reporters yelled out questions about the murder kit and materials found in the cab, but Riley evaded the questions. Even with Cooper dead, I was certain we had to be careful about blaming him without enough evidence. Away from the camera and press, though, local law enforcement and even Sanders considered the case closed. Cooper had been dubbed the Wallace Lake serial killer, and possibly one with many victims from other areas of the Midwest. Police departments all over Cooper's trucking routes scanned their cold cases for murders that matched his MO.

Wilma Henderson's image filled the screen as the female reporter talked about the brave prostitute, followed by crime scene recordings and past news broadcasts of the victims found along the Powell River. And then there was Harvey, caught by a gaggle of reporters in the police department parking lot. Microphones were shoved into her face. Instead of backing away from the press coverage as we'd all been trained to do, Harvey leaned in to it. She smiled and flipped her bangs away from her eyes. She enjoyed every moment of her filmed *no comment.*

"Cooper. That motherfucker."

I turned to find a waitress unloading a tray full of empty beer steins behind the bar.

"That he is," I said. "Do you recognize him? Has he been in here before?"

She put her fist on a hip and examined me a second. "You a cop?"

"Got me." I smiled.

"Figured." She wiped her brow. "Yeah, I've seen him. Not often. One of the townies serviced him a few weeks ago."

I handed her my card. "Pass this along to her. I'd like to talk. She's lucky to be alive, huh?"

"We're all lucky to still be breathing in some way or another," the waitress said and loaded up with a fresh round of beer for the crowd.

Now, in the hotel room, I held my spinning head and took a deep breath to gather my bearings. I caught sight of the murder board, which needed to come down soon since I was leaving the hotel in the morning. I'd contemplated taking it down earlier because it wasn't really working for the case any longer, but the deconstruction of it felt so definitive. The act itself declared that all questions were answered and the case was closed.

I still had questions. Rhonda had them, too. We couldn't be the only two; everyone else, it seemed, simply turned a blind eye to those nagging discrepancies. It would have been nice to talk these questions over with Bennett, but she was staying in Kentucky to examine Cooper's body and until his truck could be thoroughly examined.

I leaned over to untie my boots and almost fell off the chair. I was drunker than I'd realized. Suddenly, a cop's knock rapped on my hotel door, that familiar confident pound of knuckles.

Through the peephole, Detective Alison Harvey smiled at me, her arm around a bottle of rum and a two-liter of Coke.

"I thought we could hang," she said as I let her in the room. "Celebrate a little more before you have to go."

"I'm still drunk from Gary's," I said. When she passed by, the smell of liquor followed her. I understood Harvey's appeal and why women fawned over her. Attractive and built, there was a lot to look at.

"Me, too," Harvey said. "It's a celebration, though. More liquor is in order. Nice room, by the way."

I'd only been in the hotel a few nights, but it already felt more comfortable than my place in Columbus. I wasn't ready to go back to that depressing grunge of an apartment building full of neighboring college students.

Harvey put the bottle on the desk and smacked her forehead. "I forgot glasses." She held up a wrapped plastic cup. "I guess we're stuck with these." She flashed her perfect white smile and laughed a little too long. Like me, Harvey was beyond intoxicated.

I sat down on the edge of the bed and took the plastic cup Harvey handed me with a lot more rum than Coke. She'd taken me for a hard drinker; Harvey didn't know I was a beer girl through and through.

"Cheers," I said, tapping my plastic to hers.

Harvey sat down beside me and took a drink. "Cheers to closing the case. You don't seem pleased about it."

I shrugged and tried not to notice her muscular body or the heat of her next to me. "Cooper is dead—how is that justice?"

She swished the liquid around in her cup. "I can tell you think there's something more here."

"Yeah."

"Everything was inside Cooper's cab."

I turned to get a better look at her. "That's just it—*everything* was in his cab, even antifreeze. Wouldn't long-haul truckers need bottles of antifreeze for winter driving? I'm not saying Cooper is innocent of crimes, but what if he didn't kill the four women we've been working with?"

Harvey finished her drink off. "It's over, Hansen."

"There's just one problem."

"What's that?"

I finished off my drink in one large gulp. "The tattoo. Cooper doesn't have it anywhere on his body and there is no drawing or replica of it in any of his belongings."

Harvey got up to refill our glasses. "Maybe the tattoo doesn't mean anything."

"Come on," I said. "You only *want* to believe that."

Harvey shrugged. "Cooper might not have had the tattoo on him, but he was known to have been with at least two of our four victims. How much more of a connection do you need?"

I shook my head in frustration. The cases of our four victims and that of Wilma Henderson weren't connected, but I couldn't put into words exactly why I felt that way. The high level of alcohol singing through my veins didn't help.

Harvey handed me a refill and noticed the murder board.

"Whoa." She stood before it. "You've been working hard."

"Too bad the board hasn't helped me much with the case."

Harvey stood in front of the board, her fingertips grazing over the photographs I'd posted of the Heart to Heart flyer and each of the individuals we'd worked with. The noise of *Law and Order* filled the room. When she turned back to me, her eyes had teared up.

"Harvey, are you okay?" I moved closer to her.

"Alcohol makes me emotional." She blinked hard a few times and cleared her throat.

Strands of hair had come loose from my braid and fallen around my face. Harvey reached out and tucked a patch of dark hair behind my ear. She let her fingertips graze my cheek before she pulled away. The sudden warmth of her touch sent a shot of desire through me like electricity, waking up every cell in my body.

Once I caught my breath, I asked, "What are you really doing here, Harvey?"

"I'm not sure," she finally said. "I guess I wanted to make sure everything was okay between us. You know?"

I wasn't completely clear on her meaning. We'd had a rocky start, yes, but since then we'd worked well together. She wasn't entirely to blame for our bumpy start, either. It was the job of a rookie to make mistakes, and I had made an entire lifetime of it.

"It's okay," I said. "I understand you want to rise up the food chain. We all do. Just be careful of who you trample along the way. Shit has a way of coming back around in our world."

Harvey stared at her hands as if I'd scolded her, and popped her knuckles.

"And stay away from those cameras."

"I'm sorry." Her eyes were wet again. "I just wanted to learn how to use my instincts like you do."

I shrugged. "You might be better off without it. Sometimes gut instincts are nothing but reckless."

Harvey apologized again, the alcohol speaking through her.

"No need for apologies." I sat beside Harvey, curling my arm around her shoulders. "We've got a bottle of rum to get through in this celebration, right?"

Harvey wiped her eyes and lifted her chin. Her intent gaze held mine while our lips were no more than two inches apart.

I could look away, I told myself. *I could tell her to leave and stop this before it happens.*

I didn't move. And Harvey didn't look away.

❖

The morning sunlight blasted through the hotel curtains, and the familiar cleaning cart rumbled past the door. I heard Housekeeping knock a few rooms down. I tried to roll over, but my body felt leaden. My tongue might as well have been glued to the roof of my mouth, and as I turned my face away from the harsh sunlight, a searing pain shot from above my right eye toward the back of my skull.

Shit. I drank way too much.

I concentrated on slowly opening my heavy eyelids as images of the night before flashed across my mind. The celebration at Gary's. The tequila shots. The cheers for law enforcement from the topless dancers. There had been free lap dances. Then there was the hotel and the rum. And Harvey.

She was there in bed beside me, the sheets pulled up to her lower back, her naked shoulders spread wide against the mattress. I jumped out of the bed and wrapped a blanket around myself when a sudden burst of nausea sent me running to the toilet.

When I came back to the room, Harvey was sitting up. She finger-scrubbed her short hair. "You okay?"

I wound the blanket around me tighter. I sat on the edge of a chair, my world spinning. "You need to leave, Harvey."

"Why?"

Harvey finally got out of the bed to search for her clothes when I didn't answer her. She stood in front of me without the least bit of concern to cover herself. "Look, we both had too much to drink. It was a crazy case, you know? We were just blowing off steam."

On some level, Harvey was correct; I definitely was blowing off steam and the celebration got out of hand. That happened sometimes, when I drank. I'd had a few one-night stands, and while inebriation always played a large role in them, I'd never hooked up with someone I worked with. I watched Harvey pull on her pants and shirt, knowing this wouldn't be the last time I'd see her. Ohio's law enforcement community wasn't that large, which made it likely we would run into each other again somewhere down the road on another case. While I couldn't remember much of what we'd done together the night before, sudden flashes of memory told me we'd done way too much. There had been her strong hands and hungry mouth trailing over the ridges and valleys of me, her hips rocking against mine, and my open invitation to it all.

"It's okay, Hansen." I watched Harvey lace her high-tops. "This will stay between us. Besides, you're leaving today."

My thoughts flashed to Rowan. I could hear her telling me the night we broke up, *I can't take the emotional reactions, Luce, the emotional behaviors that destroy you. Destroy us.*

Harvey filled her pockets with her phone, wallet, badge, and keys. She walked over and leaned down to kiss me. I turned away before her lips met mine, and she kissed me on the cheek instead. "It didn't mean anything, Hansen. Don't worry about it."

My gaze fell on the nightstand and on the stone Bennett had given me after our kayak down the Powell River. I felt the weight of my body sinking, the edges of water swirling up along my face and filling my ears. Slowly the rising water swallowed me whole, and I sank into a bottomless mass of its heavy safety.

After some time, I got up and locked the door behind Harvey. I let the blanket fall to the floor and stepped into the shower. The hotel bathroom stank of vomit. The water pounded against my face, and I turned it hotter and hotter as if I were trying to scorch myself. Scouring my body clean, I washed every centimeter of skin, every place where the fractured memories of last night still lingered. I scrubbed my hair three times to be sure the smoke and stale beer smell was out of it and thought of Bennett. She'd given me cryptic warnings about Harvey, but I'd dismissed them. What was it she'd said? *Harvey could be difficult.* And I knew there had been something between those two, something that didn't end well. No matter how many times I told myself the night with Harvey didn't matter, I knew it would come back to bite me someday. Then again, what exactly did Bennett and I have together, anyway? Nothing more than an acknowledgment of the undeniable attraction between us followed by a promise to see one another after the case ended. I leaned against the wet shower wall and let the water beat down on me long after it grew cold.

I couldn't fool myself. That promise I made to see Bennett again after the case meant something—to both of us. *Typical,* I told myself. *Screwing up any chance of a relationship before it ever gets started.* I felt helpless against my self-destructive self, and it wasn't long before I did something I hadn't done in much too long—I cried.

CHAPTER FIFTEEN

Day Seven: 8:00 a.m.

Director Colby Sanders considered me from across his desk as I told him about the findings from the Wallace Lake case.

"Once I left Wallace Lake, I didn't hear anything from you," Sanders said. "It's unacceptable."

"My apologies," I said. "I had very little to report."

Sanders rubbed his brow where the tanned creases of skin folded together. "You can't go out on your own again, Hansen. I won't have you going after serial killers without backup like you did in Willow's Ridge. Protocol is there for a reason. For fuck's sake, use it."

"I didn't want to bother you with the minor details," I said.

"Hansen"—he groaned—"it's your job to bother me with everything, and it's my job to decide if those details matter or not. Period."

"So," I said, leaning back in my chair, "I guess now would be the time to tell you what I've been thinking about."

"In regards to this case?"

I nodded. "Remember that interview I did with you when I was still in the academy? You talked to me about the Linda Clarke case."

"Oh God, how could I forget Clarke? Why is she on your mind?"

"I can't explain it all, Sanders, but Cooper isn't the killer we've been looking for. We should be looking for a woman."

"Lord, it's that spidey sense you got going on." He rolled his eyes, but indulged me. "All right, tell me."

"Think about the use of poison. The group tattoos and the stab wounds from behind—it leads to a female killer. And then there's the location of the bodies. Why dump the victims on such a popular river if you don't want them to be found?"

Sanders turned a pale blue Bic lighter over and over in his hand. He swiped the ball and let the flame glow a few seconds. "Okay, Hansen, I'll play. Let's say it is a woman who killed our victims. Why would she kill these aging drug addicts? What's in it for her?"

"Money. Just as it was for Clarke."

"These victims weren't the type to have investment portfolios, Hansen. I doubt they could scrape together the money for rent most months. Life insurance payments would have been out of the question," he said.

"Yes, but someone could have been paying the premiums for them. And most insurance companies pay double if a person is murdered."

He lit the flame of the lighter again. "Heterosexual serials tend to kill the opposite sex. Are you thinking she's a lesbian?"

"No, I'm thinking that the women killed were easy targets. Our killer went for those in desperation and those that would not be missed. Besides, poison was involved. The victims were stabbed in the back, for God's sake. How much more of a female kill can you get?"

"That's an interesting take on the profile, Hansen, but remember, Cooper wasn't exactly the manliest man of them all. He had the gear in his cab, and he always had antifreeze handy. Who says he wasn't a chickenshit and didn't stab the women from behind?"

"He didn't do that with Henderson. He attacked her face to face."

"He was pumped up on heroin, Hansen. Feeling much stronger than he really was."

"He was a junkie, Sanders. He was always pumped up on something. I just can't make Cooper work."

Sanders gave me a half smile, and shrugged. "Here we are, Hansen, back to you not being able to let a case go, despite all the evidence."

"It doesn't add up." I tried to continue my argument, but Sanders had me. There were only my unsettled feelings about the case—nothing more. Feelings amounted to nothing in the court of law. Without my father to stand by my side in the investigation and help me make a sound argument, I was going nowhere fast.

"Only to you," Sanders said. "Look, if it makes you feel better, run the social security numbers again. Contact insurance agencies. But I can already tell you what will pop up." Sanders made a zero with his ring finger and thumb. "A whole lot of nothing."

Neither of us said anything for a few minutes. There was only the sound of his plastic lighter edges hitting the desk.

"Damn building regulations," he finally said. "Join me outside for a smoke?"

The sun shone bright, and I leaned against the third-story balcony railing while Sanders lit up beside me. An old ashtray sat between us overflowing with cigarette butts, mostly from Sanders. His weathered hands rested on the old rail. Out beyond us were the prison grounds, a medium security unit for males that neighbored our agency building. Fields surrounded us in most directions—rows and rows of corn now tall and waiting to be cut down at the end of the season.

"I need your word, Hansen. Once I get the final reports from you today, I need you to end your investigation at Wallace Lake and begin your next assignment, gut feelings or not. Do I have it?"

I nodded. There was a strange dichotomy going on between Sanders and me, and I'd recognized it ever since the Willow's Ridge case ended. He was my boss, my superior, but the Willow's Ridge case had broken down many of those authoritative walls. He'd told me time and again that my skills sometimes outmatched his. Most days we jumbled back and forth from a friendship to a superior-subordinate role without much warning. I never knew what to expect, and I figured our relationship was just as confusing for him as it was for me.

Sanders took a long drag on his cigarette. When he finally blew the smoke through his nostrils, he started again. "The thing is, Hansen, your silence from Wallace Lake felt personal."

"It wasn't."

"No?" He gave me a hard look. "This isn't about how things went down after Willow's Ridge? Again?"

I shook my head.

"Look at me," Sanders said. His eyes held mine—slate blue and full of no nonsense. "I fucked up. I shouldn't have used you in the Willow's Ridge case. It was too personal—I realize that now. I'm sorry, but I can't keep apologizing." He looked away from me then, out across the cornfields. "You're going to have to make a choice here, Hansen. You bury that grudge you're hauling around and we get back to the way things were, or you move on. I can search out another director for you."

His words took me by surprise. It took me a moment to digest what he'd just said. "You've never really apologized, Sanders. Thank you."

He nodded. "Give my offer some thought, Hansen."

"I will."

When I turned to go back to my office, Sanders said, "You did good work, Hansen. Be proud of that. You finished the teaching career of a child molester and shook up the drug culture that has found a stronghold in Wallace Lake." He ground out the butt of his cigarette. "Sometimes these cases just don't pan out like we expect. Have the closed case file on my desk by five."

I sat behind my desk drawing endless looping circles on my case notes. I'd been back in Columbus for less than twenty-four hours, and I couldn't stop thinking about the center of my Wallace Lake circle: Joan Marco. The computer cursor blinked before me with a reminder of all the reports I still had to write. The truth was

I didn't have much to report other than the arrest of Cody Allard. Everything else boiled down to suspicion about Joan and Henry Marco along with the victims' shared tattoo. I'd run the four victims' social security numbers again and found nothing. If someone was making life insurance money off the deaths of these women, there wasn't a paper trail for me or anyone else to follow.

I thought about Rhonda's insistence that there was more going on beneath the surface. *Secrets in our town aren't buried very deep,* she'd said. What was she so afraid to come out and tell me? It all sounded so metaphorical. I was a cop, not a literature professor. How was I supposed to make sense of that?

I'd spent my first day back in Columbus doing laundry and cleaning my apartment. Everything, it seemed, was filthy. Sanders had given me a head start by collecting the trash in the TV room and kitchen as well as doing some of the dishes. Still, I'd let everything go for months. When I opened the apartment door and stepped in, all I wanted to do was shut that door and walk away. I wanted to go back to my hotel room in Wallace Lake and keep digging on the case. I wanted to escape the memory of these past few months inside the apartment's darkness. I wanted to forget how I'd been sucked into the hole of depression. I wanted to be stronger than the drink that now beckoned to me.

So I got to work cleaning. I hauled mounds of clothes down to the building's basement laundry room and changed out my sheets and towels with freshly laundered ones. I opened the only window in my place to let in some fresh air and started a grocery list. A grocery list! I couldn't remember the last time I'd been to the grocery. I also downloaded the Zillow app to my phone and began the search for a new place to live. I did everything I could to not think about what was eating me up inside—what I'd done with Alison Harvey.

A part of me felt like it was really Rowan I'd betrayed that night. Rowan, who had given so much of herself to me until she didn't. Rowan, who'd wanted to move on but, for some reason, still contacted me.

I'd have to tell Bennett what happened with Harvey and soon. If she found out any other way, it would only destroy what little chance I still might have with her. But when her text message flashed on my phone around ten p.m.—*Thinking of you*—I didn't tell her. Instead, we exchanged texts about Cooper's autopsy reports. We discussed the dirt and debris found in this cab that matched the soil around the Powell River. We planned a meeting for Sunday in the tiny town of Springrock, a location halfway between our two homes. We planned to hike the trails that would lead us deep into the wooded landscape and then dine in a little mom-and-pop restaurant on their local steak and potatoes. I went along with her plans for a day together as though nothing had happened, as though I didn't have this guilty secret lodged so deep inside my throat that it felt like a jagged piercing boulder.

CHAPTER SIXTEEN

Day Eight: 7:30 p.m.

It had been a little over a week since Sanders came barging into my apartment, and we started working on the Wallace Lake case. One week ago I had been so depressed I could hardly move. I'd been reliving every second of my relationship with Rowan over and over in my mind. Now, I had three women on my mind: Bennett, Harvey, and Rowan. How did I let myself get into this place? I wanted to kick myself as I pushed open the door for the sushi bar.

The restaurant was empty save for the back booth where she waited for me. The explosion of curls swallowed her slim shoulders, and I caught the familiar glint of her nose ring in the overhead light.

Rowan stood to greet me and she pulled me into an awkward hug, our arms and shoulders bumping until we both gave up the attempt and sat down.

Rowan flashed that radiant smile of hers. "Thanks for meeting me."

"Sure." I reached for a menu even though I hated everything there was to hate about sushi. I knew Rowan loved it, so I agreed to meet her there. We'd come to an impasse in our relationship regarding food: I hated most of what she loved and she hated most of what I loved. To avoid the long lecture about my lack of taking care of myself, I usually relented to wherever she wanted to go.

"You look good, Luce. A little on the thin side, but good."

I shrugged. "I miss your cooking, that's for sure."

The waitress took Rowan's order and mine for a beer and a bowl of broth. Then Rowan smiled and patted the box beside her.

"Thanks for bringing it to me," I said. "I didn't want to come to the house."

Rowan collected her mass of curls at her shoulders and tied them back. "Of course," she said. "It's your childhood in a box. You need to have it with you."

I thought about everything the box contained. It had many of my childhood mementos and photographs that my dad had saved over the years. He'd even saved some of my soccer and softball team medals. I'd played both until I was nearly sixteen. And then, I'd met Marci Tucker through the One True Path organization and everything changed. Nothing more went into the box. I reached up and clasped the Irish cross pendant around my neck, just to be sure it was still there.

"The dogs are doing great. I know they'd love to see you."

I didn't answer. I didn't want to talk about Toto and Daisy. Not yet, anyway. I was surprised to find that I wasn't nervous. In fact, it was the opposite: Rowan was reaching to fill the gaps of silence between us and speaking too fast, a sure sign she was uncomfortable.

"The case in Wallace Lake has been all over the news," she said. "Congratulations on closing it so fast. I keep thinking about those poor women. And that bastard trucker."

"I just love the poetic justice of it all," I said. "The hired hooker killed him with his own gun in his own cab. Dumb-ass."

Rowan laughed, and we joked about the craziness of the Cooper case as well as the media's appetite for anything and everything about Wilma Henderson. The topic helped both of us to loosen up.

"Maybe you could do speaking engagements about the case, Luce."

I nearly spit my mouthful of water at her. "Me? Give lectures?"

"Why not? Didn't Sanders do a lot of lectures about that woman he chased for so long?"

"The BWS Killer. He did, but you're forgetting one important thing. I don't know how to give a lecture."

Rowan shrugged. "You could learn."

"*Right,*" I teased her.

Rowan shrugged. "I'm just saying—you're really good at your job, and people are really interested in this dark shit. Go public with it. Then someday when you're old and sick of investigative work, you could teach at the academy."

I groaned. Rowan was always pushing me to do better, to be better, to improve everything about me. Her constant life planning for Special Agent Luce Hansen exhausted me.

"Anyway," she said. "Are you happy the case is over?"

I reached for my glass of water. "I'm glad we got Cooper off the streets."

Rowan sipped her iced tea and watched me closely. "Uh-oh," she finally said. "I hear a big *b-u-t* coming."

I couldn't help but laugh. I missed Rowan calling out what was really going on with me, sometimes before I even recognized it myself.

"I think there's more to the case," I said, "*but* I can't prove it."

"What does Sanders say?"

"He says to drop it." I took a long pull on my beer.

A darkness crossed Rowan's face. Was it worry? Or was it the outward appearance of what she must have been thinking: *Here we go again.* "Just be careful, Luce. Don't get pulled into another hole you can't get out of."

I wanted to roll my eyes at her but refrained. I didn't need another warning—what I needed was someone to listen and talk through it with me. Besides, I wasn't even sure I could trust my instincts anymore. Everything pointed to the case being over— maybe I needed to trust in that.

"Why did you want to meet with me, Rowan? I mean, you could have dropped the box off at the office."

She sat back in the booth and waited until my eyes met hers. "I wanted to see you. I wanted to be sure you're okay."

"I'm okay. And I'm glad to see you are, too."

"Really?"

"Really," I said. "You look…happy."

"There are reasons for that."

I tried not to take Rowan's answer as insensitive. It had been a long time since we'd seen each other, and I had no right to expect she wouldn't find someone else.

After the waitress brought our food, I listened as Rowan told me about Sydney, another artist working in Columbus, and how the two of them met. As she talked and I sipped my soup, I realized that, in a weird way, Rowan was seeking my approval. She didn't need it, of course; we were done. I was touched, though, that she wanted it. And I realized that I was okay with Rowan moving on. I never thought I would be. Now that the time was here, though, I was strangely fine with it all. "I'm happy for you, Rowan."

She took a breath of relief. "You are?"

"I am. It's good to see you happy."

She nodded and teared up. A few tears slipped down her cheeks. "There's been so much between us, Luce. I don't know what happened, you know? Sometimes I think it was the intensity. All that pressure of the past. Have you let those ghosts go, Luce?"

I watched the tears fall from Rowan's eyes. I wanted to be able to tell her I'd found peace with my past, and that I'd finally laid all those ghosts to rest. I wanted to, but couldn't. "It's not that easy, Rowan."

I recognized the look in her eyes—I'd seen it far too many times. It was the look Rowan always gave me when she found herself face to face with that enormous wall inside me, that impenetrable wall that kept her out.

After a few minutes, Rowan wiped her eyes. "You were always my friend above all else. Can't we get back to how we started? With friendship?"

I rolled my eyes and handed her a fresh napkin for her tears. "So you want to be the stereotypical lesbian exes who are still BFFs, huh?"

Rowan laughed and dried her eyes. "I do. Not BFFs, per se, but FFs. We were always better at that, anyway."

I had to agree with that statement.

When the bill arrived, Rowan grabbed it. "You can get it next time, Forever Friend."

We chatted a little longer about her latest painting project and how she'd recently painted the barn in bold chartreuse. I told her about my shithole apartment and the girls next door who regularly stole all the hot water from our shared tank.

"I also wanted to talk to you about something else."

"Uh-oh," I said, "sounds serious. Do I need another beer for this?"

Rowan nodded. "Don't worry, I'm not pregnant."

I chuckled at the old joke between us, our staple line whenever the other said they had something important to say. We always fell back on the pregnancy joke and blamed the other for forgetting to use a condom.

I uncapped my beer. "What is it, Rowan?"

"Well, I've been doing a lot of thinking since we split. I decided to make a change and try something new."

"Not men, I hope."

"Funny." She shook her head at me and smiled. Then she pulled out a rolled-up paper from her oversized bag, unbanded it, and laid out the plans lengthwise before me.

"This is Pranam, a yoga and meditation retreat I'm designing for the house and land that surrounds it."

The sketches across the table were of the land and the home we'd selected and lived in together. We both had wanted country, and Rowan had purchased it in the nick of time. Columbus grew and continued to grow rapidly, so there weren't many places with that much land available any longer. I didn't have a lot of money, and Rowan had received an inheritance from a recent death in her extended family. She put up the funds while I put in the labor and sweat of restoring the house and barn. The old property needed a lot of attention. By the time I moved out, the house was well on its way to becoming my work of art. Technically and legally, though, it all belonged to Rowan.

"It will be a business, one I run between my art projects, or possibly in tandem with them. I recently earned my license to teach yoga, so I'm thinking of offering three-day retreats. Yoga will be a strong part of it, but I also want to focus on meditation. I'll use all the skills I learned from my studies in India. In the beginning, I'm sure I can fill the retreats with artists, and hopefully the word will spread. What do you think?"

"I think it's interesting."

"Good," Rowan grinned, "because I want you to join me in a business venture. I'd like you to be one of the partners."

I stared at her incredulously. "What are you talking about? I don't know anything about business or yoga or meditation."

"No, but you do know this house and this land better than anyone else. I need someone who can handle repairs and someone I can be certain won't take advantage of me. I can trust you, Luce."

"Rowan..."

"Shh, don't say anything. Just think about it."

I looked at the plans before me once again. The penciled designs were highly detailed and Rowan had placed a photograph on the table of the new sign for the business. She'd been carving the sign from wood. She'd hollowed out the letters on the nameplate and filled them in with a golden paint that shone against the deep blue background. Stars glittered around the business name. "What does Pranam mean?"

"Roughly, it means to honor and respect another so much that you bow to her feet. Some translations show it as a divine reverence to God."

I nodded, but the truth was Rowan's experiences and practices with yoga and meditation from her time in India were far beyond me. Just give me some water—a pool, a lake, a river, an ocean—that's where I found my God.

"You're saying you want me to help caretake the land and home. How would we share the business, and who else would be involved? You know how consuming my work can be."

"We can get to the business details later. I found a lawyer to work with who deals with businesses like this. He can walk us through it."

I stared at her, not at all sure what to say. I'd expected Rowan to say quite a bit at our dinner, but nothing like this.

"Look, Luce, I know it's a lot. All I'm asking is that you think about it." She looked down at her hands as she balled the paper napkin between her fingers. "It's just that we picked this place out together and I know you put your heart into it. It feels like even though we're no longer a couple, we should still be together on that land."

"And what about the new woman? Sydney? Will she be cool with all this togetherness on the land?"

"It's a business, Luce, and a friendship. Whoever we are with will have to live with it. Period."

I thought about how much I loved that old house and the land that surrounded it. Spending time there again meant that I could be with the dogs I missed so much. I finished my beer. "I'll think about it."

She put her hands in prayer position and bowed her head to me. "Namaste, Luce. Namaste."

"*Please.*" I laughed.

Rowan giggled with me as she collected her things. "Would you like to see the dogs?"

"What, now?"

Rowan nodded. "Toto and Daisy miss you."

She didn't have to say another word.

CHAPTER SEVENTEEN

Day Eleven: 6:00 a.m.

The country road wound its way around the edges of Wallace Lake. It was a single lane used regularly in the summer by hikers and the lake enthusiasts. This time of year, though, only locals like Albert Finley and his three-year-old mutt, Gus, regularly walked the three-mile path. They'd walked the long stretch every day, rain or shine, since Gus was a pup. Today the two walked at a slow and steady gait side by side, Gus sometimes falling behind if he caught a whiff of a good smell, Albert sometimes falling behind if he needed to stretch his ever-tightening calf muscles. Both of them needed the daily routine of their walk, and it kept Albert's joints moving and lubricated even if he required a midmorning nap afterward.

The sun was up, and the crisp air felt good against Albert's face. Winter was edging closer, but he still had at least a month of fall weather before he'd have to worry about ice and snow. Albert spotted a collection of leaves ahead. With a little bounce in his step, he kicked the pile, letting the leaves rain down on Gus who snorted and tossed his head back and forth against the leaf attack. Albert chuckled; he knew Gus was all show. The dog loved the way the colorful leaves crumpled beneath his feet as much as Albert did.

As they neared the farthest point in the path from home, the fenced-off location along the road beside the Davidsons' cornfields, Gus suddenly got a burst of energy. He ran ahead, sniffing his big wet nose along the fence line. The dog slipped out of Albert's sight, rounding the bend. Soon Albert heard Gus's frantic bark—a series of three shrill screams that the dog only used to get his owner's attention.

"Gus?" Albert picked up his gait to follow.

Albert struggled to see what Gus had found. The dog stood along the edge of the path looking up at a large object that had been tossed across the top of the six-foot fence. It looked like a mannequin. Was it a scarecrow or something from the field meant to keep animals out of the corn?

He moved closer to the fence and called for Gus. The dog slowly backed toward Albert. The object looked like a person draped over the top of the fence at the waist. Could it be a Halloween trick? Some sort of doll meant to give everyone a start? He'd never known the Davidsons to take part in decorating for Halloween. Some of the kids in this area had a rough sense of humor, and Halloween was just around the corner. Still, who would do such a thing? Albert moved even closer, his heels leaving the berm of the single-lane road. He stared at the figure resting facedown with its arms stretched long and the fingertips reaching for the ground below.

Albert stood inches from the fence while Gus sniffed the ground all around Albert's heels. Albert saw the tangled hair falling for the ground in much the same way as the fingertips. He moved to his right to get a better look. Underneath all the hair, the woman's face was turned to the side, a face that had been beaten black and blue. But it was the open eye that told him what he needed to know, that wide open glazed stare. He stepped back and took a deep breath, all at once smelling the odor of decomposing flesh.

It was real: a dead female body.

Albert's stomach turned, and the vomit came on hard and fast. Once everything was out of his stomach, he could breathe again. But something Albert couldn't quite explain held him in his position. He could have stood there all day staring at the dead woman if it hadn't been for the dog that came to his side and rubbed his wet nose against the old man's hand.

When Albert emerged from his initial shock, his mind crackled with sudden thoughts and memories. He thought about how much he loved his home, so much that he'd never left the small town. He thought about his mother and how she'd loved to hike the forested land around Wallace Lake and her words to him: *Take care of your homeland, and it will take care of you.* He thought about how much Wallace Lake had changed in the last fifteen years, how drugs had infested everything associated with Wallace Lake and how his own police station hadn't been able to stop it. Crime had set in and taken root. All destruction, Albert knew, had a main source. For Wallace Lake, it wasn't heroin or any other drug, as most believed. Albert's eyes stung with sudden tears as he looked at the dead woman again. He knew why she died, and he knew what caused it. Albert also knew that if he wanted to take back the town he'd loved all his life, he'd have to make a stand. He'd have to go against the unspoken rules of Wallace Lake.

Albert searched through his wallet until he found the card the female investigator had given him at Gary's. He tapped the edge of the card over and over again, and then ran his fingertips across the embossed card with the official looking seals. He wondered about the thin woman with her long dark braid down her back. She didn't fit Albert's idea of a cop. He knew he should call someone, but the woman he'd met seemed so small to take on something so large and destructive. He thought again about her bright eyes, her wit, and her pressing questions at the bar. Whoever the woman was, she wasn't afraid of the truth.

But what could a small female investigator from the state actually do? After all, she was from the outside.

Strength, Albert finally decided, sometimes came from the most unexpected places. And, he reasoned, it was time for the destruction to end in Wallace Lake, Ohio. He couldn't end it alone—he needed help. And Special Agent Luce Hansen.

CHAPTER EIGHTEEN

Day Eleven: 10:00 a.m.

Bennett and I stood a few yards from the fence taking in its gruesome display. Gus, Albert's dog, sat quietly at my side. I held on to his leash even though he didn't need it, occasionally resting my hand on the dog's warm head and petting his soft ears. A neighbor would be arriving to look after Gus, and until then, his leash rotated through officers. Bennett and I both arrived on the scene after word spread throughout town about another dead woman. Wallace Lake PD had set up multiple roadblocks on the single-lane country road by the time I arrived, and everything was cordoned off within a quarter mile of the body. Captain Riley engaged most of his force at the scene in an attempt to keep out the press and the curious—the last thing any of us wanted was a photograph gone viral of the dead body slung over a six-foot fence. The surrounding cornfields swam red and blue with the churning lights as emergency workers combed the scene. Two officers had been sent to speak to the Davidsons, the owners of the property. Others searched through the corn rows with cadaver dogs as the tall end-of-season stalks swished around them.

Clad from head to toe in Tyvek suits, every movement of our bodies sounded like crunching paper. Bennett crossed her arms across her chest. "When I asked you to spend Sunday with me, Hansen, I didn't have a dead body in mind. Or this sexy onesie paper suit."

I laughed. "Who says Tyvek isn't sexy? Dead bodies, though"—
I grimaced—"don't make for a good date."

We stood shoulder to shoulder, mine much shorter than
hers, observing the different angles of the crime scene. A cadaver
recovery dog barked somewhere out in the cornfield. I reached
down and gave Gus a good rub behind his tall ears, and I suddenly
missed having a dog at my side. It felt like eternity since I'd lived
with Daisy and Toto, the dogs who now roamed wild at Rowan's.
Gus's smile told me he still had some pup left in him and that his
extra-sensitive nose had probably gotten him into trouble more
than once.

"God, Hansen. This is…" Bennett shook her head, unable to
finish the sentence.

I helped her. "This is a fucking horror show. That's exactly
what the killer intended it to be."

She looked over at me, the dark frames of her glasses
highlighting her inquisitiveness. The Tyvek hood held back all of
her hair, and I was struck by how she managed to look fantastic even
in that getup.

"What do you mean?"

"This entire setup is meant to scare everyone, Bennett. It's
some kind of message. Look where we are—in the middle of
nowhere at the edge of a cornfield. How many horror films use this
same backdrop? And the positioning of the body? You can't tell me
the killer didn't plan its placement down to the exact direction the
fingertips are pointed. It's a horror show meant to scare the shit out
of everyone."

"Okay, so the goal is to incite fear. What's the message?"

I stepped closer to the body. The paper booties over my own
boots gave me the sense that my steps were unsteady. "I don't know
yet. Are they done with the initial crime scene photos? Let's get a
closer look."

Once I handed Gus's leash off to a nearby officer, Bennett and
I moved toward opposite sides of the body. "Where is Harvey?" she
asked.

"I don't know." My body stiffened at the mention of her name. The last person I wanted to see was Harvey. "Has anyone IDed the body?"

"Not yet. Albert's pretty torn up, and he didn't recognize her."

Only a few hours ago, Albert's shaky voice hitched with sobs had come across my cell. He had to repeat himself a few times for me to understand. *A woman,* he'd said, *naked and thrown across a fence. She's beaten so bad, Agent, I don't know if anyone can recognize her.* I told Albert to wait on the scene until I could get some officers and an EMT out to him. By the time they arrived, Albert was in shock and needed medical attention. He'd been taken to the ER before I arrived on the scene so that doctors could regulate his heartbeat and breathing. The poor guy had quite a start to his day.

The crime scene techs moved away so that we could examine the body. There were ladders set up on both sides of the victim— the six-foot fence didn't make it easy for us. With gloved hands, I gently pushed the blood-clumped hair away from the victim's face. Albert's description had been accurate—the woman had suffered severe trauma and her face was even more distorted from hanging upside down for hours. She had multiple blows to the head and the swelling was so severe, I could only make out the shape of her lips and the white of her teeth. One eyelid had peeled up over its glassy iris revealing the lifeless eye. I couldn't pull my gaze away from that eye—something about her was familiar.

"We're going to need extra help getting her down," Bennett said. "The metal spikes of the fence tore into her body under the weight. She's already developed a significant amount of rigor mortis."

I weaved my hands through the woman's long hair until I found what might have been the worst wound—a hard blow to the crown that cracked the skull.

"There's an old scar," Bennett called from the other side of the body, "along the neck."

My breath caught with a vague recognition. "How old?"

"Many years. The skin has puckered and lost the white crosshatchings we usually see with newer scars."

I moved my ladder closer to see. I followed the scar on the victim from her neck and down to her shoulder. *It's from a fire, when I was a kid.*

I looked down at her wrists. There was the double-hearted tattoo on the left inner wrist.

"Shit, Bennett. I know this woman." I jumped down from the ladder and paced until I caught my breath.

"How do you know her?"

"She works at Gary's Girls. Rhonda—the bartender who was afraid to talk to me."

Recognition crossed Bennett's face. "Oh, God. I remember her, too."

Bennett examined Rhonda's extended arms and hands while I called the captain. The team needed to get more photographs of her scar, but at least we had a first name and a place of employment. It wouldn't be long before we had an official ID.

We waited for additional techs to finish recording the scene and help us remove the body. It would be tricky to get the body down without disturbing evidence, but there was no way for Bennett to do her preliminary exam with Rhonda folded facedown over a six-foot fence.

Bennett grabbed the edge of her lower lip with her teeth, working the flesh white with worry. "What a terrible way to die."

"Was she alive when they put her on the fence?"

"I need to examine her to be sure, but the extension of her fingers tell me it's very possible. There is also lividity in her hands, and that usually happens with hanging victims."

Dear God. No one deserved to die like this.

"Did she say anything the other night to make you think she was a working girl?"

I shook my head. "She was the bartender at Gary's, though. I hate to make generalizations, but a lot of those girls work the streets." I thought about my conversations with Rhonda. She'd mentioned

Sadie. Now that the case was officially reopened, I needed to follow up with her at some point in the day.

"Holy hell!" Both Bennett and I turned to see Harvey coming toward us. My stomach tightened and my shoulders stiffened at the sight of her. "What happened?"

Bennett used a hand to shield her eyes from the sun and looked up at Harvey. "It's another woman from Gary's. We'll need your help to get her down."

Harvey gave me a quick look from head to toe. "Another girl? What's going on?" she asked.

"It's not over, Harvey." I couldn't look at her as I spoke. "Not even close."

It took the three of us and three crime scene techs to lift Rhonda off the fence and onto the gurney. Bennett wasn't kidding about the severity of the rigor mortis. Rhonda's body would not lie flat against the rolling gurney, and it was as if her arms were frozen above her head. Bennett positioned Rhonda on her side in order to do the preliminary exam, and I watched Bennett's fingertips move quickly over the body. There were multiple abrasions, and the blood pooling caused a lot of the bruising to the face and limbs. Rhonda had been stabbed in the back twice. I wanted to grab something to cover Rhonda on the gurney; I wanted to help keep the damage to her body her own so that she could keep some semblance of dignity in this enormous mess. I turned away when Bennett punched the thermometer through Rhonda's skin to get the temperature of the liver.

"She's been dead anywhere between ten and twelve hours."

Harvey looked at me. "I wonder if she was working last night."

"Probably. Saturday nights are busy, and this would have been somewhere around one a.m. Seems early for her to knock off for the night."

"Maybe she was with a john," Harvey said. "Someone she met at Gary's. We need to review the security footage from the bar."

I looked closer at the stabs to the back. It was the same MO we'd been following with two of the other four victims. Could it be that the stabs represented the metaphorical saying—a stab in the back?

"The wound to the crown of the head left her unable to defend herself," Bennett said. "It didn't kill her, but knocked her out. I doubt she ever regained consciousness."

"What about her hands?" I asked. "You said I could be wrong about the positioning of them. She could have been reaching for the ground?"

"Most likely that was the body's way of fighting death on its own. When a person is rendered unconscious, the body will sometimes take steps on its own to save itself." Bennett glanced up at me. "I'll need to run more tests, but I doubt she felt much of anything after she fell unconscious."

That, at least, was some good news. I never wanted victims to suffer and I hoped that Rhonda slipped painlessly into the grace of death. That was about the best anyone could hope for, given the circumstances.

Harvey and I stood by and watched as Bennett and the techs loaded the folding gurney into the van. We needed to meet with Captain Riley, and while we waited for him to spare a few moments, Harvey paced back and forth around me. She'd buzzed the back and sides of her hair since I'd last seen her, leaving her blond bangs long. She had them gelled away from her face, combed so carefully I could see the teeth tracks. She looked at me with her strong chin jutted out and hands on her slim hips. "Are you going to talk to me?"

"This proves Cooper didn't kill those girls."

Harvey rolled her eyes. "I meant about what happened. With us."

"There's nothing to say, Harvey."

When she began an apology, I stopped her. "We're both to blame. I had too much to drink. It's all good, okay? Let's just focus on the case."

Harvey stared at me incredulously. "Why can't we discuss it?"

I ignored her question. I refused to get personal with her at a crime scene. "It wasn't Cooper, Harvey. He might have killed other girls, but not our women."

Harvey, realizing she couldn't change my mind, finally joined me in the work conversation. She looked back at the fence where Rhonda had been found. "Why the change in the positioning of the bodies? Why wasn't Rhonda found in the river?"

"Because her death was a threat. It was a message to the Wallace Lake community. Her murder screams, *If you stab us in the back by talking to the authorities, you'll meet a similar tragic fate*."

Harvey ran her fingers through her gelled hair and looked around the crime scene. "As far as we know, the only authority Rhonda spoke to was you. Someone was watching at Gary's the night of the celebration."

I nodded. "Or someone watched the bar's security recordings. Rhonda knew—she was terrified, Harvey."

"We'll need to get a formal statement from you for the record."

I popped my knuckles one at a time, thinking through the last few days I'd spent in Wallace Lake. "The bar was open to everyone on the night of the celebration. But our people and his employees made up at least ninety percent of the crowd."

Harvey nodded. "I see where you're going with this. You think one of our people leaked the information."

"It's possible."

"Hansen, I don't even want to go there."

A loud whistle came from somewhere in the cornfields. Barking dogs followed with the rustle and spread of corn stalks as an officer forced a path in the overgrown field.

"Get me an evidence bag!" an officer shouted. "I found a purse."

I followed Harvey through a cornrow, the leaves of the stalks smacking against us as we headed toward the voices. Photographers followed. The drop location of the purse was probably the length of a soccer field from the fence line, and by the time Harvey and I arrived, a crime scene tech had already set up the numbered evidence markers for the photographs.

The worn purse was made out of blue jean material and reminded me of some sort of eighties fashion where everything was made out of parachute material or stonewashed denim. Once the photos were taken, I reached down for the purse with a gloved hand and slowly unzipped it. The photographer snapped off shots every few seconds.

There was nothing remarkable inside the purse: a half pack of cigarettes and a lighter with Gary's Girls printed on it, a slim wallet with eight dollars and some change along with an expired driver's license for Rhonda Betterly of Wallace Lake, Ohio, two four-by-six photographs of a child no older than ten, a pack of gum, and keys on a Daytona Beach keychain. I pulled out a patch of receipts from a side pocket, mostly for fast food and groceries, and lastly a folded but very familiar flyer.

Trying to kick a bad habit? Lost all your family and friends because of drugs? Need help and support? Heart to Heart Recovery is hear for you!

While the officers recorded all the contents of the purse and bagged it as evidence, my mind whirled with possible connections. Rhonda knew Joan Marco. She knew about the so-called sober living home. She knew Wilma Henderson, who had also been involved with Heart to Heart. It was possible that Rhonda had been helping Joan locate women for her sober home through the bar.

I'd spent time with Rhonda. Only a few minutes, yes, but enough for me to get a read on her. Rhonda struck me as an honest woman giving everything her best shot. She didn't stand out to me as someone who would willingly send sick and needy addicts into the throes of a sober living home that might hurt them in some way. Her words to me in the bar had been laced with fear, but there was also something else: guilt. In order for her to take part in something she seemed to feel so guilty about, Joan Marco must have had *something* on Rhonda. Rhonda had to have done something she felt terrible about, possibly something illegal, and Joan most likely used it as a threat against her. That threat was probably made real for Rhonda once she realized that if she talked and Joan Marco found out, Rhonda might not see her child again.

Maybe I'd been giving Rhonda's cryptic message too much thought; perhaps I was overthinking the simple. The secret she referred to could be hers.

Secrets aren't buried very deep.

Was it possible that the message could have been a lot like the stabs Rhonda received in her back—literal, not figurative?

CHAPTER NINETEEN

Day Eleven: 6:30 p.m.

Deceased bodies, Bennett told me, are full of great stories. I'd spent the late afternoon and evening in the coroner's lab watching Bennett take Rhonda apart in order to listen to the stories her body had to tell. From the time Bennett unzipped Rhonda's death bag to the moment Bennett stitched the body back together, Bennett translated for me the stories this body held.

Rhonda Betterly was only forty-three, which surprised me. I'd taken her for much older, and Rhonda's life had apparently ground the youth out of her. Rhonda's body, according to Bennett, contained all the signs of a woman who worked hard and played even harder. Drugs had a way of festering inside the soul and taking their time letting go. Bennett found scarring and damage typical with heroin abuse. Rhonda might have given up the drugs, but Bennett found evidence of active alcoholism through the severe swelling of Rhonda's liver and the burns to her esophagus and stomach lining. In so many ways, Rhonda was very similar to the women who had been found along the Powell River: she worked at Gary's, she had the matching tattoo, had been in some sort of recovery from drugs though continued to struggle with addiction, and she was known to sell her body for extra money. It was the very distinct difference in Rhonda that interested me most: she was much younger than the others. This fact left me with one of my nagging gut feelings that

Rhonda Betterly had been important to the killer, at least at one point in time. Then something happened, something changed.

My suspicions were at least partly confirmed when Rhonda's nine-year-old daughter was brought into the station by her aunt. The child spent most of her time at her Aunt Rebecca's home, a preschool teacher at the local Presbyterian Church. To aid with the questioning, Captain Riley called in a child psychologist to interview her. Harvey, Riley, and I stood outside the one-way window and listened as the little girl detailed for the psychologist observations of her mother's life. She knew her mother did bad things with men, and that she drank too much. The girl talked about her mother's frightening drinking binges that ended with her mother coming into the girl's room in the middle of the night and waking the child. Rhonda insisted on sleeping in the girl's bed, holding the child tight in her arms, and sobbing into her neck slurred promises to keep the child safe. These episodes usually ended with her mother vomiting and/or blacking out, at which time the child crawled onto the floor to sleep. She knew her mommy needed help. She also knew her mommy wasn't well, and she talked to the psychologist about her mother's death much like an adult in a small body.

Rhonda's daughter confirmed for us what I had already guessed: her mother had been close with Joan Marco until they had some sort of falling out a few years back. The child remembered Marco and her funny husband because she was nice and always gave her sweet treats like brownies and homemade cookies. She also remembered Marco taking her to a fresh patch of earth in her backyard and helping the woman to plant a garden full of tomatoes, zucchini, and squash. Her mother was happy with Marco, the girl said, and she finally stopped sticking needles into her arm. The girl and her mother regularly spent the night at the Marcos' until one day they left and never went back.

"Why?" the psychologist asked.

The little girl shrugged. "Mommy said something bad happened. She said she needed to keep me safe. So I started staying with Aunt Becca a lot after that."

"Do you know where the bad thing happened? Did you see something bad?"

The girl paused, holding a doll in her arms like a baby, and said, "Outside in the night."

"Outside the house?"

The girl nodded. "In the yard. Only my mommy and Joan came back."

"What do you mean? Who was left behind?"

"The man," the little girl said, rocking the doll back and forth in her arms. "The funny man."

Harvey stepped away from the window and gave me a look.

"Yep," I said. "I heard it, too."

"What's going on?" Riley asked.

Harvey explained to Riley about the absentee husband Joan had explained away during our visit.

Riley turned to me. "You think he's buried in the backyard?"

"Joan Marco fits the general profile of a black widow," I said. "They generally keep their victims close to gloat over what they've done. And the house is located in a relatively new development. No one would question why the Marcos were working on the house or the yard."

"We'll need a warrant. I'm sure she won't agree to let us dig up her place without one."

"She'll be pleasant to work with, though," I said. "It's all smoke and mirrors with that one. Look for a money trail. See if the husband is still getting any sort of assistance checks."

He shook his head. "Richardson ran a zoning check—you were right, that property is zoned for a recovery residence. But where was the money coming from for these residents? Someone had to be paying for the women. Why would the Marcos open their home to these women if not for money?"

"That's what we are working on, sir," I said.

Riley groaned. "We'll need a warrant for the Marco property, and it's Sunday. You know how hard that will be," Riley said. "We have the girl's statement and yours from the interview—it's flimsy and generally wouldn't fly with the judge, but given the new murder victim and the press crawling up our ass, we have a chance."

While Captain Riley made a call, I stepped closer to the window. I watched the little girl playing with the doll on her lap. Her mother had clearly gone to the Marcos' home to get clean—the timing made sense based on Bennett's autopsy findings. Marco must have offered some sort of shelter and makeshift safe house to these women to kick drugs. Quitting heroin or any form of opiate was never pretty, and I doubted Joan Marco simply offered her home up to these women out of the goodness of her heart. She wanted something from each of the residents in return. Maybe that had been the cause of the falling out Rhonda had with Joan—Rhonda wasn't willing to do what was asked of her.

There was only one person I could think of who could possibly answer some of these questions. I left Harvey and Riley, both on their cells, and made my way to one of the occupied holding rooms. Once again I was defying Sanders's orders, going off and working alone. At least I had the good sense to flip on the room's recording devices.

Rebecca Betterly looked up when I pushed through the metal door, her face swollen and red with grief. She gratefully accepted the cold bottle of water I offered and immediately put it against her cheek.

"I can't stop crying," she told me from across the table. "I can't decide which is worse—losing my only sister like this or my niece saying to me that she wasn't surprised her mommy had to leave this world. She expected it—that's a lot for a little one to live with."

"It is." I took a drink from my own bottle of water. "She's so lucky to have an aunt like you. I'd be willing to bet if Rhonda knew she was dying, she found great comfort in the fact that you were taking care of her daughter."

My words provoked a fresh set of tears from Rebecca. "I'm so sorry," I told her. "Rhonda didn't deserve this. The only way I know how to make sense of it is to look for the person who did it, and to find some kind of justice for your sister. Will you help me?"

Rebecca dabbed her cheeks with a tissue and looked at me. "What do you mean? How can I help you? I don't know anything."

"Well," I said, "I need to know more about what has been going on in Rhonda's life these past five years or so. Did you know that your sister was an addict?"

After a moment, Rebecca finally said, "How did you know?"

"Her body. She has many of the signs of long-term alcohol abuse and there is damage from heroin abuse. When did she finally kick the heroin?"

"I'd say it's been about five years now. I heard it was bad—I never knew because I was away at college. When I came back, she was living with the Marcos."

"And she got clean there?"

Rebecca nodded. "From what I could tell, both Rhonda and my niece were happy and healthy living with the Marcos. I was grateful to the couple for all their help."

"What caused them to leave the Marcos' home?"

A darkness crossed Rebecca's face, a shadow regarding the past. Her brow furrowed. "Do you think the Marcos are involved with what happened to Rhonda?"

"I don't know," I said. "When someone is murdered in such a horrible manner, it generally is about something personal. I need to look at all the relationships in Rhonda's past, so I'm starting with where she got clean. There's a reason, though, why your niece isn't surprised her mommy is dead. What did Rhonda tell your niece? What did she tell you?"

Rebecca worried a tissue to shreds in her hands. I could almost see the gears in her mind turning, evaluating the risks of whether or not she should talk to me. I waited her out from across the table, sipping my water, and tapping my boot against the carpeted floor.

"She always told both of us if something ever happened, I was to take care of her daughter. She said that Gary's Girls could get rough, and some of the johns she went with didn't respect her rules. She tried to be selective, you know, but it didn't always work out."

"How is Joan Marco related to Gary's Girls?"

Rebecca looked surprised. "Sorry, I thought you knew. Joan got my sister the job at Gary's. She paid for the bartending course so that Rhonda could make more money and take better care of her daughter."

Rebecca had all my attention now. "What did Joan Marco want in return?"

Rebecca shrugged. "Nothing that I know of."

"Come on, Rebecca. Marco must have wanted something. Tell me what your sister told you."

Rebecca started to protest, but then realized I was far beyond listening to any bullshit. "She complained to me a few times that Joan wouldn't leave her alone. Joan insisted that Rhonda owed Heart to Heart for getting her sober. It was a large amount of money, and my sister didn't have it. Eventually, Joan asked Rhonda to introduce her to the girls who worked at the club who were strung out without any family. I thought it was because Joan wanted to help these girls, you know? But my sister said she didn't want to get involved because Joan was using the girls for money."

Rhonda knew Joan who knew Gary. Most likely it was Gary who'd informed Joan about my conversation with Rhonda. The pieces were finally adding up. "How did Joan make money from these girls?"

Rebecca shrugged. "All I know is that Rhonda tried to stay out of it, but Joan threatened her. That's when she made a will and the talk began about me caring for her daughter."

"She was scared."

Tears began to flow down Rebecca's face once again. "My sister was terrified. She started drinking again and I didn't know what to do to help her."

I reached across the table for Rebecca's hand. "You're caring for her daughter. You've helped her more than you'll ever know."

I waited for Rebecca to collect herself before I asked, "Did you know the Marcos before your sister moved in with them?"

"Mrs. Marco was our school counselor, but I didn't really work with her because I knew I wanted to go to college. She worked with the kids who didn't go on with college, so I only knew her name and face."

"What about Mr. Marco? I've heard he was disabled. Do you know if he ever worked?"

Rebecca gave me a questioning look. "Disabled? That must have happened after my sister left their place. He was fine when I visited. He worked for some kind of insurance company."

Rebecca had all my attention. "He sold insurance?"

She nodded. "I think so. That was how my sister was able to pay them for Heart to Heart."

"Henry Marco got your sister some sort of insurance coverage?"

Rebecca nodded. "He had to. Rhonda was broke."

❖

It had been a long day, so long that one of the only restaurants still open in Wallace Lake was the Waffle House. Bennett sat across the booth from me, her curly hair tied back from her face in a faded red bandana. We were both exhausted, fed up with waiting on the warrant to dig in the Marcos' yard, and starving—we finally had some time to eat our first meal all day.

We'd both been strongly warned to stay away from the Marcos until Captain Riley had the warrant. Every bone in my body wanted to drive over to their home and tear it apart board by board. But I knew it would ruin everything, and the stakes were too high. One mistake on our part, and the Marcos could get away with everything.

"You know what really bugs me about Rhonda's case?" I asked, pouring more syrup on my waffle.

"Hmm?" Bennett said between bites.

"I wonder why she stayed in Wallace Lake. If she was so worried about her daughter's safety and had gotten clean, why stay in this threatening place? Especially if the fear of it was so great it drove her to drink. She broke her sobriety."

Bennett chewed a bite of omelet and considered my question. "Her sister said she was threatened by Marco. She was afraid of losing her daughter and her sister."

I held up my cup for the waitress to give me a refill of coffee. Once she left, I said, "The threats indicate Rhonda knew something that could bring Joan Marco down."

"Well, if Rhonda helped her kill her husband, isn't that enough to bring someone down?"

I agreed. "It's more manipulative than that. She needed dirt on Rhonda so she wouldn't go to the police. She was probably physically forced to help Joan kill her husband. That way, if Rhonda did go to the police, she would also have to serve time for helping Joan. I think she played on Rhonda's sense of guilt."

We were quiet a moment, focused on the food before us. Finally, Bennett said, "I keep thinking about when you talked to me at the very beginning of all this about the wandering spider case. How did you see the signs so early?"

"I'm a profiler, remember?" I gave her a quick wink.

"A good one, too." She grinned at me, remembering our similar exchange on the Powell River. "This case is getting to you."

"It is." I rubbed my tired eyes. "I can't stop thinking about it. I *know* the pieces fit, I just can't see how yet. More players have to be involved in this than Joan Marco."

"Cody Allard?"

I really could have used my dad's help. This was exactly the sort of thing he would have loved talking through with me, and together we would have at least gotten closer to some sort of answer. Where was he? I understood that his ghost only came around when I needed help with cases, and this would have been a great time for his assistance. I wasn't sure I would be able to put all the pieces together alone.

"Allard," I said, "seems to have a strong relationship with Joan Marco. He must know something."

"Maybe she helped him get that job so she could keep the connection with the school."

I smiled at Bennett across the booth from me. Talking through hypotheticals on the brink of exhaustion was never easy. She'd brought up a good point with Allard, though, so I continued. "What could Allard bring to her table?"

"Well, he kept her connected. And he's a weight lifter."

Something clicked. "Youth and strength," I said.

"Yes." Bennett emptied her coffee cup. "She's an older woman who leans toward frail. She needed the help with something... maybe moving the bodies? Allard's a lot like Rhonda was when she lived there—young and strong."

I revisited a possible connection. "Rhonda went there to get clean. Allard could have needed Marco for the same reason, and he would have been indebted to her as well."

I understood why Joan needed the connection to Gary's Girls to find marks, but why the high school? What was she looking for in the teenagers?

"Maybe the focus shouldn't be so much on the dead but the living," Bennett said.

"I need to talk to Allard."

I reached across the table for Bennett's hand. Her fingers wound through mine. I wanted nothing more than to slip over to her side of the booth and kiss her, but my eyes burned with exhaustion, and what I really needed was some sleep. "You're good at this crime reconstruction stuff, you know?"

She chuckled. "I'm a detective of the dead, Special Agent Hansen, and a storyteller at heart. I can spin scenarios with you all night long, if you like."

I wished I had the night to give Bennett, one where I wouldn't instantly fall asleep on her. Bennett fascinated me, and I felt the mistake I'd made with Harvey even more. My father's presence would have helped me in so many ways with this case, but I began to see another possibility. Perhaps I was losing my dad as a partner to talk through various crime scenes, but it was possible he wasn't completely abandoning me. Maybe, just maybe, he sent Dr. Harper Bennett to take his place.

CHAPTER TWENTY

Day Twelve: 11:30 a.m.

A collection of law enforcement officers from Wallace Lake County and the OBCI gathered on the Marcos' lawn. Despite the blockaded neighboring roads, we were all on high alert for anyone who might have infiltrated the barriers. Everyone hoped to get the first photograph of the latest dead body found in Wallace Lake, and the story of the serial killer in small town Ohio had gone global, filling the lineup of crime shows like *Dateline* and *48 Hours*. Our fears became reality when an aerial photograph surfaced of us removing Rhonda's body from the fence. Those images only fanned America's thirst for more details on the case, and we were bombarded with questions regarding Cooper. *Was he really the killer? Had we gotten it all wrong? Was the general public really safe?* The team resented these relentless questions, which not only implied that we were inept at our work, but also that the public could no longer trust us to solve the violent crimes. These questions only incited fear in an already simmering local environment, the air so charged it felt like the right word or accusation could ignite the entire town.

Sanders had called in Dr. Frank Duffy, a forensic anthropologist and crime scene recovery specialist, with ground-penetrating radar. Duffy, who had a tuft of a bushy gray beard and an even longer ponytail, set up his boxy device that looked a lot like a manual lawn mower. An attached computer screen showed any anomalies or disturbances in the soil, which could be anything from a dog toy to a buried skull. Duffy used the computer to map the scene and document surface objects before he carried out the full scan of the earth below.

Subpoenas of Henry Marco's banking and insurance records verified that social security disability checks continued to be regularly issued to Henry Marco and deposited into a joint checking account held with Joan. Furthermore, in the last nine months there had been no insurance claims for medical visits or physical therapy submitted in his name, but prescriptions had been regularly refilled for Henry by mail and sent to their address of record.

After issuing a tristate BOLO for Henry Marco, and now armed with a possible missing person and governmental fraud, Captain Riley requested, and obtained, a search warrant for the Marcos' home and property.

When the cavalry descended on the Marcos' home, Joan answered the door and politely offered the crew coffee. Dressed in her usual grandmotherly attire with an adult Disney shirt, elastic-waist jeans, and rubber-soled shoes with great arch support, she rendered all sorts of stories about where her husband had been for the last year. Ultimately, she couldn't produce her husband or give an account of his whereabouts; all the coffee and the homemade cookies didn't change those facts. Joan eventually resorted to dramatic tears and claimed Henry had left her months ago, taking off like a thief in the middle of the night. Riley arrested her on the spot for fraud.

Once Joan Marco was removed from the property, the search intensified. We started with the places Joan valued and tended to most. Her home had been well cared for and was the perfect picture of domesticity—a mirage meant to hide what simmered beneath. When we searched under the polished wooden floorboards and behind the bright floral wallpaper, we found only the cavernous hollow space of a false life. Everything was set up for show, including Henry's house slippers tucked neatly beneath the edge of the bed and his crisp button-down shirts lined up in the closet. The home office revealed a collection of driver's licenses under different names and a corresponding variety of insurance cards. Officers confiscated any records related to insurance, disability, or medical claims and packed up the computer to search for hidden files.

"Be sure to leave a mess," Harvey instructed, clearing a shelf of books onto the floor. "Let her know we've been through everything."

Commotion arose in the backyard, and the sound of voices filtered through the windows. Suddenly, every officer's radio in the house crackled with the news: Dr. Duffy found something in the ground.

The indoor search continued, and I joined Harvey and Bennett at the edge of the Marcos' property. Harvey crossed her well-muscled arms over her chest. Dark sunglasses shaded her eyes. "Did you check back into the same hotel?" she asked.

When I nodded, Harvey said, "They might as well have given you the same room. Too bad you took the murder board down."

Officers dug one shovelful at a time, each collection of earth sifted and searched thoroughly. Then, finally, a bone fragment turned up under the zucchini plants and another under the tomatoes. Excitement mounted across the yard, and crime scene techs photographed the dig from every angle. Techs complained of the hard earth and picked around the bones with small trowels. Once the bones were placed on a tarp, Bennett examined them.

"These don't appear to be human," Bennett finally said. "I'd feel better if we could find the rest of the skeleton, though."

"We'll keep going," Duffy said.

Bennett bagged and tagged the two fragments to send them with a tech to the lab. Duffy continued to sweep his machine along the yard, and Bennett scribbled a quick sketch to document where the bones had been located in relation to other objects on the property.

"Scavengers make our work so much more difficult," Bennett said.

Captain Riley joined us. "Madame Marco won't talk."

"Big surprise," I said. "Is she in the holding tank?"

Riley nodded. "With our smelliest and loudest Frequent Flyer. There will be an indefinite delay before we move her out to general population."

The thought of Joan Marco in such a situation brought a smile to my face.

"It's possible the kid gave us a false story about Henry," Riley said.

I shrugged. "It's possible, but she seemed sincere. Of course she couldn't see what was happening once everyone went outside."

"I just hope this isn't all for naught and a complete waste of resources. We have so many eyes on us."

I felt those eyes, too, but Riley's words made me consider something else: while the yard was secluded and most neighbors were away, it still seemed absurd to bury a body in the backyard of a neighborhood home. Joan Marco was brazen, but certainly not stupid. With her strategic planning, she knew her home and property would be searched, eventually. Were we simply falling into Joan Marco's master plan?

The fall sun beat down on us, and with each sweep of the yard, Duffy narrowed the space he still had left to search. Forty minutes after he found the two fragments, when we had all but lost hope he'd find anything more, Duffy gave a shrill whistle. Everyone who'd been fighting for a spot in the shade rushed into action. This time the shovels dug much faster.

"It looks like the bones are all together," Duffy said. "Don't disturb them until we get a series of photographs."

Bennett squatted beside the hole, and then called out to the rest of us who couldn't get close enough. "We have a skull, but it's not human." She threaded her pen through the eye socket and held up the skull for everyone to see. "A dog. From the looks of the skull and the depth of its burial, he's been here a long time, probably before the Marcos moved in."

Groans erupted and Riley cursed beside me. Crime scene techs reburied the dog's bones, and my thoughts turned to where we needed to go next as well as the techs' complaints of the hard earth.

"We need to check one more place before Duffy packs up."

"Come on, Hansen," Riley said. "We need more evidence before we start scanning everything."

"The clearing," I said. "Just give me the clearing, and I'll let it go."

"The place where you found the teenagers and the teacher?"

I nodded. "It was obviously a part of their plan to get rid of evidence. Why not another body? Bennett told me the ground is softer around the river, making it an easy hiding spot. The clearing is public property, but private, safer, and above all, much easier to dig into."

"Answer this for me, Hansen. Why would they go to the trouble of burying the body in the first place? Why not put it in the river like the others?"

"Easy," I said. "We are dealing with two separate killers with different MOs. The killer who buried the body wanted to hide what they had done—shame dominated this killer. The other wanted the bodies found as soon as possible. This killer had a strong sense of compassion and wanted the bodies returned to the families."

Riley sniffed beside me and rocked back and forth from his heels to the balls of his feet. He grunted after a moment and called out to the crew. "Wrap it up! We're moving to one additional location."

❖

The clearing wasn't large enough to hold the full crew, and most waited for any findings along the dirt road where I'd found Cody Allard and Sadie Reid. I followed behind Riley, Duffy, Bennett, and Harvey single-file down to the flattened section where the local teenagers hung out. When Bennett and I discovered the killer's entry point to the river, we'd been looking for tracks and evidence someone had been along the water's edge, but we didn't look for a disturbance to the land that might indicate something or someone was buried. We fanned out across the land, and I pushed my way into the surrounding foliage.

With the sun sinking in the sky, a shadowed darkness settled in around us making it even harder to detect any changes to the soil. From the clearing we could see Dead Man's Point, that crazy bend where the river met Wallace Lake, as well as the nearby road where the bend caused so many accidents. From the clearing, there was also a direct line of vision to the land bars where the bodies had been found, and once again I thought about how perfect this location would have been to keep watch over the bodies. My theory that the killer had some level of compassion lent itself to the scenario that the killer sat in the clearing and watched over the victims. Had the killer been here that morning Ava Washington happened upon the two dead women?

I thought about the history of this location and again about my theory about why the bodies were found on the land bars. The killer must have been a local and familiar with the history and folklore surrounding this area. More evidence that the killer was hoping for a quick recovery of the bodies, and quite possibly a peaceful passage into death. A compassionate killer, of sorts.

"I think I found something," Harvey called out.

Harvey had been searching in a place so obvious, the rest of us dismissed it—the fire pit. We crowded around, but it was hard to see much of anything given that multiple logs and debris had been burned. The edges of the fire pit, though, appeared to be disturbed.

Techs made their way down to the clearing and helped to lift away the scorched wood and debris. As soon as the surface was relatively flat, Duffy ran his machine over it. The uneven ground made the reading difficult, but it wasn't long before Duffy whistled. "We've got something down there," he said and guided the techs to dig a deep, wide hole into the soft earth.

Shovels heaved away load after load of dirt until eventually the edge of a white bone gleamed against the dark earth. Duffy stepped down into the hole and used a trowel and brush to slowly pull away the impacted dirt. Gently, he investigated the area by pushing the trowel into various locations around the bone. Bennett joined Duffy near the bone and soon determined it was human.

"We've got more," he called out. "Drop the shovels," he directed the techs and handed them all trowels and brushes. A full skeleton was revealed, apparently curled in the fetal position, suggesting the person might have been buried alive.

While Duffy and Bennett worked to excavate the bones and remove them to a large blue tarp, the rest of us closed off the area with crime scene tape and collected evidence from the location. Once the recovery of a buried body began, it continued until everything had been excavated. This would be a long night for everyone, but especially Bennett and Duffy.

Close to midnight, with enormous floodlights illuminating the grave, the bones were arrayed on the tarp.

Harvey and I stood beside the tarp, our breaths little clouds in the cool fall night.

"Hello, Henry Marco," Harvey said.

"This body has been here awhile—long enough to completely decompose to only bone and hair," I told her.

"We don't know exactly when Henry went missing. He could have been gone over a year," Harvey countered.

"We know he was around for doctor and therapy visits less than a year ago."

Once the bones were fully exposed and photographed, a tech brought a gurney down to the clearing from the road. While the bones were prepared for transport back to Bennett's office, Riley called the detectives for a briefing with Bennett and Duffy.

"I know you need to run more tests, Dr. Bennett, but is there an obvious cause of death?" Riley asked.

Bennett looked to Duffy for confirmation. "We didn't see any bullet markings or obvious head trauma. This could be a case of poisoning or a stabbing. The positioning may indicate that the victim was conscious at burial and died from suffocation. A closer look at the bones will give me some clues."

Riley nodded. "Can you tell if the skeleton is male or female?"

"Female," she said.

Riley groaned. It wasn't Henry Marco, and we were now dealing with another victim.

"There is enough hair here to do a DNA analysis," Bennett said. She picked up the pelvis and held it out for all of us. "The pelvic inlet on males is heart shaped. This one is oval, and there appears to be a gap where the two pelvic bones meet." Bennett stood to face Riley. "It's a woman, and I'd say she's given birth at least once in her life."

"Hansen, you said we're dealing with two different killers here. You're losing me—how does all of this fit the profile of a black widow?"

"It's all about power," I told Riley and the group. "A black widow has the need to always be in control. In this particular case, I'd say Joan Marco knows exactly who this body is and knew exactly where this body was buried, and that knowledge gave her power."

Harvey agreed. "That's why you had Joan Marco at the center of your murder board circle, Hansen."

"Exactly, but there is one difference. I don't believe Joan had as much control over this kill as she did the others," I said. "I believe Rhonda Betterly killed this woman under Joan's direction, but Rhonda chose to bury the victim rather than place her in the river. We all know the black widow loves the drama, and this type of burial would not have been in Joan's instructions to Rhonda. We're looking at the disagreement that ended Rhonda's connection with the Marcos. Rhonda did what she needed to do to stay alive, but she insisted on doing it in her own way."

Suddenly, I felt the weight of Bennett's heavy unyielding stare.

Then it hit me: Harvey referenced the murder board inside my hotel room.

Bennett knew. And I hadn't been the one to tell her.

CHAPTER TWENTY-ONE

Day Thirteen: 1:00 p.m.

Small rural towns, at their very core, demand devotion. A protective barrier encases such places for those who belong—those who've spent the vast majority of their lives within the village. The us vs. them mentality led to the unwritten code of conduct: *What happens with our people stays with our people.* I saw the code in action when Ava's mother cautioned her not to reveal too much information about the drug issues in Wallace Lake. The code had also been a part of my interaction at the bar with Rhonda the night of the celebration. She was scared, sure, but she was also protecting someone. Guilt drove Rhonda to give me her cryptic message. She'd tried to give me enough to piece together the disjointed clues without her having to break the small town code of conduct.

I was faced with that code one more time when Harvey and I met with Cody Allard on his front porch. There was one very real difference with Allard, though, one I planned to use in my favor. He had only moved to Wallace Lake a year ago—Allard was not yet an *us*.

Sprung from jail less than twenty-four hours ago, Allard looked disheveled in his dirty jeans and sporting a three-day growth of beard. His freedom came courtesy of Joan Marco. She'd paid his bail in full the moment the judge deemed him eligible. Allard's bank accounts, however, did not have the funds to do the same for her.

"May we come in?" Harvey asked him, after his chilly greeting.

"I'd rather you didn't," he said. "What do you want?"

I looked around at the neighboring houses. People watched us closely while pretending to be busy with something, anything, in their yards and driveways. "You sure you want to do this out here?" I asked.

Allard glanced up and down his street and then finally nodded us inside. Harvey and I followed him into the dank rental home where all the shades were pulled tight and the trash bin overflowed with boxes from takeout—a way of living I could relate to. Today, however, *I* wore clean clothing; the smell of fresh laundry still clung to my collared button-down and dark trousers.

Allard swept off some papers and books from his couch so we could sit. A hand-knitted throw fell over the back of the couch, and I wondered if Joan Marco had made it. Knitting seemed like something she would do, and it fit into the persona she presented as the happy homemaker and caring mother.

Once Allard pulled up a folding chair to join us, I started. "We have a few questions for you, Mr. Allard, about your relationship with Joan Marco."

He looked at me hard and smirked. "You're looking for dirt on Joan. You won't get it from me."

"Cody," Harvey said too harshly, "climb down off your high horse. Trust me, we have more than enough dirt on Joan."

I shot Harvey a look that said, *Let me do it.* The last thing I needed was for her to argue with and alienate the one person who might be able to help us. "We're here as a courtesy, Mr. Allard. We're giving you the chance to explain the basis of your relationship with her and your role in Heart to Heart."

"And if I don't?"

I shrugged. "We'll find out on our own. But make no mistake, Mr. Allard. If we find any criminal activity between you and Mrs.

Marco that you haven't disclosed to us, you'll go down just as hard as she does."

Allard leaned back in his seat and the chair wobbled under his weight. The dark circles under his eyes revealed how much sleep he'd lost over the past few days. He considered me through a clump of unwashed dark hair that fell over his brow. "I want immunity."

Harvey and I shared a glance: Allard was willing to talk.

"Immunity?" I asked. "Why would you need something like that?"

"Don't play games with me, Special Agent Hansen. I think we're both past that."

"Immunity is not a game, particularly when you've already been charged with statutory rape and a trial is pending."

"Those charges are bullshit."

I crossed one leg over the other and pushed my heavy braid behind my shoulders. I'd had about enough of Cody Allard and his smug grin. "Don't kid yourself, Mr. Allard. You're a predator, and a skilled one at that. And I bet if I dug around enough, I'd find you've done this before. But I'm not the only one who has thought of looking into your past, am I, Cody?"

Allard's chair creaked as he shifted in it uncomfortably.

"Joan beat me to it, didn't she? She found the others and got their stories on record. She used that information to get you to do what she wanted done. She set you up for failure in this new town, a place where you swore to yourself you'd never touch another girl. But Joan paraded these two girls in front of you—one of age and one not—and gave you the choice. You couldn't help yourself—you found Sadie too old. You took Joan's bait hook, line, and sinker. And then she blackmailed you into Heart to Heart."

There was no sound in the small room. I let the silence sit between us and hoped Harvey wouldn't be the first to break it.

It took a few minutes, but finally Allard spoke. "What do you want?"

The smugness was gone. He'd only needed a little prodding from me. "I want to know about Heart to Heart. I want to know where the money came from."

Allard shook his head, avoiding eye contact with me.

"We know she fronted as a private sober living home, Cody," Harvey butted in, unable to help herself. "In Wallace Lake, no less, where so many are suffering with addiction. What did she do, Cody, promise you a job? A cut of the profits if you brought in enough women from your connections at the high school?"

Allard shrugged. "It doesn't really matter, does it?"

When Harvey started to speak again, I held out my hand to stop her. I needed verification of one fact—Harvey wasn't going to help me get there.

"There is one thing I know for sure about Joan Marco, Cody. She's a master manipulator who turns a person's greatest weakness into her weapon. She turned these women's heroin addiction into her opportunity to make money. I know Henry Marco worked out the insurance scam for the women," I said. "Here's what I don't get, Cody. Joan went through a lot of work for an insurance payout, but it doesn't seem worth it. Then, I realized there were other means of getting money from women in a sober living home."

"I don't know what you mean."

"Come on. Joan is a smart woman, and she'll put up with a lot if money is involved. So much so that she opened her home to addicts. She fed and cared for them while they kicked heroin and every other drug pulsing through their veins. You and I both know how labor intensive and unpleasant that venture can be. It's not worth insurance reimbursement, not in a million years."

"Look, you have it wrong. Joan really does care about those women. She just wants to help people who need it."

I turned to Harvey. "He makes her sound like Mother Theresa, huh?"

Harvey agreed. "Somehow I just don't see it."

Allard sighed. "This is getting really old."

"It is, isn't it? Tell me what happened, Cody. I'll do my best to protect you."

He shrugged. "She wasn't dealing, if that's what you're after."

"No, Joan was after the real money. Heroin and meth weren't enough for her and far too messy. She was into another kind of trade wasn't she, Cody?"

"I don't know—"

"She turned the women out as prostitutes," I said. "Mother Theresa gone pimp."

Beside me, Harvey's mouth fell slack. She hadn't heard the entire theory I'd been working on, and for once, she didn't have anything to add to the questioning.

"I didn't kill anyone," Cody pleaded, "and neither did Joan."

I moved forward on the couch until my knees were only inches from his. "You helped Joan negotiate payments for sex from women who were powerless to say no. You took advantage of the women's addictions right along with the Marcos." I spoke deliberately and in measured tones. "And you sexually abused a minor. It may not be murder, I'll give you that, but that's all I'll give you."

"Get out!" Allard pointed us toward the door. In his mind, he'd already lawyered up.

I sat across the table from Harvey in the busy restaurant where I found myself sharing a meal with her when I'd rather not. At least at this local eatery both Harvey and I could find something we liked. Harvey was vegan and thought the entire world needed to be as well. I stretched my legs out long in the open booth as Harvey ordered a plate of tomatoes, cucumbers, and lettuce to go along with her protein shake. I ordered the meat loaf and garlic mashed potatoes. Harvey gave me a disgusted face.

"At least the beef is coming from a local farm," I told her.

It had been a long two days. Bennett had been working since the bones were found and still had a lot of hours ahead of her. She had the preliminary forensic results that revealed the bones belonged to a Caucasian woman, most likely in her sixties. Henry Marco might have been deceased somewhere, but he wasn't in his own backyard or in the clearing near the Powell River. Riley had taken a go at Joan Marco to find his location. She refused to talk and asked for her lawyer before the officers could deliver her to intake.

Bennett wasn't returning any of my calls or texts. To be fair, though, she'd been busy with the transport of the bones to her lab and the analysis. She was nearing the second night of work to determine the manner of death and to officially ID the victim.

I'd been so stupid—not telling Bennett early on made it seem like my night with Harvey had been something worth hiding. My actions had done nothing but scream mistrust. Now I finally had the chance to ask the question I'd wanted to for a long time. "What happened between you and Bennett, Harvey?"

She looked up at me over the rim of her glass of tea, her blue eyes steady with mine. "Why do you ask?"

"I know something happened, that's all. I can feel the tension between you two."

She set her glass down. "A lot like the tension happening between you and Bennett, right?" She pushed her long bangs off her face. "Look, I know there's something there, and that's a good thing."

"It was," I said, "until she figured out what happened between you and me."

Harvey gave me a sad face. "I'm sorry, but it was only a matter of time. I swear Bennett is the most observant person I've ever met. She should have been a detective."

"Sounds like you spent more than a couple of nights together."

Harvey shrugged. "Not more than a few weeks. In case you haven't noticed, there aren't very many of us in this town. When I joined the force, Bennett and me went out a few times. She wanted something serious, something long-term. She thought I led her on, but I was just having fun."

I took a drink of my water and tried not to gag. It tasted exactly like it smelled—Wallace Lake. "Did you tell her you were just having fun?"

Harvey's shrug told me *no*. "Bennett was really disappointed, and she took it hard when I didn't level with her from the beginning."

I nodded, but what Harvey was describing didn't seem like enough to cause the reactions I was seeing from Bennett. After all, Harvey had only been seeing Bennett a few weeks. Why would she hold so much anger for such a short relationship?

Harvey must have read my thoughts. She added, "And there was this thing that happened with her med school roommate, Emily."

"Ah, the truth comes out."

The waitress saved Harvey from our discussion by delivering two plates of food. When Harvey shot her a wink, the waitress's blush spread down her neck.

"You get all the women, don't you?" I said, looking after the waitress.

Harvey gave me a guilty grin. "I have my secrets, Hansen."

I nodded. "I bet you do."

I cut open the steaming piece of meat loaf in front of me. "Tell me, Harvey, is there any woman in this town you don't have history with?"

"Yeah," she said. "Joan Marco."

We both laughed.

"About the other night, I'm sorry," I told her, reaching for the pepper. "I didn't mean to let that happen between us."

Harvey nodded and gathered a forkful of potatoes. "We were both drunk. Sometimes it just happens, I guess. We all need someone once in a while. Coppers are lonely people, you know."

I hadn't yet seen this side of Alison Harvey, the budding philosopher.

"Our job has so much pain and death involved, sometimes we have to temper that darkness with something good," she said.

"Deep thoughts, Harvey." I focused on the meat loaf in order to hide my surprise. Harvey rarely showed this thoughtful side. I understood what she meant; the darkness was strong and sometimes overwhelming. It was good to know I wasn't the only one who felt that way. "I just wish I would have been the one to tell Bennett, you know?"

"Tell the truth, Hansen. All of it. And then start over."

I would have laughed if the situation wasn't so serious to me. Here I was taking dating advice from Alison Harvey. I'd been worried that I'd feel uncomfortable with Harvey after our night together, and that our work would be filled with long unbearable silences. I'd found quite the opposite: in some ways we'd become *more* comfortable together.

Eventually, though, Harvey and I couldn't get away from the fact of *why* we were eating together, and our conversation turned back to the case. Over the course of the day, Detective Richardson had uncovered life insurance policies for the four victims along with insurance policies that covered a portion of their stay in the Heart to Heart sober home. Once Richardson knew the patterns, he uncovered similar insurance scams for other women, not only our four victims. These findings opened up an entirely new line of questioning: Were there more bodies to be found? Had some of the women escaped the Marcos and moved out of the area? Why were some of the women killed and not others? As usual, when this case answered one question, it opened three new ones.

Henry Marco had been an insurance salesperson for over twenty years. He gamed the system, buying insurance policies for women who couldn't afford their own and then banking the insurance payouts. The policies covered up to sixty days in a facility like the Marcos', just enough time for Joan to groom the women and make them emotionally dependent on her, and grateful enough to do as she asked. Gary's Girls was used as a hunting ground for prostitutes and other women down on their luck and in need of a soft place to land. All the money from the women's forced prostitution went to the Marcos—modern day pimps hiding in plain sight among the banalities of small-town life.

"So," I told Harvey, "we have adequate evidence for insurance fraud and conspiracy charges, but no evidence of murder against Joan and her husband."

"Even with another body at the freaking river."

"It will be hard without a witness, and you know Joan. She'll pull the sweet grandmother act to win over the jurors. As long as Henry is missing, she'll blame everything on him."

Proof of murder was easier said than done with a suspect as slippery as Joan Marco. I wanted nothing more than to put an end to her game of destruction and the pleasure she derived from setting into motion her wheel of horror.

CHAPTER TWENTY-TWO

Day Thirteen: 11:00 p.m.

Canal Street Park hugged the edges of Wallace Lake where its docks reached far into the dark water. During the day, the park was filled with families and swimmers with picnic lunches and bright lounge chairs scattered across its sandy beach. At night, though, the park became Wallace Lake's largest hangout for drug addicts looking to score and prostitutes looking for johns.

"No one is going to believe I'm a john," Richardson said looking into my hotel mirror.

"Keep that comb-over in place, and they will."

Richardson turned to face me in his Dockers jacket and khakis creased perfectly over his boat shoes.

I couldn't help but laugh. Since I'd met Richardson, I'd only seen him in a white button-up and black jeans. He wore stylish eyeglass frames in an array of colors that changed daily. "Perfect. Play dumb and the women will take pity on you," I teased, shoving my hair into a ball cap. "Besides, you have the perfect cover—you only want the famous hooker. I'm sure Wilma has been very popular since her story made the headlines."

We drove separately, and I stopped along the shoulder of the park's entrance road underneath the spread of a willow tree. Richardson drove slowly past and into a parking lot. From where I sat, I could see the shadowed outline of his car. He turned off his headlights and turned on the parking runners, a signal used to show he was looking for a date.

Where are they? Why aren't they coming to the car? he texted.

Be patient, I texted back. *Someone will approach.*

Thirty minutes later, a young woman finally emerged from the darkness. He called my phone and put his phone on speaker before she approached his open window.

"Hi there," the young woman said, leaning on Richardson's truck for stability. "What are you up for tonight?"

"I'm looking for someone," he said. "Wilma. You know the one all over the news?"

The woman laughed. "Wilma, Wilma," she said. "The celebrity whore. She's not anything special, buddy."

"Where can I find her?"

"I know where she is, but I think you need a young piece tonight. A tail you need to chase, not one that's already retired." I imagined her pressing her chest forward into Richardson's face. "What will you do with that granny anyway, huh?"

Richardson fumbled on his words. "I'm…I'm only interested in Wilma."

Show her the money, I directed him in my mind.

Finally, I heard him unroll a crisp bill from the roll of twenties he'd been given.

She sighed. "I haven't seen Wilma in a while. Try Gary's."

"I just left Gary's," Richardson said. "I heard she was here."

She took the money. "Well, it's a big park."

Richardson unrolled another twenty. "I'm sure you know your way around."

There was silence at the other end, and I imagined the woman looking at Richardson hard, her eyes evaluating him with pupils much too big. When she didn't move, he counted off a few more bills. "It's yours if you bring Wilma to me in the next ten minutes."

She disappeared back into the blackness of the park, and he shut off the motor.

"You got that?" he asked me.

"Yeah, hang tight," I told him. "I'm moving in."

I slipped out of my truck and moved closer to his car along the shadowed tree line. Everything was quiet save for the occasional ding of a buoy against the steel docks.

"Remember," I told Richardson, "cuff her as soon as she takes the money."

A good twenty minutes later, the familiar shape of Wilma emerged from the darkness with the young woman trailing after her. They approached Richardson's car cautiously.

"This is Wilma," the young woman said, and stepped up to the window. She held out her hand. "Pay up. I got her for you."

"It took longer than ten minutes," Richardson said, but handed her the cash. I heard the shake in her voice, a clear indication she was in need of her next fix. The money would soon be shot up her arm. She took off into the park, but Wilma remained.

"What can I help you with, handsome?"

"I'm looking for a date with the infamous woman who took down Cooper."

Wilma smiled. "You found me." She eyed the wad of cash in Richardson's lap. "Two hundred fifty bucks for the full experience." She rubbed her hands over her wide hips and breasts.

"Two hundred."

"Not for this piece."

"Two fifty is a lot of dough."

Wilma shrugged. "Celebrity inflation."

When Wilma turned to walk away, Richardson called after her. "Deal. I only pay this much for celebrities, though."

The moment her hand closed over the money, Richardson showed his badge and held tight to her wrist. He hadn't been quick enough with the cuffs. I charged through the shadows and had Wilma's hands cuffed behind her back before she realized another person was even there. Her tight skirt rode up over her thighs and she wobbled on the stiletto heels, leaning into me for balance.

Wilma spewed a thread of curse words at us, and then at herself for falling for it.

"Get in," I told her and led her to the passenger door. Once I closed her inside, I climbed in the back behind Richardson so that I could see her.

Wilma Henderson took one look at me and cursed again. "You're that agent, aren't you? The one that questioned me at Gary's?"

"I have some more questions for you, Wilma."

"Are you arresting me?"

"That depends on you. If we get your cooperation and honest answers, then no."

"I'm not doing anything wrong out here," she pleaded. "Jackie, the other girl, told me a guy in the parking lot needed some help, so I was just checking on him. I was worried he was sick or something." Her eye makeup was smeared and her bottle-blond hair a pile of knots.

Richardson held up his cell. "All recorded."

It was late, and I didn't have the patience for games. "Will you help us or not?"

Wilma spilled over in the passenger seat, her heavy arms resting on the console with her legs spread wide. She smelled of marijuana and stale cigarette smoke. "Let's go for a drive," she said.

Once the car rolled out onto a main road, I asked, "Why didn't Joan Marco kill you?"

"Huh?"

"You went through the Heart to Heart program. The Marcos hold a life insurance policy on you. And, I'm sorry, but you couldn't have been bringing in that much with prostitution. Why didn't they kill you like the others?"

"I don't know what you heard, but I didn't have anything to do with killing anyone."

"That wasn't my question, Wilma."

When she didn't answer, I directed Richardson to head to the station. "Wilma, the media's love affair with you is ending. You're on the tail end of your fifteen minutes of fame. What do you think would happen if I told reporters you weren't cooperating with our investigation?"

Wilma's jaw tightened. She'd been feeding off the media attention and didn't want it to go away. "I wasn't bringing in enough to stay at the Marcos' and I hadn't made up what I still owed them," she finally said. "They let me go because I was established at Gary's and was able to send johns their way."

"There are a lot of other women who could have done the same thing."

Wilma shrugged. "Henry had a thing for me. We went to high school together, and he had this crush. He was the one who wanted to let me go."

"Speaking of Henry. Where is he?"

Wilma chuckled. "Probably ran far away from his wife. She bossed him all around and beat the crap out of him when things didn't go as planned."

"Wilma"—I was tired and done with the conversation—"are you really telling me that this man, who Joan smacked around and belittled, convinced his wife you should live because of a high school crush?"

"You don't know what it's like!" Wilma cried. "I've got no one. My mom took Sadie, and I'm alone. The Marcos are my family."

"I'll let the reporters know," I told Richardson.

Wilma Henderson cried as the car neared the station house. When Richardson flipped on his blinker to enter the lot, Wilma caved.

"Wait. I'll tell you, okay?"

"You have two minutes," I said.

"I had this ginormous debt and my tally sheet only got bigger. No matter what I did, I'd never be able to pay it off. I needed to get out from under Joan, so I traded. I brought in three young girls who could milk johns for all their cash."

Now we were getting somewhere. "What do you mean, you brought three girls in?"

"You can't just walk away from Joan. I had to give her something worth more than me."

"Where did you find these girls? And why did they agree?"

"At Gary's. You sleep long enough on the streets and starve, you'll do just about anything for a bed and hot food."

"When was this?"

"A few years ago."

"Where are these girls now?"

"Where all the other girls go—they disappear into the night. Some run, some pay the Marcos off, and some are killed. But most just go away and hope they stay hidden from Joan Marco forever."

Richardson turned the car around to head back to Canal Street Park. The road was empty. Even with the headlights on bright, we could only see a few feet in front of us in the darkness.

"Why were some of the women killed?" I asked. "What made them different?"

Wilma sighed—she was tired of all of this, too. "They refused to pay back the debts on their tally sheet. They wouldn't do what was asked of them even though they signed the contract when they came in."

"Contract?"

Wilma nodded and held out her wrist to me. The double-hearted tattoo: a permanent contract and constant reminder of that promise etched into the skin.

I finally understood what happened with Rhonda. She helped Joan Marco kill the person we found buried along the river in order to fulfill her contract. Rhonda was let go with the understanding she would continue to bring in business. The minute Rhonda talked, though, she broke the contract and lost her life. The victims were the rebels, the ones who refused to prostitute themselves, kill, and keep quiet about the atrocities going on in that house. This new information brought me to the very real concern that the latest rebel against the Marcos was sitting with us in the car.

"How can we help you stay safe?" I asked.

Wilma gave a sad laugh. "Keep the Marcos in prison. That's the only way to keep all of us safe."

"How many others are we going to find, Wilma?"

Wilma shrugged. "I'd say most of them have already been found."

I started to question Wilma, and then it clicked for me. Of course—the bodies needed to be found in order to claim the insurance money. We needed to go back through the death records from the area for the past several years and look for deaths that appeared on the surface to be overdoses, accidents, or unsolved homicides.

I also understood why Joan Marco hadn't killed Rhonda earlier. Rhonda, and only Rhonda, knew the location of the woman she'd killed. She withheld that information from Joan—it was Rhonda's trump card, and the only card that kept her alive. Until she decided to talk to me.

Another large piece of the case fell into place. Because Joan used different women to kill for her, the manner of death regularly changed. It was possible the same woman had killed all of the four victims I was called in for, but Rhonda had killed the woman by the river. And the almighty Joan Marco had killed Rhonda Betterly in a show of her power.

CHAPTER TWENTY-THREE

Day Fourteen: 12:00 p.m.

I stopped by the hospital on my way to the station. Albert Finley had been admitted for dehydration and shock. By the time I arrived, he was well on his way to recovery. He gave me a big smile when I walked in the room and finger-combed what was left of his hair that stuck up in a variety of angles.

"They're springing me loose in a few hours," he said. "I'm in need of some real food." He pushed away the untouched lunch tray in front of him.

I laughed and pulled up a chair next to his hospital bed. "You had yourself quite a fright yesterday, didn't you?"

Albert agreed and told me how he'd found Rhonda, all the while running his fingers through his iron-gray beard and mustache.

"Once the officer told me it was Rhonda, I couldn't stop thinking of her. She was such a good girl and ran that bar like no other. Does she have family?"

I nodded. "A child."

"Poor baby. I wish I'd found her in time to do something."

"You did what you could, Albert."

I listened while he talked about Gus, his sweet dog, who was staying with a neighbor. Albert's eyes lit up when he talked about the mutt—Gus with the big nose that had to investigate everything along their walking trails. "I might not have seen her if it wasn't for Gus."

I leaned forward with my elbows on my knees. There was a purpose to my visit other than to check on his health. I'd spent a good deal of time thinking back to how I'd met Albert and my observation of his familiarity with the women who worked at Gary's. "I need to ask, Albert. Why did you call me yesterday?"

Surprised, he said, "I needed help."

"I've spent the last thirteen days of my life piecing together the crimes of the Marcos. They were running a business, Albert, something they couldn't have done alone. It would have been difficult to keep their business a secret in such a small community, particularly from the folks who frequented Gary's Girls."

The monitors beeped around us. Albert looked closely at me. "And?"

"And I'm wondering if you were a part of the Heart to Heart business."

Albert laughed incredulously. "Me? I called *you*, remember? If I was in on their crimes, why would I call the state police out to a murdered body?"

"I don't think you were involved with Rhonda's death," I said. I decided to take a gamble and then gauge his reaction. "I do think you were involved with the conception of Heart to Heart. I think you helped with the prostitution of the women. You called me for help because you knew it had gone too far. You didn't know how else to stop it."

Albert leaned back against his stacked pillows and stared at the game show on TV.

"Tell me what went down here, Albert. I'll help you the best I can."

He appeared to be watching TV, but I knew his mind was spinning. Albert was working through the consequences of what his words might bring. I waited him out.

Finally, Albert spoke. "I was born in Wallace Lake, and I never left except for short summer vacations to the South. I always loved it here. People used to ask me when I'd retire and move to Florida to become a snowbird like the other retirees from the Midwest."

"Sounds like a good retirement," I said.

"Not for me. I can't imagine my life without Wallace Lake. Even when the factories closed and the drugs moved in, I couldn't leave my home. There are so many good people here, Special Agent. The young ones deserve a clean place to grow up, and I want people to respect my town again. It needs to end."

I handed him a tissue from the side table. "I'll help you in any way that I can—you have my word. How can we finally end this, Albert?"

"It's a great start with Joan in jail, but you need to find Henry."

"Where can I find him?"

Albert continued his empty stare toward the television, and I saw the slight shake of his head.

"I need your help, Albert."

"If I help you, I will most likely be killed. I will be the next one you find hanging from a six-foot fence."

I moved in closer to the bed. "I know you're scared. I would be, too, given your situation. Trust me, Albert. When we take them both down, the Heart to Heart business will crumble."

"I might have my life, but I'll spend the rest of it in a jail cell."

There was nothing for me to say to that. If Albert had been involved, he would be charged as well.

Albert cleared his throat. He did not look at me but said, "A businessman never ventures too far from his product. Check out the old barn on State Route 710 near Bayton Bridge. There's an abandoned house out there. The local PD will know where it is."

I scribbled down the directions. "Product...is this where the drugs were kept? Or is this where the older women stayed who were recovering in Heart to Heart?"

Albert balled the tissue up in his fist. Tears filled his eyes, and he struggled with the decision of whether or not to tell me more. After some hesitation, he finally gave me his trust. "This is where the *other* product is kept. The younger women. The ones marked up and bid on."

My blood ran cold.

Young women. *For sale.*

❖

Harvey and I pushed through the overgrown grass and weeds, both nervous and unsure of what we might find. Thistles and thorns swatted against our legs until we came to the old, abandoned farmhouse near Bayton Bridge. The windows of the three-story home were broken, and chips of white paint peeled away from the wood in long shards. Creeping vines wound their way up the sides of the old home where portions of wood had rotted out. The nearest neighbor was at least a mile away. Just as Albert had said, there was also a barn on the property. We'd been inside it and found nothing other than a stray cat and her kittens along with some old farming equipment. A farmer who lived in the area was rumored to have taken over the land and used the abandoned barn to store his plow—a squatter of sorts. When we located him, he apologized profusely, terrified we'd arrest him for using land that wasn't his for profit. Once we convinced him we only wanted information, he said he tended to the crops most days, but hadn't seen any unusual activity on the land.

Harvey and I stood before the tall farmhouse with guns drawn. I'd already called in the location where the girls might be held, and Riley responded with a strict order: *Wait for backup*. Since Albert told me the girls were in the barn and we'd found nothing, I didn't have much hope there would be anything in the crumbling farmhouse. But there was always the chance—the chance Albert had told me the truth, the chance there were girls caged inside—and I couldn't let them wait any longer for help. I turned the broken doorknob. It clicked, and I slowly pushed open the heavy wooden door. I gave Harvey a signal: *Go left. I'll go right.*

I rounded an old dining room table and made my way into a kitchen barren of anything but a sink and a ceiling fan with broken blades. The floorboards creaked beneath my weight, unsteady and soft with lack of care and years of moisture. I turned the corner into a small room that was most likely used for laundry, my stance rigid with tension. A large steel tub sat in the corner, and trash littered the space along with a few overturned paint cans. When I emerged from the room, Harvey stood waiting before me. The first level was clear.

I directed her upstairs while I went down. The steep, slatted stairs led me into darkness so thick I couldn't see my hands in front of me. I flipped on a flashlight and rested it above my gun, descending slowly into the silent cellar. I finally landed on the cement flooring, which had cracked, and the pieces had grown disjointed with age. The pungent odor of mold filled the air. I made my way across the uneven flooring, scanning the space with the flashlight. The cellar was empty featuring a wide-open cavern with a small staircase to a hatch exit like the one they used to escape the tornado in *The Wizard of Oz*.

The cellar stairs creaked above me. My light beam spun around.

"All clear upstairs," Harvey said when she met me in the cellar. "Maybe Albert sent us to the wrong location on purpose."

"Or maybe they moved everything as soon as we arrested Joan Marco," my voice hardly above a whisper. My light beam scanned along the seams of the walls.

"The mold down here is enough to kill a horse," Harvey said.

"Breathe through your mouth." I dropped the light beam to scan the edges of the flooring along with their connection to the walls.

"Come on, Hansen." Harvey's voice sounded nasally through her scrunched nose. "Let's get out of here."

Just as I turned to follow her up the stairs, the light hit a section of the wall that was different—cement blocks that were painted brown to look like the rest of the heavy wooden slats. I stepped toward it, and Harvey followed. Leading with my gun and flashlight, I ran my hands along the wood and cement. The rap of my knuckles against the slatted wood sounded hollow, like there could be an open space behind it.

"Help me pull down this wood," I said.

Harvey grunted, her way of telling me she really just wanted to get out of the old house, but would appease me.

"Look for an opening in the wood, anything we can grab hold of," I said.

The wood slats were flush, but there was a give to them. We found a chipped hole near one of the corners about the size of an acorn.

Then I heard it: a small voice. Faint at first, then gathering in volume: "Help."

I turned to Harvey. I gave her a look that said, *Did you hear that?*

"Please. Get us out of here!"

Both Harvey and I leapt at the wooden wall; our hands couldn't tear at the boards fast enough. When I shone my flashlight into the small hole and told the voice to hang on, the light beam landed on the large eyes of a frightened girl. "Help us!" she screamed.

My hands dug and tore at the crevices of wood, ripping my fingernails down to the quick. When I finally found an opening that led me to a small door, the tips of my fingers chafed and filled with splinters. Huddled together in a mass of flesh were the girls—the ones for sale.

The smell of urine and defecation overwhelmed me, and I instructed Harvey to stop pulling down the wooden slats. We needed as much of the original structure in place for documentation of the scene. I called for medical squads and the entire crime scene team, directing them toward the back of the house to the cellar door where the entrance would be easier.

Harvey motioned to the women with her arms. "Come out. You're safe."

"No!" I pleaded with the young women to stay. "We can't risk moving them, Harvey. They could go into shock."

"But the EMTs will be here in a few minutes."

I called into the small space, "Is anyone hurt?"

No one responded, and in the glare of our flashlights, multiple large brown eyes stared back at us. Naked, bone-skinny, and strung out, their eyes hadn't seen light in months and fought to adjust. The oldest among them couldn't have been more than twenty years of age, and they clung to one another in a small circle for support. When one girl fell to her knees, the others lifted her back up. They turned from Harvey and me as if we might lock them back up or kill them.

I held my badge up and shone the light on it. "Police," I said. Soon the oldest spoke to the others in a sudden burst of thick language I didn't recognize. Then everyone fell quiet. The young women's muscles had atrophied with the forced starvation, and I found myself staring at their knobs of vertebrae, one over the other, like a string of pearls.

"Leave them." I directed Harvey to stay with the girls and moved over to the short set of cement stairs tucked away in a far corner of the cellar. They led up to the padlocked door where I could see a thin line of a blue sky where the two wooden doors met. I pushed against them hard, but the padlock wouldn't budge. I resorted to kicking against the doors hard a few times before the cellar door finally popped open to let in a stream of the bright sun. I savored a few breaths of fresh air, and I went back to help Harvey watch over the girls.

In the depths of the cellar, no one spoke, and no one cried.

The young women were all alive, and the sirens roared toward us.

CHAPTER TWENTY-FOUR

Day Fourteen: 7:30 p.m.

I lay across the hotel bed and listened to the TV news commentators report on the human trafficking ring found in Wallace Lake, Ohio. *In a bizarre twist to the Midwest's recent serial killer case...*Aerial photographs showed the run-down farmhouse and the collection of law enforcement vehicles surrounding it. The commentators had a field day speculating on what this latest piece could add. What the commentators didn't say, unfortunately, was that Ohio was a common stop on human trafficking routes through the United States. Most wouldn't guess those sorts of nightmares hid beneath the surface when they drove through the idyllic countryside or our friendly Ohio cities.

The four young women found in the old farmhouse had been airlifted to a Columbus hospital. While they were badly dehydrated and undernourished, all were expected to make a full recovery. We'd lost six women in the case that we knew of so far; the recovery of four gave our team something to celebrate, but it didn't balance out the bloody equation. Justice, I'd found, generally carried with it a deficit.

It had been a long and emotional day. A nurse had removed all the splinters from my hands and cleaned the abrasions. She wrapped my hands, winding around every finger, and explained to me that the community of Wallace Lake saw us as heroes. "You saved those girls," she said. "Lord knows how many others have come through our town. Your actions put a stop to it." I smiled and thanked her, all the while hoping that Sanders would see my actions in the same light. I'd blatantly ignored Riley's command to wait for backup, and while he wasn't my direct supervisor, I knew he'd report the risky behavior to Sanders.

As more details emerged about what the young women had gone through, I fought the urge to vomit all the acids churning inside my stomach. I chastised myself for taking so long to find the girls, for not asking people the right questions, and for my inability to see that the entire case could have been about human trafficking. After all, it had been me who'd initially asked Sanders about the tattoos as a marker for human trafficking. Why hadn't I followed through on that instinct?

Henry Marco, we'd learned, was arrested during a routine traffic stop in West Virginia. He'd been speeding seventeen miles over the limit, and the officer recognized him from the BOLO. Henry was in transport back to Wallace Lake where he'd join his wife in a separate holding cell. They had been the perfect cover for a human trafficking ring: an older, retired couple with spotless records and the façade of a welcoming home. The more I learned about the Marcos, the more I saw the carefully created image they strove for—everything, including their careers, were part of their invisibility from law enforcement. What made them invisible from the police, though, made them desirable to women of all ages struggling with addictions and financial troubles. After all, who would question a retired guidance counselor or the grandmotherly type who baked fresh cookies and pies? Who could imagine the friendly retired couple down the street as pimps and human traffickers? The entire scenario was simply absurd—and the perfect cover.

My cell rang.

"I found something, and I'm not sure exactly what it means," Richardson said.

"God, Richardson, you're relentless."

Richardson chuckled. "I just wanted to check into a few more things. I was running a search for the recently deceased in the area and for some reason an adoption petition came up."

"Adoption?"

"Glitch in the system, I guess. I found a record that shows Joan and Henry Marco tried to adopt Sadie Reid two years ago."

I sat up. "What?"

"Sadie was sixteen years old at the time."

"Why would the Marcos want to adopt her?" I asked.

"I don't know, but it looks like the adoption never went forward. Wilma Henderson signed the documents, but I can't find any signature from the grandmother."

"The grandmother didn't know." I thought about what Rhonda had said: Sadie was staying with Joan. Why had Rhonda even brought Sadie into that conversation?

"Remember Wilma said she owed the Marcos. She said she gave them three girls as payment from Gary's," I said. "What if Wilma traded her own daughter for freedom?"

"We've found no evidence that Sadie has been involved with any of this. Sure, she could be prostituting for the Marcos, but they didn't need to adopt Sadie for that."

I thought about the leather band one of the officer's found at the river and the mistake of *hear* for *here* in the Heart to Heart flyers. I thought about how Sadie kept her wrists hidden when she spoke to me about her mother being missing. Sadie Reid, like her mother, had the tattoo.

Suddenly, I understood.

Rhonda had been trying to send me a signal, and I completely missed the message. Sadie Reid was the latest victim of Joan Marco's sick game. Ava Washington had been a red herring planted by Joan Marco. And we bit on that bait. Hard. Marco knew that as law enforcement officers, one of our biggest jobs was to keep minors safe. While we were focused on Ava and the process of removing her from Allard's life, Joan hoped we'd overlook the other teen that desperately needed our help. Sadie, under Joan's strict orders, had killed our four victims posed on the Powell River land bars.

❖

My fist banged against the trailer's front door. "Ava!" I called. "Open up, Ava!"

A pair of eyes peeked out at me through a glass cutout in the door. Ava's mother opened the door. "It's late, Special Agent."

"Please, I need to see your daughter."

She sighed. "Is this about Allard?"

"No. Sadie Reid."

As soon as I mentioned Sadie's name, Ava pushed her mother to the side. "What's happened to Sadie?"

"I'm not sure. I need your help."

Ava opened the door farther and motioned for me to come in. I followed Ava over to the couch where I'd questioned her thirteen days ago. Her mother shook her head. "I *told* you that girl was no good."

I held up my hand to her; I didn't have time for a petty argument with a mother. I needed to find Sadie.

"Don't tell me to shut up. A woman was killed for talking to you, and now you are in my house. You are putting us all in danger."

News of Rhonda's death had made its rounds through town. I turned to Ms. Washington. "We are doing our best to make sure *everyone* is safe. We have officers patrolling neighborhoods around the clock. Time is of the essence, Ms. Washington."

Ava spoke up. "I'm sure she's fine. Sadie does this sometimes, when she's really upset."

"Does what?"

Ava shrugged. "It's Sadie's thing. You need to ask her."

"I'd love to, Ava, but I can't find her," I said trying to hide my frustration. "That's why I'm here."

Ava flipped her long blond hair over one shoulder. "Sadie disappears. She checks out on life for a few hours."

"Where does she go?" I already knew Sadie wasn't at her grandmother's because I had been there. Officers were dispatched to the dirt road near the river where we'd found Allard and Sadie, but they found no signs of her there or on the Powell River.

"I'm not sure she'd want me to tell you."

"Ava!" her mother warned, hands on her hips, and lips pursed in anger.

"Wallace Lake, okay? I only know because I followed her once and tried to go with her on the boat. She wouldn't take me with her."

"What kind of boat?"

"She rents one from the marina," Ava said. "You know the ones that look almost like canoes but have a little motor on the back?"

A rowboat. With a motor, she could make her way almost anywhere on the lake if the water was calm. It would be slow going, but doable.

"Where does she go on the lake?"

"I don't exactly know where," Ava said. "But she told me it makes her feel close to her dad."

"Her dad?" Ms. Washington said. She turned to me. "Do you know about Sadie's father? He passed when Ava was still in diapers."

I'd heard the story from Sadie's grandmother. "He drowned in a fishing accident on the lake, right?"

"That was the official story," Ms. Washington said. "Word around town was that Eric took his own life. He was mixed up in the beginning of the drug trade here in Wallace Lake and was out on bail. He was looking at jail time, and I think he was afraid of what might come out in the trial."

Sadie Reid's disappearance made sense to me now. She knew it was only a matter of time before we determined she was the killer. Once we found her, Sadie knew she'd be arrested. Sadie wasn't planning to pay homage to her deceased father when she took the motorized rowboat out on Wallace Lake to where her father drowned; she planned to take her own life and sink into the same watery grave where her father passed.

The water lapped against the sides of the rescue boat, and I yelled to the lake safety officer to push the motor as hard as it would go. We had two boats on the water—Harvey and I were on one, with Riley and another officer who regularly worked Wallace Lake manning the second. Our speedboats traveled in opposite directions with the bright search lights scanning the dark waters around us. Wallace Lake wasn't as large as Lake Erie or Lake Michigan, but it was vast enough for someone to hide on, particularly because of all its small canals and wooded shorelines.

Detective Richardson pulled the case file on Eric Reid, Sadie's father. The body had washed up on an eastern wooded grove about two days after he died, and officers had sketched the approximate location of his fishing boat at the time of the accident. From the records, we learned that Eric Reid's accident happened almost dead center of the lake. He'd cut the motor about five miles from the marina and let his fishing boat drift. The watercraft didn't have the required lights for night boating, so he was invisible to the safety officers who regularly patrolled the lake. Eric fell overboard sometime during the night, and his boat was found abandoned the next afternoon by patrolling safety officers. The chief ME at the time determined the cause of death as drowning while intoxicated along with heat exhaustion. Reid had been on the lake most of the day consuming alcohol and very little water. He lost his balance, the report read, and fell over the side. Reid did not have the strength or the sobriety to get himself back into the boat and eventually drowned.

I thought about what Ava's mother had said regarding Eric Reid's legal issues. Had he committed suicide on the lake? He'd been involved with the early trade of meth in the Wallace Lake area, and I wondered if he too was wrapped up in business relations with Joan Marco. Richardson pulled Eric Reid's arrest record, but there was little information other than his charges, and there was no way to tell exactly whom he might have been working with. Given that the mother of Eric's child and his daughter, Sadie, were both involved with the Marcos, the chances of his involvement with the Marcos were strong, too.

Harvey stood beside me with her PFD pulled tight against her chest. She gripped the overhead rail for stability. "I can't swim very good," she said in my ear.

"Seriously? You were snorkeling for evidence in the river when I met you."

Harvey shrugged. "I could easily make my way to the bars where I could *stand*. We're so far out right now, I bet the bottom is a hundred miles down." She gave a nervous laugh and moved closer to me. I thought about the rubber rescue rafts without motors Riley had used that day. It was possible the river wasn't very deep in those places. At least Harvey's fear served me well in this instance—I didn't have to fight her for the lead.

Our boat roared on. The spotlights swept across the smooth surface of the water, but there was no sign of a rowboat. After a few minutes, the officer slowed our watercraft down to a gentle rumble. "We are approximately in the center of the lake," he called back to us.

Riley's voice crackled through the radio—they'd found nothing, either. We could see the lights from their boat, which had traveled the northern parts of the lake and then turned back toward us. "We are heading west toward the canals," Riley said.

"Go toward the thickest tree line," I told the officer. Perhaps Sadie decided to go to the location where her father washed up—a thick wooded grove on the eastern edge of the lake.

The officer gave the boat more gas, and we veered toward the southeast. Above us, the stars shone clear in the night sky, and the loss of the sun chilled the night's temperature. The edges of winter weren't far away.

Once we neared the wooded groves, the officer idled along and I rotated the large lights to see into the wooded corners with the deep lake beneath. We found all sorts of abandoned fishing equipment caught up in the far-reaching branches, but no rowboat.

Finally, we saw a dim light waving with the current about one hundred yards from the tree line. I motioned the safety officer toward the dimming light, and he edged our boat closer to where a dying battery-operated lantern rested on one of a rowboat's benches. A shadowy figure sat beside it.

"I'm here to help, Sadie," I called out to her.

The officer set the motor to a soft hum and did his best to get as close to the rowboat as possible.

Sadie looked up as if she fully expected to see us out on the lake at night. Her face was ghoulish with the glow of the lantern highlighting her chin, cheekbones, and eyebrows. Long dark hair fell about her shoulders in sheets, and her knees bobbed up and down. Empty bottles of liquor lined the bottom of the steel rowboat, and I could smell the alcohol all the way from where I stood.

"I won't go to jail!"

"We can talk about that, Sadie, but we need to get to shore first. Will you follow us?"

"I'm staying here with him." She spoke fast, and her words slurred. Sadie had taken something else besides the sedative of alcohol, something that had revved her up.

"Sadie, I know you didn't want any of this to happen. You just didn't know how to stop it."

Behind me, Harvey radioed Riley for backup. The safety officer had already tied a rope to the rescue flotation device. "We'll tug you to shore," he called to her, carrying the float to the edge to throw it to her. "Hold on to this float. Ready?"

Sadie ignored him and spoke to me. "You don't know what you're talking about."

The tip of our boat now floated only inches from hers. "Joan Marco is a psychopath, Sadie. She and Henry are in jail. You are safe."

I moved closer to the edge of our boat. If I could somehow get into Sadie's, I could subdue her and drive us to shore.

Sadie tossed her head from side to side. "What will happen to Joan?" she screamed. Her actions were frenetic, her voice too high-pitched. She'd taken meth, and from the looks of it, too much. We needed to get her to shore and restrained before her behavior turned into excited delirium, a state some users went into that gave them superhuman strength and caused them to fight.

"How about I help you into this boat? Or I join you for the ride to shore?"

"No!" she cried. "I'm not going back."

"Sadie, please."

"The others are coming, aren't they? You told them where I am." Paranoia laced her words. Suddenly she stood, and the small boat rocked with the shift in her weight. The edge of her boat knocked into ours.

"I'll make a deal with you," she shouted. "If you promise me nothing will happen to Joan, I'll come with you."

"I can't promise that." I understood that Sadie was so far enmeshed in Joan Marco's grasp, she couldn't see clearly. She didn't recognize how much control Joan had over her. "She's not who you think she is," I said.

"I won't turn on her. She needs me."

Our exchange wasn't going anywhere, and I needed to get to Sadie. With a deep breath, I stepped up on the lip of our rescue boat and jumped into the center of her rowboat. It rocked wildly underneath me, and it didn't help when Sadie moved to the opposite side of the boat. She was off balance and near the edge. It didn't take much for the shifting boat to dip hard and throw her over the side.

"Sadie!"

Harvey used one of the light beams to scan the water where Sadie had gone down, but there were only the air bubbles that floated to the surface.

Without a second thought, I dove into the dark waters. I knew the safety officer had the rescue equipment ready, and Harvey had already called Riley for backup. Still, I'd broken standard protocol that everyone studying water safety learns first: don't jump into the water to save a drowning person—her panic could pull you down as well. In all my years of training, though, I'd never received any information on what to do for someone *trying* to drown.

The rush of the cold water engulfed me and its darkness—its blackness—swallowed me whole. When I surfaced, there was only the wavering light of the rescue boat. Sadie was underneath the surface, lost somewhere inside its blackness. In order to save her, I had to give up my sense of sight and use only my touch. I reached down, but she was too far below.

Something splashed beside me: a round floatation device. "Hold on to the floater, Luce!" the officer called to me.

I knew that he and Harvey intended to pull me onto the rescue boat. I refused to go without Sadie.

Slipping under the glassy surface, the familiar grasp of the water's strong arms held me. A part of me wanted to sink into the heavy safety of the water—the pure cool comfort of it. Then I felt the wide kick of my foot touch the bony edge of Sadie, possibly her shoulder. I dove deep and fought to lock my arms around her chest. Sadie wasn't going to go easily, though. She kicked me hard in the stomach, and I sucked in a large mouthful of lake water with a scream. I refused to let go of Sadie, and I kicked hard and arched my back sharply until we both buoyed to the surface. I held her tight with the bend of my arm under her throat, sputtering and coughing from the swallowed water.

"Let me go! Please," she begged. "Leave me with my dad!"

"I got you, Sadie. Lean in to me." I tried to maneuver her in the water to begin the rescue crawl toward the safety boat.

Sadie twisted in my arms and yanked against my grip. Her legs kicked me hard, and suddenly my forearm screamed with pain. Sadie bit down until she drew blood and didn't stop until my arm released around her chest. We battled in the water as I tried to get ahold of her and she tried to stay away from me. The air felt heavy so close to the water's surface, and my lungs screamed for a full breath of oxygen.

Harvey yelled from the side of the rescue boat. "Get out of the fucking lake, Hansen! Now!"

I looked up and caught sight of the black gun she pointed toward Sadie—a Taser.

"No!" I screamed. "Drop the Taser!"

The safety officer turned and realized Harvey had the Taser pointed at us. He knocked it out of her hands. Harvey didn't consider that using the Taser in water could create a dangerous shock.

Sadie pulled me under the surface again. She scratched, kicked, and bit me, finally resorting to yanking my braid. We fought hard, flipping over one another without anything solid to ground us in the deep lake. Another round of water flooded my windpipe, and I knew we couldn't keep up this fight for long. My body would most likely give out before Sadie's, as I suspected she'd already slipped into a delirium from meth. I did the only thing I could think of: I fisted a patch of her long hair, broke the surface for a breath, and held Sadie by her hair above the water.

Suddenly I heard the sound of Sanders's voice from the interview I did with him. *Linda Clarke's methodical*, he'd said. *She plans everything.* Had Joan Marco planned Sadie's suicide? Was it possible she'd booked the boat for Sadie and provided the alcohol and meth? There had been no reports of Sadie struggling with drugs or alcohol, and it would be in Joan's best interest for Sadie to die—she held all of Joan's secrets. I couldn't let that happen. In order to save her, I had to hurt her. Everyone who was supposed to help and take care of Sadie in her life, save her grandmother, let Sadie down. She never had much of a chance. I wanted to be the one to give Sadie a chance now by putting an end to this thing once and for all.

I let go of Sadie. Once her body began to slip underwater, I pulled my fist back and punched her as hard as I could on the right cheekbone. Her head flung back with the force of the punch. Then her head lolled. What I didn't take into consideration was how fast she'd go under. Coldcocked, she sank like a bag of cement. I reached for her, and suddenly we both went down as Sadie pulled me into the water's darkness with her.

For a moment, I couldn't gather my strength to pull Sadie above the water. I closed my eyes to center myself, and when I opened them, I saw the image of my dad wavering in the dark water. "You don't need me anymore, Luce," he said. "You've always known exactly what to do."

I reached for him, my fingertips spilling through the lake's thickness and grabbing hold of nothing. My father's image was gone just as quickly as it had emerged.

Soon I found the perfect grip on Sadie and scissor-kicked hard until I lifted her unconscious body to the surface. Without having to contend with Sadie's delirium, it was easier to move her body through the water. My arm swept across her upper chest, and I leaned back into the rescue crawl while hearing bits and pieces of Riley's voice barking orders. I felt Sadie's warm breath on the crook of my arm—she'd regain consciousness soon. I reached for the rescue device. Once I got ahold of the floater, the safety officer pulled Sadie and me toward the rescue boat under its bright spotlights.

Harvey tossed a harness down to me. As I maneuvered Sadie into the straps that wound around her legs and shoulders, I pulled close to her ear hoping somewhere inside she could hear me. "I won't let you go through this alone," I told her. "I promise."

Harvey and the safety officer hoisted Sadie up, water running from her dangling arms and legs in rivulets. They positioned Sadie on her back against the floor of the rescue boat. I climbed up the boat's ladder and my exhausted body soon came to rest beside Sadie.

CHAPTER TWENTY-FIVE

Day Fifteen: 10:00 a.m.

The incessant beep of the hospital monitors kept me awake most of the night along with the uncomfortable drip of antibiotics and extra fluids through an IV. And then there was the painful bloat of my belly. I'd swallowed more lake water than I realized in the fight to save Sadie, and every part of my body ached. The doctor kept me overnight for observation after stitching the wounds in my forearm where Sadie had taken a good-sized chunk out of me.

After a short rap on the door, Harper Bennett pulled the curtain back. She was dressed in heels, navy pants, and a simple off-white blouse—clothes that told me she'd been in court, not examining bodies along the riverbank.

"How are you feeling?" she asked, pulling open the drapes across my window.

"Like I'm carrying a child." I pulled the sheet down for her to see my stomach's swell.

"Ah, I have just the thing for you." Bennett reached into her shoulder bag and pulled out a bottle of water.

I laughed. "You can't be serious."

"I am serious. It sounds ridiculous, I know, but you need to take in fluids to expel the water from your system." She put the bottle on the bedside table. "So drink up."

I felt exposed in the hospital gown and pulled the covers up to my shoulders. The tilt of the hospital bed rendered my body useless except for my hands—a very uncomfortable position for someone like me who thrived on the physicality of her body.

"How is Sadie?" I asked, hoping to take the focal point off me.

"She's hanging in there, though I suspect she's not very happy with you." Bennett pulled up a chair to the bedside. She sat down, crossing one leg over the other. I noticed for the first time that she was wearing makeup, a hint of dark eye shadow with a brush of mascara.

"I just left the courthouse. Joan Marco's hearing was this morning. No surprise, old Judge Neelan kept her without the possibility of bail. They are moving her to a facility for females in Columbus since she can't be in the same jail as Sadie."

"What did Marco plead?"

Bennett gave me a look that said, *Do you really have to ask?*

"Not guilty because of what? Insanity?"

"The defense didn't go there. They only pleaded not guilty and offered no explanation. Word is she's blaming Henry and Sadie for all the murders."

I guessed that was coming. A woman like Joan Marco would never admit to the evil deeds she committed no matter what the consequences. Just like the infamous Brazilian wandering spider, Linda Clarke, Joan Marco expected to use her charm to manipulate her way out of the consequences.

"Joan has a tough judge. Thomas Neelan is the toughest, really. He won't fall for her lies. There will be justice in this case, Luce."

"Maybe there will be some justice for the murdered women and the girls caught up in human trafficking. But what about Sadie? She's only eighteen. What kind of justice will there be for her?"

There was nothing more to say regarding Sadie, so we sat in silence while the monitors beeped around us. We both knew Sadie would be charged with the murders. The circumstances that led up to the murders didn't matter much in our court of law, particularly since Sadie was the one who delivered the poison and fatal stab wounds. Sadie would be charged for the four murders no matter who told her to commit them.

Finally, Bennett broke the silence between us. "The talk all around the station is about how you saved Sadie. Impressive, Luce, but you could have drowned with her."

I knew the lectures from my superiors would be coming soon. Jumping in after Sadie had been a tremendous risk, and my body was paying the price for it. I'd gone out on my own again, and Sanders would only be more than happy to remind me of how these behaviors were my biggest fault as an investigator.

"I heard you gave Harvey quite a scare."

I grinned at the memory. "She learned it's best not to use a Taser on the water."

Bennett chuckled. Then, she said, "Why didn't you tell me?"

I wanted to play dumb with Bennett to avoid the conversation, but we were way beyond pretending. I needed to come clean if I ever wanted to be something more than her co-worker.

"I tried to, but it never seemed like the right time. I'm sorry, Bennett. We were both so drunk."

"That's a lame excuse."

I agreed. "If I could take it back, I would."

Bennett stiffened, and then re-crossed her legs. "I trusted you."

"I'm sorry," I said again. "I never meant to hurt you."

Bennett shook her head and looked past me out the hospital room's window. Her eyes took on an unfocused and distant look. "You don't owe me anything, you know? Not even the truth." She folded her hands in her lap. "Maybe I just *wanted* us to have some sort of a connection."

"There is a connection between us," I said. "The intensity of this case brought out the worst in me at times."

Bennett continued as though she hadn't heard me. "It's just that it was with *her*. Of all the people, *Harvey*."

The conflict between the two women made more sense to me, but I also sensed there was no point in bringing Harvey into the conversation. Bennett's continued anger implied she still cared for Harvey—perhaps I'd been the one to misread the connections going on around me.

"I owe you the truth, Bennett, and I hope you'll accept my apology."

Bennett stood up. "Most of this is about me—I'm sure you know that. What you don't know is that I was in a long-term relationship headed for marriage until I found out about the cheating. It had been going on for almost two years, and I never suspected."

"Bennett…"

"All of this"—she waved her hand in my direction—"has shown me that I'm not ready to see you or anyone else."

Bennett pointed to the bottled water on my hospital tray. "Drink up, Hansen, and take care of yourself." She pulled the door closed behind her.

I'd broken the trust I'd developed with Bennett and found myself in an awful position. Trust was a funny thing—once lost, sometimes you could never fully regain it. I was at the mercy of Bennett and her willingness to let me back in, just as Sanders was at my mercy while he waited for me to let him back in.

CHAPTER TWENTY-SIX

Day Twenty: 2:30 p.m.

I rapped my fingertips against the thick glass of the oversized window, and the female guard gave me a tired look until I pressed my badge against the glass. The guards, I figured, must have been exhausted from the press who'd camped outside the front door of the Wallace Lake County Jail. I'd had a difficult time weaving through the gaggle of reporters, and it didn't take long for one of them to recognize me as the lead investigator on the serial case. *Are you here to talk to Sadie Reid? What is Sadie saying about the case? Did she confess?* The assault of questions and recordings went on until I found safety from them inside the jail doors. Everyone wanted Sadie Reid's story. Since her arrest, Wilma Henderson had lost the limelight in the tabloids, and her daughter had taken over. Sadie was the subject of news broadcasts and internet reports across the country. Because Sadie refused to speak to the press or her lawyer, it led to reporters' speculations of what her role could have been in the murders and the human trafficking case.

The jail had been busier in the last seventy-two hours than it had been probably in the last ten years. A guard with a mound of paperwork buzzed me through the heavy steel door. Once inside the locked gates, I placed three books and a pen on the counter and then removed my gun and badge. While I signed in, the guard locked my gun in a safe where it would stay until I checked out of the facility. No weapons were allowed inside the jail, a rule that always made me feel much safer inside those gated communities. Anything could happen when guards carried guns on the inside, and I always trusted my hands and body as my very best defense.

When the metal detector didn't buzz, the female guard handed me my badge. "You here to see Reid?"

"Yes." I took a temporary ID from her and clipped it to my shirt collar. "How is everyone holding up?"

The woman gave me a wave of her hand, thick with too much sitting behind a desk. "The media's a bitch, but we're getting on."

"They'll go away as soon as the next story hits. Won't be long," I said. "How is Reid?"

"No trouble from her yet. We moved her out of solitary and into general population."

"That's good news. A glimmer of it, anyway." I hated that Sadie had to be held in solitary for the first forty-eight hours. Most incoming young inmates stayed in solitary longer than that, until they could be certain the inmate was ready to join the general population. Their decision to move Sadie told me that she was acclimating as well as could be expected, and she'd kept her mouth shut—a golden rule in America's penal institutions. Sadie would only stay in the Wallace County Jail until her trial, and then she would move to one of the larger female prisons in Ohio once her case had been heard, a prison meant for long-term incarceration rather than only a few months' stay.

The guard waved the wand detector over the books. She opened each, one at a time, and flipped quickly through the pages. She cleared them and pushed the books across the counter to me.

"There's a visitation room down the hall and to the left." She pointed the way. "I'll alert a guard in Reid's pod to bring her down."

"Thanks. Where are the vending machines? I'd like a soda and a candy bar for Reid."

"You're mighty generous today, Special Agent."

I shrugged her comment off. Most officers only doled out sugar when they needed answers to solve their cases, but I remembered seeing Sadie with a Mountain Dew before everything happened. I guessed she really could use one about now.

"Vending machines are outside the visitation rooms."

I stepped into the first holding area and the heavy steel door banged shut behind me. I waited for the door in front of me to buzz and unlock. I knew somewhere in the jail complex an employee watched me through a camera and ID'd me through Ohio's law enforcement system. Once I'd been cleared, the door buzzed and I pushed through.

After I had the goodies from vending, a guard in visitation led me to a small room lined with shatterproof windows used for inmate visits with lawyers or police. The rooms had a door that closed and a camera to monitor inmate behavior since some inmates were known to get violent when they didn't receive positive news about their cases.

I waited inside the room for Sadie, uncomfortable on the hard steel stool secured to the floor. I thumbed through the books I'd brought—a Stephen King collection of stories that included the original story used for the film *Shawshank Redemption*, a small collection of essays and stories from female inmates who had served time in American prisons, and a new journal just waiting for Sadie to write her first words in it. She had a lot of time on her hands now, and it would move faster if she kept her mind busy.

It took a good fifteen minutes for a guard to finally appear with Sadie. She stood next to him in a crumpled orange jumpsuit with her wrists bound. A thick thatch of dark hair fell over her eyes. She shuffled along beside the guard in her thick-socked feet and thin prison flip-flops.

"You wanted Reid?" the guard grunted at me.

I nodded. "Take the cuffs off, please."

The guard eyed me. "Sure?"

"I'm sure."

Once the cuffs fell away, Sadie rubbed her thin wrists where the heavy metal had been. The guard waited until Sadie was seated across from me.

"I'll be outside. Any problems, just wave."

I looked at Sadie, whose face I could hardly see through her curtain of hair, and then back at him. "There won't be any problems."

Once he left, we sat together in silence. Finally, after a few minutes, I pushed the Mountain Dew and candy across the table to her. "I figured you'd be hungry for anything resembling real food by now."

Sadie looked up at me but said nothing. Her neck and arms revealed the bruises from our water battle, and in the orange jumper she looked much smaller than I remembered. Sadie reached for the soda can and wrapped her hands around its sweaty coldness.

"I'm leaving town today, and I wanted to see you before I left," I said. "I brought along a few books and a journal for you. Something to pass the time."

I didn't know quite where to begin with Sadie. The two of us had been through so much, both in the lake and outside it. I felt guilty for not seeing the clues of Sadie's involvement much earlier in the case. I kept going back to that leather bracelet Harvey had found in the river the day I arrived in Wallace Lake. Why didn't I see it then, put the pieces together that matched Sadie? I couldn't blame it all on Joan Marco. No law enforcement officer *wants* to find out a teenager has committed a crime, but I hadn't given it enough consideration as a possibility. Ultimately, I let Sadie down by not doing my job—carefully considering every possible suspect.

"I'm sorry, Sadie."

"For what?"

"The situation you're in. You've had a rough go of it in life. That isn't fair."

She didn't respond to me, but popped the can's tab and took a full swig of the cold, bubbly liquid. The hint of a smile crossed her mouth. Her eyes made contact with mine for the first time. "I need to see Joan. Is she somewhere in this jail?"

Joan Marco. I should have guessed Sadie's first questions would be about the woman who'd manipulated her into killing. Sadie was dependent on Joan, not much different than the girls we'd found in the farmhouse. I was looking at a true-blue loyalty, though sick and twisted through manipulation, in Sadie Reid's devotion to Joan Marco.

"She and Henry have been moved to other facilities. Legally, the three of you must be separated. You aren't allowed any contact with either of them until the trial is over. At that point, the judge will most likely rule that the three of you are to have no contact for the rest of your incarceration."

Sadie stared at me incredulously. "What? Why?"

Rather than answer her question, I switched tack. "You were stuck in this situation for a while, Sadie. Why didn't you ask someone for help? Call 9-1-1 and leave an anonymous tip? Tell a teacher or Ava's mom? Somebody. Anybody!"

"Really?" Sadie glared at me. "Joan Marco *was* my guidance counselor. Do you really think I'd tell another teacher where Joan worked?"

"There were opportunities to tell someone."

Sadie shook her head. "You don't understand. I need to talk to Joan."

"You and Joan are done communicating. Period."

"That's stupid!" Sadie tossed her empty soda can against the wall.

The guard jumped at the sound, but I waved him off when he opened the door.

"What is it you need to say to her, Sadie?"

Her eyes welled up with tears, but she didn't answer my question. Instead, she said, "What will happen to Joan?"

"I don't know." I wanted to tell her that whatever happened to Joan wouldn't be enough. I wanted to say that sometimes the legal system isn't fair, and that sometimes bad people get away with murder and rape and selling other humans despite our best efforts. At least we had one solid murder on Joan Marco—Rhonda Betterly would put Joan in prison for many years.

Sadie reached for her candy bar. "Joan has some health problems. She's been complaining lately about the arthritis in her knees. Will they take care of her in here?"

"You have been worrying a lot about her." I waited for Sadie's nod and then said, "What about you? Aren't you at all concerned about your trial and the murder charges against you?"

I shifted in the hard seat with my frustration. *Close your mouth,* I warned myself. The last thing I needed to do was alienate Sadie with my anger toward Joan. I wanted Sadie to know she could talk to me, and I had to remember that the brainwashing Joan did with this young woman ran deep. It took years to groom Sadie into the person she was today, and no one would be able to help Sadie break free of that in only a few days. Sadie needed intense therapy. She needed people around her she could trust. I had every intention of being one of them.

"Joan was like my mom."

"But she *isn't* your mom. You have a mother. Every press outlet in America billed Wilma Henderson as a hero," I said. "Anyone who takes down a serial killer is a hero in my book."

Sadie shook her head. "She's an addict and a whore who never gave a shit about me."

"She's been working with police, Sadie. Give the woman a break—Wilma is doing the best she can by you right now."

"Give *her* a break? Are you serious?" Sadie ripped open the packaging of the chocolate bar. "Where was she when I was little and needed her? Where was she for all my school functions or to pack me lunch everyday? What about when I graduated? I'll tell you where: Wilma was high and with her johns. Joan Marco was there for me."

I shook my head. "It was your grandmother who took your mother's place. Not Joan."

Sadie wasn't listening; there was nothing I could say at this point that would change her mind. The intense pain of her mother's betrayal showed on Sadie's face. Tears streamed down her cheeks. I stood and handed Sadie the box of tissues from the windowsill. Sadie took a tissue, and I waited patiently for her tears to stop.

When she finally blew her nose and wiped her eyes, I said, "It's okay to love the people who have hurt you. It's okay to love the people you trusted to take care of you even when they didn't. You can love them, Sadie—that doesn't mean those people shouldn't receive consequences for their vile behavior."

After a few minutes, Sadie swallowed the rest of her candy bar. The guards wouldn't let her leave the room with any uneaten food or drink. "I won't see you again, will I?"

"Why do you say that?"

Sadie shrugged. "It's what people do."

"I'll be back to visit you, and I'll be there for the trial. You can count on it." I tapped the journal. "My address and cell number are inside."

I'd inscribed the journal for her with the same Virginia Woolf quote I'd seen in Bennett's office: *Arrange whatever pieces come your way. Stay strong, Sadie.*

"I doubt you'll answer."

"Give me a chance, Sadie."

The guard rapped on the steel door and opened it. Our visit was over.

I watched as the guard shackled Sadie, a young woman who had been forsaken by so many people in her short life. I promised myself I wouldn't be another one for her to add to that list.

"I have one more question for you," Sadie said. She looked over at me. "Why didn't you let me go?"

"What do you mean?"

"Out on the water. Why didn't you let me drown?"

Her question took my breath away. It took me a minute to gather my words. "Everyone deserves a second chance, Sadie."

Sadie shook her head slowly back and forth. She let her hair fall over her face when the guard reached for her arm for the escort to her cell.

"You should have let me go. You should have let me sink to the bottom of Wallace Lake."

Chapter Twenty-seven

Colby Sanders didn't have an ounce of Irish in him, but most nights he could be found with a beer in hand watching a baseball or football game at our local Irish pub. He waited for me in the near-empty bar with the ever-present cigarette in hand. This pub had an underground reputation of ignoring the no smoking in public facilities law, so die-hard smokers like Sanders frequented it. I was able to survive the stale smoky smell because I met him before the bar got too busy. Generally, Sanders was the only smoker in the house early in the evening. Later the place would be foggy with smoke.

Sanders grunted hello as he pulled out the stool next to him. His silver hair shone ghost white in the bar's lighting. "You eaten yet?"

When I shook my head, he signaled to the bartender for a menu and gave me a wink. "You can always count on the burgers here."

Sanders and I were part of a diminishing crowd of meat-eaters in our office and we shared that like a dirty secret. It wasn't only Harvey who had had her go at me about it. I understood the urgency to go vegetarian—everyone in our office saw too much death and destruction every day. We didn't want to also face it on our plates. I gave it my best a few times, going meatless, but always found myself eventually craving a juicy burger or the salty crunch of bacon. Tonight Sanders and I had both: bacon cheddar burgers washed down with rounds of beer.

"You did good work on the Wallace Lake case, Hansen." He nudged the half-full bowl of mustard-flavored pretzels toward me. "I should have trusted your judgment that the case wasn't over."

I took a swig of my beer and let the cold liquid coat my mouth. Finally, I said, "I haven't given you much of a reason to trust me in the past few months. For what it's worth, I'm sorry, too."

"For what?"

"For making you worry about me, but mostly for the royal grudge that's been sitting on my shoulder ever since the Willow's Ridge case. I've given you a really hard time, Sanders. You didn't deserve that."

He took a pull from his bottle and nodded acknowledgment that he'd heard me. Sometimes it was hard to read Sanders who was the proverbial hard-boiled detective with so many years on the job he'd lost count. As the director, he'd perfected the act of barking orders and asking questions later. With me, though, he'd always been generous with his time and knowledge. I assumed he felt he owed it to my father to keep me under his watch and make sure I didn't completely self-combust. I appreciated his attention although I'd completely ignored it these past few months.

"We've come a long way together in a very short time, Hansen. You can be a pistol to work with, but you're the best. I won't forget that."

"Forget?"

Sanders reached into his coat and pulled out an envelope sealed with the FBI insignia. He pushed the envelope across the bar. The letter was addressed to both Sanders and me through our office address.

Sanders watched me closely. "Open it."

I slid my finger along the sealed edge and unfolded the paper. I read the letter carefully, then once more. Amongst the praise for my work was the job offer I'd been waiting for. The FBI.

I stared at the letter a long time, as if I couldn't make sense of the words. This job offer was the entire reason I'd wanted to become a serial profiler. This was the job I thought would make everything okay for me, the move that would finally make sense of my world. I folded up the letter slowly and slipped it into my back pocket.

"Congratulations," Sanders said. "I'm going to miss you."

The bartender placed steaming burgers in front of Sanders and me. The smell of bubbling bacon and cheese made my stomach growl. I folded a fry into my mouth. "I knew you wrote the recommendation for me."

"I wasn't happy about writing the letter, but I did it," Sanders said. "We'd just wrapped up the Willow's Ridge case, and I wanted to keep you onboard in Ohio. You asked for this, though, and I knew you really wanted it."

"Thank you." I flipped the cap of the ketchup bottle and offered it to him. The fact that Sanders thought beyond his needs and considered what I wanted meant the world to me. "I've given my work a lot of thought the last few days. I've decided to stay on in Ohio. I'm happy to be a part of your team."

Sanders nearly choked on the bite of burger in his mouth. "What?"

"If you still want me, that is."

"You wanted DC so much. What made you change your mind?"

"I'm an Ohio girl, Sanders, through and through. I've spent my entire life in this state and I belong here. Besides," I said, "serial crimes are on the rise in the Buckeye State—my people need me as much as I need them."

Sanders had been back in Ohio for five years now, and I couldn't imagine him leaving, either. The slope of his shoulders and his quiet acceptance told me he understood exactly what I meant. He often said that Ohio had a way of claiming people for its own. I guess Ohio had claimed both of us.

"I thought this new job might be just what you needed to get away from Rowan. A new town. A new position. And a new beginning."

Sanders's thoughtfulness amazed me sometimes. As much as I didn't want to admit it, Ohio wasn't the only thing that had claimed me as its own. I belonged to Colby Sanders in many ways, too. "I've already started over."

He gave me a suspicious look over his burger.

"I'm moving out of the apartment and into something away from the city. I'm looking for a nice quiet place in the country."

"Thank God," Sanders said. "That dump you've been living in is enough to put anybody in a catatonic state of depression."

I chuckled. "Know this, Sanders, I'm never going to be able to get that image of you cleaning in those purple dish gloves out of my head."

"Hey, that was one of my finest moments!" He laughed with me over the pathetic highlights of my apartment and joked it was exactly the stereotypical building where we'd expect to find a serial bomber.

"And Rowan?" Sanders finally asked.

I shrugged. "She asked me to be her partner in a new yoga and meditation retreat business she's building. She wants to run it on the land and use the house as a type of bed and breakfast."

"Hmm…business partner. That's different."

"I thought so, too. I told her I'd help out when I could, but we're better friends than any sort of partners."

Sanders nodded.

"So I can stay?"

Sanders polished off the last of his burger and leveled his intense gaze with mine. "Under one condition."

I groaned, imagining what dreadful rule he was about to impose on me.

"You move up to be an assistant director of the OBCI. You'll have full authority to open and clear cases. A pay increase will be in order, of course. Something to help you with that new place in the country."

Could I have really heard him correctly? I shook my head, trying to understand. "Why are you doing this for me, Sanders?"

"You deserve it." He reached for his pack of cigarettes and lit one. "Besides, as you said, we keep catching more and more serials, and I need your help. And there is the fact that I'm becoming an old man."

"No," I teased him. Sanders had recently turned sixty, and the OBCI couldn't run smoothly without him. He was as essential as the bricks and mortar of our building.

Old man or not, I wanted Sanders by my side in any case. "Deal."

"Excellent." He tipped his beer bottle at me. "So tell me about this perfect place you're going to find in the country."

❖

I had to walk almost three blocks to my apartment building; all the parking spaces were taken and the city streets were metered. I finally found a spot on a neighborhood street. Free and ample parking was definitely something I looked forward to in my new place of residence. The cool night air felt good against my face after the warmth of the beer and my discussion with Sanders. For the first time in a long time I felt a strong sense of calm. I folded my hands inside my jacket pockets and felt the tail end of fall tinged with a taste of what the winter would bring.

The entry of my building was littered with twentysomethings all milling about to organize which clubs they'd spend the night trolling. I elbowed through them and took the stairs two at a time. I couldn't wait to shed this temporary home and move on.

As I neared my front door, I saw a shape against the wall in the hallway's darkness. Someone was waiting for me.

"Bennett?"

She stood up to greet me and the dog beside her bounded toward me and licked my hands.

"Gus!"

"I hope this is okay," Bennett said. "I probably should have called."

"It's fine," I said, walking closer with Gus tailing me. "It's good to see you both." I rubbed Gus behind his soft folded ears and his tail wagged so hard, it smacked the wall behind him. "Why is Gus with you?"

"He wanted to take a ride with me to see you. Can't you tell he loves you best?" Gus licked my hand over and over again.

Bennett shifted back and forth on the thick edges of her trail shoes, and finally her soft brown eyes turned up toward mine. "I wanted to say something to you, Luce."

"Me, too. You go first."

I waited, noticing how perfectly her worn jeans fit her athletic frame and the way her flannel collar rested against the taut skin of her neck which still showed the last traces of her summer tan. She'd rolled the sleeves up a few turns, and a silver watch that looked like it logged everything possible sat on her wrist. A worry line formed between her dark brows and I wanted to reach out for her, to hug her, but she spoke before I could move.

"I overreacted. I'm sorry."

"Me, too. I should have told you immediately. It just never felt like the right time, and I didn't want to hurt you."

Gus licked my hand and rubbed against my leg. "Are you caretaking for this handsome little man?" I asked.

"Albert has been arrested, and he'll do some time," she said. "His neighbors can't take the dog long-term. Albert asked if you would."

I knelt down and stroked Gus behind the ears. He looked like he was grinning at me.

"I know this doesn't replace the dogs you left with Rowan, but this little guy needs your help," Bennett said.

"How can I deny this sweet guy a home?"

"You can't," Bennett declared. "Here's his stats: forty pounds, about three years of age, completely healthy, and he's been well cared for. The vet says he is a mix of Lab and beagle."

"Gus had me with his first lick," I said.

I unlocked my apartment door and turned back to Bennett. "I'm really glad you're here, and not just because of Gus. Just a warning: you're stepping into an old pit of mine. I'll be moving soon."

Bennett smiled and pulled me into a big hug, the dog between us at our feet. Our lips met, searching each other at first and then hungry for so much more.

"I'm glad I'm here, too," Bennett said.

Epilogue

The Powell River loomed wide and blue against the April sky. For our first float of spring, the riverbanks and surrounding forest brimmed with wildflowers and lush green leaves. I edged the tip of my kayak past Bennett's, cutting through the calm waters still cold from the winter months.

"Don't get overzealous there, hotshot." Bennett paddled hard until her kayak pulled ahead of mine.

Bennett, I'd learned, couldn't stand to lose. In the past few months, our strong-willed personalities clashed in a few battles, but we always found our way through it. Today, I wasn't going to let her lead. Once my kayak pulled ahead of hers again, the healthy competition commenced. We edged each other out, first her and then me, in a race to see whose kayak would lead. Our paddles frantically circled the figure eight as river water sprayed across our bodies.

I'd had some practice with the paddle since my first kayaking experience with Bennett, and I had a good start to filling my very own stone jar. In January, we traveled together to the Florida Keys for a two-week kayaking adventure where we floated our way along each of the island's edges and watery marshes. We kayaked early in the morning, and then took refuge inland from the brutal midday sun. Throughout our travels in the Keys, we toured the towns, investigated the history of the islands, and lounged together under ceiling fans where she read and I napped to the soft sound of her turning pages. In the evenings, Bennett and I took to the water again where we watched many fiery sunsets from our little plastic boats.

Traveling to the Keys wasn't the only adventure Bennett and I had been on together. On one of the coldest days of the year, we embarked on a daylong meditation retreat at Pranam, Rowan's retreat center. It had been Bennett's idea, a way to show support for Rowan's business since I declined her offer as a business partner. While I helped out with some repairs and other small duties around the house and land, I was rarely in the area and Rowan was forced to find other handywomen. Despite her disappointment in my decision, Rowan blessed us with hemp smoke and sang blessings for our souls throughout the daylong retreat. Her toe rings clicked against the barn's wooden floor, and her bare feet showed one toe visibly missing, a terrible reminder of the suffering Rowan endured because of me during the Willow's Ridge case. Truth be told, that was why I was willing to sit on the hard floor fighting the lotus pose and listen to what she had to say about karma. Rowan had regularly talked to me about karma when we were together; she used the promise that what goes around comes around as a way to soothe my pain over the death of Marci Tucker and my experiences in the One True Path ministry. In some ways she was correct—there were aspects of crime that couldn't be settled in a courtroom and were better left up to the laws of karma. Many times, though, I needed more than karma—I needed justice.

Justice, for the most part, had been served in the Wallace Lake case. Everyone involved with the crimes had been held legally accountable and would serve some type of sentence. Both Joan and Henry Marco would spend the rest of their lives behind bars. Legally, Joan would only answer to human trafficking, fraud, and the murder charge of Rhonda Betterly, though I believed she should answer for so much more. She would never see the outside of prison again, and I believed serving hard time was more of a punishment than the death penalty. I found solace knowing that things would not be easy for Joan Marco on the inside—Heart to Heart had touched many in the drug community, and Joan would soon come face to face with some of the women she'd pimped out. Cody Allard's life would never be the same again. He was sentenced to a year in prison. He lost his job at the Wallace Lake High School, and the sex offender label sentenced him to the life of an outsider. Justice was also served in the cases of Sadie Reid, Henry Marco, and Albert Finley for their parts in the crimes. I was torn, particularly for Sadie, whom I understood was guilty of murder. I also understood there were extenuating circumstances that led to her involvement. And I'd grown fond of Albert—I didn't want to see him suffer. Bennett liked to remind me that I couldn't pick and choose who got justice. After all, Bennett liked to say, the statue was blindfolded for a reason.

"Hansen! Bennett! Wait for us!"

Bennett and I slowed down the kayaks so that the group could catch up. I floated beside her with my oar resting across the boat.

"Teenagers." Bennett rolled her eyes. "Slowpokes."

Ava Washington finally came into our view with a slew of teens in kayaks following behind her. Bennett and I regularly appointed Ava as the team leader for our day trips and excursions into nature.

After the case closed, a new teen center opened in Wallace Lake County, a place where kids who had been affected by the opiate epidemic or the sex trade could find safety and a listening ear. Almost every person in this part of the state knew someone who struggled with these types of addictions. Most knew at least one person who'd died from it. The center offered group discussions and educational classes on health and well-being to help teens either break free of their addictions or to stay away from dangerous substances and behaviors. They also offered many group activities, some of which Bennett and I led. We'd taken groups kayaking on the Powell River, fishing on Wallace Lake, and led many hikes through the wooded terrain of Wallace Lake County. I loved the activities because they gave Bennett and me a chance to spend time together and also allowed us to get to know the teenagers in the area.

It had been a good five months since everything went down in Wallace Lake, and Ava Washington still struggled. It wasn't only the fallout of her relationship with Cody Allard, but she also dealt with feelings of guilt. Ava believed she should have asked Sadie more questions, and she should have helped the friend she idolized before it was too late. Something told me that no matter what Ava would have done, Sadie wouldn't have accepted help. The trick was helping Ava to realize that.

My life had significantly improved since the beginning of the Wallace Lake case, and I found myself most grateful for the little bungalow I bought in Springrock. It was far enough from the Powell River not to flood every time its waters rose, and close enough to the shore to hear the constant flow of the currents. My new country home was about forty-five minutes from the OBCI headquarters and two miles from Bennett's place. I often ran the distance between our homes with Gus pulling me along behind him.

Bennett and I had made a commitment to each other. This time around, though, I was doing things differently. Instead of moving in together after only a week like I had with Rowan, Bennett and I determined we each needed our own space. For the time being, at least, we kept the separate residences. I was still learning it was okay for us to be physically apart and still be together. Even though we were happy, I was still me—my Berlin Wall was still in place and self-destruction was never far away. Lucky for me, Colby Sanders was never far away and Bennett showed me nothing but understanding.

My father's ghostly presence, though, had appeared very little since the Wallace Lake case ended. I trusted that he would be back when I had a case large enough to warrant his help, but for now he appeared to be in retirement. In his absence I'd realized he was right yet again—I didn't need his help as much as I thought. I was certain, though, that my dad would have loved my new home, and he would have taken on remodeling projects with gusto. He would have loved the crickets that sang to me on my early morning runs and the complete blackness of the country night as much as I did. He would have encouraged me to spread out in the wide-open fields of Springrock and explore the thin country roads that wound like ribbon throughout the surrounding forest. Most of all, my dad would have been happy to see my roots growing deeper into the rich Ohio soil.

In many ways, I'd come home to Springrock. That bungalow brought me full circle to what balanced me most: water. Sometimes the currents of the deep river and lake were peaceful and calm. Other times they roiled with angry whitecaps and raged against their hard stony edges. There was no way to ignore the living presence of the river in Springrock, and I listened for its quiet guidance every morning. Those rolling waters anchored me, a lifelong companion that sometimes saved me, sometimes threatened me, but remained the constant element in my life and had never forsaken me.

About the Author

Meredith Doench teaches writing at a university in southern Ohio. Her work has appeared in literary journals such as *Hayden's Ferry Review*, *Women's Studies Quarterly*, and *Lumina*. She served as a fiction editor at *Camera Obscura: Journal of Literature and Photography*. Her crime thriller, *Crossed*, was a silver winner for the 2015 IndieFab Book of the Year Award in Mystery. Learn more about Meredith at: www.meredithdoench.com.

Books Available from Bold Strokes Books

Forsaken Trust by Meredith Doench. When four women are murdered, Agent Luce Hansen must regain trust in her most valuable investigative tool—herself—to catch the killer. (978-1-62639-737-8)

Her Best Friend's Sister by Meghan O'Brien. For fifteen years, Claire Barker has nursed a massive crush on her best friend's older sister. What happens when all her wildest fantasies come true? (978-1-62639-861-0)

Letter of the Law by Carsen Taite. Will federal prosecutor Bianca Cruz take a chance at love with horse breeder Jade Vargas, whose dark family ties threaten everything Bianca has worked to protect—including her child? (978-1-62639-750-7)

New Life by Jan Gayle. Trigena and Karrie are having a baby, but the stress of becoming a mother and the impact on their relationship might be too much for Trigena. (978-1-62639-878-8)

Royal Rebel by Jenny Frame. Charity director Lennox King sees through the party girl image Princess Roza has cultivated, but will Lennox's past indiscretions and Roza's responsibilities make their love impossible? (978-1-62639-893-1)

Unbroken by Donna K. Ford. When Kayla and Jackie, two women with every reason to reject Happy Ever After, fall in love, will they have the courage to overcome their pasts and rewrite their stories? (978-1-62639-921-1)

Where the Light Glows by Dena Blake. Mel Thomas doesn't realize just how unhappy she is in her marriage until she meets Izzy Calabrese. Will she have the courage to overcome her insecurities and follow her heart? (978-1-62639-958-7)

Escape in Time by Robyn Nyx. Working in the past is hell on your future. (978-1-62639-855-9)

Forget-Me-Not by Kris Bryant. Is love worth walking away from the only life you've ever dreamed of? (978-1-62639-865-8)

Highland Fling by Anna Larner. On vacation in the Scottish Highlands, Eve Eddison falls for the enigmatic forestry officer Moira Burns, despite Eve's best friend's campaign to convince her that Moira will break her heart. (978-1-62639-853-5)

Phoenix Rising by Rebecca Harwell. As Storm's Quarry faces invasion from a powerful neighbor, a mysterious newcomer with powers equal to Nadya's challenges everything she believes about herself and her future (978-1-62639-913-6)

Soul Survivor by I. Beacham. Sam and Joey have given up on hope, but when fate brings them together it gives them a chance to change each other's life and make dreams come true. (978-1-62639-882-5)

Strawberry Summer by Melissa Brayden. When Margaret Beringer's first love Courtney Carrington returns to their small town, she must grapple with their troubled past and fight the temptation for a very delicious future. (978-1-62639-867-2)

The Girl on the Edge of Summer by J.M. Redmann. Micky Knight accepts two cases, but neither is the easy investigation it appears. The past is never past—and young girls lead complicated, even dangerous lives. (978-1-62639-687-6)

Unknown Horizons by CJ Birch. The moment Lieutenant Alison Ash steps aboard the Persephone, she knows her life will never be the same. (978-1-62639-938-9)

Divided Nation, United Hearts by Yolanda Wallace. In a nation torn in two by a most uncivil war, can love conquer the divide? (978-1-62639-847-4)

Fury's Bridge by Brey Willows. What if your life depended on someone who didn't believe in your existence? (978-1-62639-841-2)

Lightning Strikes by Cass Sellars. When Parker Duncan and Sydney Hyatt's one-night stand turns to more, both women must fight demons past and present to cling to the relationship neither of them thought she wanted. (978-1-62639-956-3)

Love in Disaster by Charlotte Greene. A professor and a celebrity chef are drawn together by chance, but can their attraction survive a natural disaster? (978-1-62639-885-6)

Secret Hearts by Radclyffe. Can two women from different worlds find common ground while fighting their secret desires? (978-1-62639-932-7)

Sins of Our Fathers by A. Rose Mathieu. Solving gruesome murder cases is only one of Elizabeth Campbell's challenges; another is her growing attraction to the female detective who is hell-bent on keeping her client in prison. (978-1-62639-873-3)

The Sniper's Kiss by Justine Saracen. The power of a kiss: it can swell your heart with splendor, declare abject submission, and sometimes blow your brains out. (978-1-62639-839-9)

Troop 18 by Jessica L. Webb. Charged with uncovering the destructive secret that a troop of RCMP cadets has been hiding, Andy must put aside her worries about Kate and uncover the conspiracy before it's too late. (978-1-62639-934-1)

Worthy of Trust and Confidence by Kara A. McLeod. Special Agent Ryan O'Connor is about to discover the hard way that when you can only handle one type of answer to a question, it really is better not to ask. (978-1-62639-889-4)

Amounting to Nothing by Karis Walsh. When mounted police officer Billie Mitchell steps in to save beautiful murder witness Merissa Karr, worlds collide on the rough city streets of Tacoma, Washington. (978-1-62639-728-6)

Becoming You by Michelle Grubb. Airlie Porter has a secret. A deep, dark, destructive secret that threatens to engulf her if she can't find the courage to face who she really is and who she really wants to be with. (978-1-62639-811-5)

Birthright by Missouri Vaun. When spies bring news that a swordswoman imprisoned in a neighboring kingdom bears the Royal mark, Princess Kathryn sets out to rescue Aiden, true heir to the Belstaff throne. (978-1-62639-485-8)

Crescent City Confidential by Aurora Rey. When romance and danger are in the air, writer Sam Torres learns the Big Easy is anything but. (978-1-62639-764-4)

Love Down Under by MJ Williamz. Wylie loves Amarina, but if Amarina isn't out, can their relationship last? (978-1-62639-726-2)

Privacy Glass by Missouri Vaun. Things heat up when Nash Wiley commandeers a limo and her best friend for a late drive out to the beach: Champagne on ice, seat belts optional, and privacy glass a must. (978-1-62639-705-7)

The Impasse by Franci McMahon. A horse packing excursion into the Montana Wilderness becomes an adventure of terrifying proportions for Miles and ten women on an outfitter led trip. (978-1-62639-781-1)

The Right Kind of Wrong by PJ Trebelhorn. Bartender Quinn Burke is happy with her life as a playgirl until she realizes she can't fight her feelings any longer for her best friend, bookstore owner Grace Everett. (978-1-62639-771-2)

Wishing on a Dream by Julie Cannon. Can two women change everything for the chance at love? (978-1-62639-762-0)